DIAMOND DREAM

DIAMOND DUET
BOOK 2

ANNA COLE

Copyright © 2024 by Anna Cole

All rights reserved.

No part of this publication may be reproduced, stored in, or introduced into a retrieval system, distributed, or transmitted in any form or by any means, including photocopying, recording, or other electronic or mechanical methods, without written permission from the author, except for the use of brief quotations in a book review and as permitted by U.S. copyright law.

This book is a work of fiction. The story, all names, characters, and incidents portrayed in this publication are fictitious. No identification with actual persons (living or deceased), places, buildings, and products is intended or should be inferred.

Cover: Maria @ Steamy Designs

AUTHOR'S NOTE

Dear Reader,

Thank you so much for your interest! **Kat and Nik's story begins in book one, Diamond Don. Please make sure to read it before diving into Diamond Dream.**

Scan the QR code below to get Diamond Don:

CONTENT WARNING

Dear Reader,

Please be aware that this book contains graphic scenes meant for a mature audience.

Trigger Warnings: dubious consent, kidnapping, explicit scenes, and descriptions of violence.

MAILING LIST

Sign up to my newsletter for exclusive bonus content and updates on upcoming releases! **New subscribers get an exclusive epilogue.**

Scan the QR code to subscribe:

1

NIK

"THERE YOU ARE, darling. As delicious as ever, might I add," a familiar female voice says behind me.

Kat and I turn around to face the woman addressing me.

"Edna, you're too kind," I say in greeting. "It's been a while."

"Too long, darling. Far too long. Although I suppose it's always a good thing when a man in your line of work doesn't need someone in mine. But I wasn't talking to you, Nikolai. Katherine, it's been ages. I never properly thanked you for giving me a hand with that nasty Brussels business. Lovely dress, by the way."

I glance at Kat, surprised to learn she and Edna are familiar with each other.

Kat smiles warmly at the woman in front of us. "How are you, E?"

Edna Smith is a very peculiar person. Barely five feet tall, she always manages to look down her nose at all of us made men, even through her black-rimmed glasses. She has to be at least in her late fifties, but she doesn't look a day over thirty. The woman can be a bit abrasive, and her many quirks can grate on anyone's nerves, but she grows on you.

Regardless, Edna doesn't care if people like her. Truthfully, it doesn't matter to her one bit. After all, anyone in my line of business needs her now and then, so we can't afford to get on her bad side. That's the privilege that comes with being the best in the field. God knows she isn't afraid to wield it.

Like Kat, Edna is a renowned independent contractor in our little *demimonde*. But unlike my bewitching date, Edna is in what we call the clean-up business.

"Now, I heard the rumors, but I confess I didn't take them for much more than meaningless gossip until now," Edna says. "It made little sense to me that Nikolai Stefanovich—the all-mighty *pakhan* of the Russians—and Katherine Devereaux, my favorite cat burglar and con woman, would be romantically involved. After all, you two are polar opposites of each other, as I know very well. What could have possibly brought the two of you together?"

"What, indeed?" Kat asks me with a mischievous smile, winking at me.

I narrow my eyes at her, and she blows me a kiss. Lord, have mercy on me. With a small sigh, I sip on my whiskey.

"I see it now, of course," Edna adds with a delicate shrug. "Pure, animalistic sexual attraction, obviously."

I almost choke on the liquor, fire burning in my throat and even in my nostrils as I cough uncontrollably. Kat rubs my back, softly laughing.

"I couldn't have put it better myself," Kat says as my coughing fit subsides.

"And it's great timing on your part, too. There's nothing like the promise of new love to help keep the sorrow and grief of losing a loved one at bay. I was horribly sorry to hear about Maxim, Nikolai," Edna says, flipping her short hair back. She always liked him.

I nod in acknowledgment. "I appreciate that, Edna."

"I've been very curious about a few details concerning his death, though, so I'm glad I ran into you tonight. What's this nonsense I hear about his body disappearing?"

"Nothing to worry about," I say, giving her a smile that doesn't quite reach my eyes. "It's just a small mix-up with the funeral home. I'm sure it'll be worked out soon enough. Nothing but an oversight."

Edna doesn't seem convinced by my response. As a matter of fact, the little woman raises her thin eyebrows so high that they disappear behind her bangs. "What are you talking about, Nikolai? What kind of oversight leads to a body going missing? There's something weird going on here. I'd know, of course. Making corpses disappear is my bread and butter, as you're aware."

I carefully consider my answer as I take a deep, fortifying breath. Truth be told, I'd love nothing more than to ask Edna to fuck off and mind her own business. But as the *pakhan* of the *bratva*, I can't even consider the possibility. She's far too essential to our operations. I can't risk offending her.

"What can I say, Edna?" I ask with a smile, shrugging. "We're working on it, and I'm confident this issue will be sorted out sooner rather than later. While we're at it, you wouldn't have any information you'd like to share with me, would you? I can only imagine what a woman in your position could do for a man in my unfortunate situation. As always, I'd make it worth your while, of course."

Edna scoffs. "Nikolai, please. Don't insult me with your vulgar suggestions. You know how fond I was of that boy. I'd never play any part in any shenanigans involving his body.

That poor thing. Is it true that he was strangled to death? With a garrote, I hear? Well, at least it was quick, I suppose. In your line of work, one can never be too grateful for these small blessings."

Next to me, Kat gasps, but I don't let my polite smile fade away. I know Edna doesn't mean to insult. This frankness of hers is just one of her eccentricities. I can't say I blame her for being so desensitized to discussing the practicalities of death.

"Was an autopsy done?" she asks.

I shake my head. "Not yet."

"Well, it's best to assume it'll never be done. Even if you miraculously recover his body, it'd be pointless. He'll likely be too far decomposed by now. I think we can safely assume that anyone who'd steal his corpse wouldn't be concerned about keeping it fresh. Even if they don't have any other nefarious goals besides hiding evidence of their crime—which, trust me, isn't a given."

My stomach churns a little, and Kat shoots me a concerned look, a cute little frown wrinkling her brow. She clutches my hand, and I return the gesture.

I manage not to say anything to Edna, focusing my energy on not letting the mental image of Maxim's decomposing remains tossed in a ditch overtake my brain. It's a better use of my strength than choking the life out of Edna.

"To be perfectly candid with you, Nikolai," she adds, "you might as well give up hope of finding your friend's body. It's for the best. Take it from someone who does this sort of thing professionally—the odds of you finding anything you can even remotely attempt to put to rest are very slim. Any person who'd dare to steal the corpse of the *bratva*'s *pakhan*'s best friend isn't messing around."

Kat interrupts Edna's tirade with a polite smile. "Thank

you for the advice. We appreciate your professional opinion and insight."

"Well, you're welcome, of course," Edna says with a dismissive wave of her hand. "Now, of course, if anyone can pull off such a feat and find a rotting corpse after so long, that's your man Nikolai. But I'm just not sure it's worth the effort. Maybe you're better off burying an empty casket as a symbolic gesture and moving on. I am, of course, more than used to the reality of putrified body parts, but I understand it can be an upsetting experience to many—which is why I advise against this pointless pursuit."

Unable to restrain myself, I clutch my whiskey glass tightly before forcing my hand to relax. The last thing I want is the damn thing shattering and cutting Kat as she leans against my side, caressing my arm.

Still, the image of Maxim's blue eyes turning into oozing, decomposing fluids as his skin breaks down to reveal the contents of his body is hard to shake.

"We'll definitely give that some thought, Edna," Kat says in a pacifying tone. "I must ask—where did you get that bag? I just love that color."

Edna chuckles, blushing with pleasure at Kat's well-placed compliment, meant to distract her. "Oh, this old thing? There's this fabulous little shop in Rome, my dear. Remind me to give you the address later. Now, about Maxim's death, let me ask you this—"

Kat cuts her off, straightening next to me, her voice as striking as a lashing whip. "Edna, I've been delicately trying to let you know how insensitive and rude you are behaving, but I realize my attempts at polite subtlety are wasted on you. I'm afraid I must ask you to stop asking these pointed questions or making graphically gruesome comments about Maxim. I insist, actually. Please don't talk about him at all.

You're being incredibly indelicate and hurtful. Nikolai's too much of a gentleman to tell you to have some tact, but I don't mind saying it at all."

Edna's head snaps back as if Kat had struck her. I'd be willing to bet a lot of money that no one's ever talked to her like that. As her shock subsides a little, she looks down her nose at Kat in that supercilious way of hers. With an insufferable air of superiority, Edna says, "For old time's sake, I'm going to pretend you didn't talk to me like you just did. I'll give you an opportunity to ask for my forgiveness."

Kat laughs, sipping her drink. "Come now, Edna. You've always been a practical woman. Don't lose your grip on reality now."

Edna squints her eyes so tightly I'm not sure she can see anything. "Nikolai, please talk some sense into this girl. She's lost her mind. She must not know who she's speaking to."

Before I have time to say anything, Kat interjects. "It goes both ways, Edna. You must've forgotten who you're speaking to as well. After all, I know all about your little incident back in Brussels. Maybe you'll need my services again., so I'd be nice to Nik and me if I were you. Or I might be inclined to not pick up the phone next time you call me."

I expect Edna to chew Kat off for speaking to her like that. I know for a fact that made men—armed to their teeth and with over a hundred pounds on Kat—will cower at mere hints of Edna's displeasure. Instead, she stares at Kat, her mouth slightly ajar, looking stunned.

Honestly, I can relate. I know just how she feels. I suppress a nervous laugh, torn between feeling ecstatic and horrified. Horrified because I don't even want to imagine the consequences of pissing off Edna for a man in my position. Ecstatic because Kat took me by surprise by being in my corner like that. I don't know where this version of Kat came from, but I like her—a lot.

Still, I study Edna, trying to devise a way to salvage this disaster. "Edna—" I say, unsure of what to tell her.

To my surprise, she chuckles. "You know, I've always liked you, Kat. You're just my kind of girl. No bullshit. You're right, of course. I forget myself sometimes. You mustn't take it to heart, darling."

My head pivots to Kat, and I'm relieved to see in her expression that she will accept Edna's olive branch.

"Oh, I would never, E. Don't give it another thought," Kat says.

"And I didn't mean to offend you, *Don* Stefanovich," Edna says, showing me deference for the first time in the decade I have known her. "You know I loved that boy. You must forgive me. At the end of the day, I'm nothing but a crazy old woman who spends way too much time in the company of corpses. I forget these things."

"You have nothing to apologize for, Edna," I say, lying to her face with a smile.

Out of nowhere, Edna jumps up excitedly. "Oh, if it isn't that handsome rascal Garrett I see! He used to work for me, you know. I must bother him mercilessly. If you two will excuse me..." She waves her goodbyes to us over her shoulder, walking towards the poor man.

Kat and I watch her leave in a flurry of motion. I glance in Kat's direction, and she shoots me a curious look.

"What?" she asks with a frown. "Why do you have that look on your face?"

"My knight in shining armor," I say with an exaggerated sigh.

Kat rolls her eyes, but her lips curve in a slight smile. "I just—I couldn't take it any longer. It was like watching a car wreck. Somebody had to tell her to stop." She shrugs, but I'm not so easily fooled.

I sigh again as I pull her into my arms, unable to restrain myself any longer. I need to feel her body against mine. "My hero."

Kat looks at me with exasperation, but she doesn't resist me. I place my hand on her hips, pulling them against mine, and the feel of her flesh makes me want to growl in possessive pleasure.

Mine, mine, mine.

She wraps her arms around my neck, shooting me an aggravated look. "I won't have anyone else messing with you like that. If anyone gets to put you in your place, it's me."

"Try it and see what happens. Try it, I'm begging you. You'll make my day."

"*Miliy*, please," she says with a mock sigh. "We both know you're all bark and no bite when it comes to me. I'm as safe as a kitten as far as you're concerned."

I can't even pretend to look displeased. Not when she calls me by that pet name in Russian.

"You talk a big game for a girl ready to throw down with Edna fucking Smith to spare my feelings. That woman knows how to dissolve bodies in a vat of acid, Kat." I shudder in mock horror. "It's okay. You can admit it. You're a little fond of me." I wink at her, and she rolls her eyes, even as her smile grows.

"That's for me to know and for you to wonder about," she says against my lips, and I go from zero to sixty in a millisecond. She raises an eyebrow, smirking as she feels me harden against her stomach.

"Two can play this game, you know," I say against her ear, nipping at it.

"Aw, Nik, don't threaten me with a good time," she says, repeating her words from what feels like a lifetime ago.

"There you are, Kat. I've been looking for you," McGuire says, his rancid voice reverberating behind my back, the last place I want him to be.

Well, second last, at least. Anywhere but in Kat's vicinity will do.

Kat shoots me a scorching hot look that promises me things I've only dreamed about before removing herself from my arms and turning to face the Irish mobster.

"Here I am, Patrick," she says.

"Would you like that tour of the house now?" he asks with a smile, offering her his arm. He doesn't invite me to tag along, of course.

Kat glances at me briefly, giving me the tiniest apologetic shrug. McGuire and anyone else would've missed it, but I'm so attuned to this woman and the slightest vibrations in her body that it could never escape me.

I give her a slight nod in response, in understanding.

Yeah, Kat, I was enjoying myself, too. I agree it sucks that this asshole interrupted us. And yes, I understand that we have a job to do, so you should go with him, even though it makes me die inside a little whenever I see you even breathing the same air as this miserable prick.

As McGuire leads Kat away toward the doorway, she looks over her shoulder at me and blows me a small kiss that he doesn't even notice.

I wink at her, somehow managing to stop myself from killing the man right here and now, if for no other reason than for lusting after what's mine.

2

KAT

"I still think we should give it a go," I say over my champagne flute.

Nik sighs wearily. "I thought we had an understanding," he says as he runs his fingers through his hair, making it my turn to sigh. His glossy, dark hair is my weakness. Although, at this point, maybe it's more accurate to say that his *everything* is my weakness.

"No. You did your best to lay down the law, and I acted like I agreed with you then, fully intending to make you see things my way once the right moment presented itself. *This* is the right moment," I say with a whisper, even though it's probably unnecessary. As the night goes on and the liquor is freely poured, McGuire's guests become rowdier and rowdier. Even the band our host has hired for the night is having a hard time competing with the crowd's noise.

"It's too risky."

"Oh, come on, Nik. What's the worst that could happen? Look at where we are." I wave my hand, gesturing to all the women and men surrounding us on McGuire's luxuriously built terrace. The warm night was too alluring, so the party moved outside.

"Make no mistake, Kat. This gathering won't stop McGuire from doing whatever he wants if we piss him off. It surely wouldn't stop me." Nik shrugs, sipping his drink.

"Come on. He won't think anything of it."

Nik scoffs, giving me a look that doesn't hide the fact that he doesn't share my beliefs.

"He really won't," I say. "He told me all about Erin when he gave me the tour of the house. Even if he spots me speaking to her—which is a big *if* considering the size of this crowd—I'm sure he'll assume I'm curious about the girl after hearing so much about her. Trust me."

Nik sighs again. "You're not going to drop this, are you?" he asks under his breath.

I give him my best smile. "Nope. See, you know me so well already, *miliy.*" I rise on my toes to kiss his cheek.

To the man's credit, he does his best to look reprimanding, but I guess I know him pretty well by now, too—because I see through his menacing act in an instant.

"No need to sweet-talk me, Kat. You already got what you wanted," he says, but his right hand rests on the small of my back as I brush a kiss against his lips. "Go talk to Erin. But, for the love of God, be careful. We're outnumbered at least two dozen to one tonight."

"Your wish is my command."

Nik grips my wrist. "I'm serious. Don't tell her anything you wouldn't want McGuire to know."

"I won't. Don't worry, I've got this. I'll be right back."

Nik stares at me for a moment longer before letting me go.

I try to appear casual as I approach McGuire's daughter. Erin is leaning against the terrace's ornate balustrade, with her soft brown hair displayed over her back in long waves. She doesn't see me approach as she stares off into the distance.

"Hi there," I say in my most friendly tone as I lean against the railing beside her. "You're Erin, right? Your dad was just telling me all about you. I'm Kat Devereaux."

Erin McGuire stares at my outstretched hand, looking slightly startled and confused. After blinking her big, green eyes at me a couple of times, she takes my hand and shakes it. Her firm grip surprises me.

"Oh, hi," she says. "It's nice to meet you."

"The pleasure's mine, I assure you," I reply with a smile. "Your dad mentioned you've been spending most of your time here since the renovation was completed. I must say, I'm jealous. You live in a beautiful home."

"Thank you. That's very kind of you to say." Erin's tone and expression are thoroughly polite, but it's clear her mind is elsewhere.

"Of course. I don't blame you for not wanting to go back to the city. I wouldn't want to spend my summer away from this place, either."

The aloof beauty nods absentmindedly before giving me a polite smile. "Yeah, I think I'll be here for a while. I can't go back yet." Almost as an afterthought, she sighs.

"No one would blame you for wanting to say. I'm sure there's so much to do around these parts in the summer. Obviously, your dad's into sailing, but what about you? What do you like to do for fun?"

"Fun?" she repeats with a frown, blinking. "I guess—I walk a lot. I mean, I take long walks by the water. Sometimes I swim, too."

"So you're the outdoorsy type, huh?" I smile. "Well, that sounds like a good time."

"You'd think." She shrugs. "I saw you earlier with Nikolai. Are you his date?"

"I think you could say that. Do you know Nik well?"

"Oh, I wouldn't say that. But we've known each other for a while. He's a good guy."

"I'm starting to think so, too," I reply, and she gives me a mystified look.

"Have you been together for long? I don't think I've ever seen him bring a date anywhere before." I file that interesting tidbit of information for later.

"No, not for long. To be honest with you, it's been a bit of a whirlwind affair."

"Oh." She frowns slightly, blinking at me again. Her eyes are a fascinating shade of pale green. "That's...a little unexpected, I think. That doesn't sound like him, but I guess you must be very special."

Erin McGuire has the good manners and social graces of a princess, but it's obvious she's a little out of practice when it comes to socializing.

I laugh. "I guess I must be. Thank you. I think."

With a shake of her head, she sighs. "I'm so sorry. That was indelicate of me. I didn't mean to—you must forgive me."

"Oh, no need to apologize. You didn't insult me or anything. Besides, you do have a point. It doesn't sound like him, does it? I guess I *am* special."

For the first time tonight, she smiles. It's the slightest, almost imperceptible twitch of her lips—but a smile, nonetheless. "Yeah. I think you are."

"Well, that's sweet of you to say, Erin. I'm sorry, but I have to ask—for someone who claims not to know Nik well, you seem to know a lot about what sounds like him or not. Anything I should worry about?"

"Oh, God. No. Not at all. I swear, it's not like that at all. It's complicated, I guess. I feel like I know him, but I don't. Not really. I just used to know somebody who did."

In the softest of tones, I ask, "Do you mean Maxim?"

Erin McGuire's eyes widen as she gasps. For some reason, I get the feeling that no one has dared to utter his name to her in a long, long time.

"Yeah, I mean him. He used to talk about Nikolai so much that I feel like I know him myself. But you see, we've only spoken a handful of times. I barely know the man. Obviously, you have nothing to worry about if the way he was acting around you earlier today is any indication. Maxim would've loved to see it."

Erin's smile turns sad as she turns away from me, staring off into the distance again.

"You miss him. Maxim, I mean."

After a moment of hesitation, she nods, her eyes brimming with unshed tears. Her voice cracks as she says, "Yeah, I do. I really do."

My heart breaks a little—this poor, poor girl. "Oh Erin, I'm so sorry for your loss. I can't imagine what you must be going through."

Erin nods, her tears running down her face. I search my clutch purse for my pack of tissues and offer it to her.

"Thank you," she mumbles before clearing her throat.

"Don't mention it."

"You're the first person to say that to me. That you're sorry for my loss, I mean." She discreetly sobs, trying to conceal her tears from the other guests.

"What do you mean?" I ask her in disbelief. "What about your friends? Your family?"

"No one would dare say it. They won't even acknowledge that he's gone, let alone that I might be grieving his loss. It's taboo. Because of my dad and everything that happened back then."

I shake my head, horrified. "I can't believe this. You poor thing. You lost the man you loved, and no one has even offered you a shoulder to cry on."

"It's worse than that. We're barely allowed to say his name. It's almost like he never existed. Almost like his death isn't real."

I shake my head in sympathy. "Oh, Erin, I'm so sorry."

She nods, drying her tears. She does her best to compose herself before patting my hand on the railing. "Thank you for your kindness."

"Of course. You don't need to thank me for acting like a decent human being."

"No, I do. I really do. I'd also appreciate it if you didn't mention my outburst to anyone else. My dad can't hear about it."

"It'll stay between the two of us. But Erin, there's something you should know." I glance around us for anyone who might be eavesdropping before lowering my voice to a whisper. "Your dad might pretend Maxim never even existed, but his death is very real to Nik. I assure you, he hasn't forgotten about it. If there's anything you are aware of that he should know, don't be afraid to share it."

Erin's eyes widen, and Nik's warnings about the risks of approaching her spring to the forefront of my mind. After all, the girl is clearly under her father's thumb. Still, I can't believe this brokenhearted woman would betray the memory of her lover by harboring any secrets that might benefit his killer. Whatever sins Erin McGuire might be guilty of, she's still deeply in love with Maxim.

She opens her mouth to speak. Then, seeming to hesitate, she chews on her bottom lip. She glances around us before leaning closer to me. "I don't mean to offend you," she says so quietly that I can barely hear her. "You've been so incredibly kind to me tonight. But I don't really know you enough to know that I can trust you."

"I get that. But you know Nik. Or at least, you knew him through Maxim. I never knew Maxim, but if what I see in Nik is any indication, then the two of them shared an unbreakable bond—an undying one. If I know this after such a short period with Nik, then you must know it, too. So trust Nik. And know that I speak for him when I ask you to help us do right by Maxim."

Erin stares at me for a long moment before nodding. "I wouldn't dare tell you everything I know right now. Not here, where the walls have ears. But you should know—and Nik must know—that my dad was behaving strangely the day Maxim passed away. He even had his right-hand, Connor, brought to him out of nowhere. He sent Connor two states away a couple of nights before to handle some issue with a shipment. But he changed his mind that day and had Connor hurry back to attend the gala with him. I overheard them arguing on the phone."

"What else did you hear that day?"

"Not much." She shrugs. "Dad had me locked away here. He put a full regiment of guards in place and everything. There's one other thing, but I'm not sure we should discuss it here."

I want to moan with impatience and frustration, but I manage to ask, "When can you meet me? And where? Just tell me the time and the place."

Erin glances around again before saying, "Meet me by the front door at midnight. We'll go for a walk, and I'll tell you everything I know."

"I'll be there. Now smile, here comes your dad."

Startled, Erin looks over her shoulder, spotting her father a moment after me. Unfortunately for us, she's not half the actress I am, so I must overcompensate for her shortcomings. I'll have to do my best to distract the man from his daughter's contemplative mood by flirting with him.

"Should I be concerned that the two women who are always on my mind these days are now on talking terms?" McGuire asks, winking at me.

I give him my best fake laugh, and his smile deepens. Erin, however, doesn't even pretend to enjoy her father's attempt at humor. After excusing herself, she walks away.

"Are you enjoying yourself, Kat? Is there anything I can do to make your night better?" McGuire asks with a suggestive glint in his green eyes.

Once again, I laugh, faking my amusement at his flirtation. "Oh, Patrick, you'll get me in trouble."

"I'm game if you are," he says, too close to my ear. "Just lose the Russian, and we can have a good time."

I try to cover my discomfort at his closeness. "You make it sound so simple."

"It can be. What's stopping you?"

I force a sigh. "Well, Nik can be a handful. I wouldn't dare do anything to cause his anger."

"I can protect you, sweetheart."

"Can you? I just can't be sure. It's too much of a risk."

"No, no, darling. Tell me how to show you I can protect you from him."

"Well, there's one thing..." I say, eyes wide, doing my best to feign concern. For a moment, I worry that I'm laying it on too thick and that he'll see through my dramatic display. But his eyes glaze over, focusing on my lips, and I realize my hook is in place.

I take a deep breath, mentally calculating the best way to suggest to McGuire that having proof that he took Maxim's life would show me he's capable of taking on Nik.

Just as I'm about to reel the man in, a familiar, large hand wraps around my waist. A heartbeat later, I'm pulled back against a broad chest. I look up and see Nik's face, his dark brown eyes searching for mine.

"Hi there," I say, curious about the timing of his interruption.

"Hi. I've missed you."

I turn to fully face him so McGuire can't see my expression. I shoot him a look of disbelief. I can't understand what's going on inside his thick skull. Why would he interrupt us just now? I was so close...

Nik ignores my frustrated expression as he coldly addresses our host. "McGuire."

"Nikolai," the other man says with a smirk. "We were just talking about you."

"Were you now?" Nik asks, raising his eyebrows.

"Indeed. But if you'll excuse me, I see my guests are waving me over. I have a feeling I know what it's about. There's this card trick I know that they just love. You must let me show it to you later, Kat. We'll continue our conversation then." He grins at me.

"Sounds like a plan." I wink at him.

With a smirk, McGuire trots over to where a dozen drunk men cheerfully await him.

Nik doesn't waste a second before wrapping his hand around my wrist and dragging me away to a secluded, darkened corner by the railing. He forcefully turns me until I'm facing him. "What the hell was that?"

"I could ask you the same thing. What were you thinking? I was so close to getting him to tell me everything! We'd have a recording of his confession right now if you hadn't interrupted me."

Bemused, Nik glares at me for a moment before shaking his head. "McGuire wouldn't confess to Maxim's murder in the middle of a party. He sure as hell wouldn't do it when I'm within hearing distance."

"I'm not so sure about that, Nik. He flat-out told me to ditch you for him just now. Believe it or not, he even went as far as promising me he could protect me from you."

"*He did what?*" Nik shouts. He glances over my shoulder, his head swiveling from side to side, undoubtedly searching for McGuire.

"What are you doing?" I ask him through gritted teeth. "What's wrong with you?"

"What's wrong with *me*? How the fuck can you ask me that? It's one thing for him to flirt with you in front of me—that's just him trying to get a reaction out of me, and I can handle that. But openly trying to steal you from me? When I'm right fucking here? That's just too much, Kat. He's asking for it now. Let's see how well he can protect *himself* from me." Nik grabs me by the waist, trying to move me out of his way.

"Nik—" I say as loudly as I dare. The last thing we need is to attract any undue attention to us right now. "Have you lost your mind? You were just talking about how badly outnumbered we are. This is his home. Pick a fight with him, and you'll get yourself killed."

He smirks darkly. "I'll take him with me. It'll be worth it."

Horrified, I gasp. I grab his jacket's lapel and drag him back into the secluded dark corner with me, pulling his enormous body as hard as I can. I don't want prying ears or wandering eyes picking up what I'm about to tell him. Lucky for me, he doesn't resist me too much.

"How can you say something like that? What about me? What will happen to me if you get killed in a brawl with McGuire and his men?" I ask him, my voice breaking.

He finally seems to notice my dismay. Rapidly blinking, he frowns. "*Milaya*—" he says with a sigh, tenderly caressing my cheek. His eyes finally connect with mine. The crazed look in them slowly dissipates, melting into something much more tender. "No, no, *milaya*. Don't be upset. Please. I can't stand to see you upset. I didn't mean to make you sad."

"What did you think would happen when you announced you were going to throw yourself at them? All by yourself against dozens of men! What were you thinking?" I shake him by his jacket.

"I—I wasn't thinking," he says with a confused look on his face.

I scoff. "Well, we can agree on that. I just don't understand you sometimes."

Nik sighs wearily. "Since I've met you, I don't understand myself sometimes." He shrugs. "But is it really such a big surprise that I'm struggling to curb the impulse to kill him after everything he's put me through?"

"Well, no. But there's a reason you have restrained yourself so far. You don't want to start a war, remember?"

"Less and less by the minute."

"Nik," I say through gritted teeth, shaking him once more for good measure. "I can't believe you're risking everything you've worked for. Especially now when we're closer than ever to nailing McGuire. I haven't even told you what Erin said to me. That's how crazy you're acting."

"You think I'm crazy now? Wait until you see what I'll do

if I have to tolerate another minute of him flirting with you or touching you."

"What about Maxim? What about your plan to make his killer pay? Have you forgotten about all that?"

That crazed look returns to Nik's beautiful eyes. "No, but maybe I've just had enough. Maybe I just want to watch everything burn, consequences be damned. If McGuire wants war, maybe I'll give it to him."

"You don't mean that," I whisper.

"You're sure about that?" he asks, raising an eyebrow. "Because I'm not."

"You wouldn't want all that death and chaos. You wouldn't do that to your men. You're their *pakhan*. They trust you to lead them."

"Well, maybe I'm tired of always being the *pakhan*. Maybe I want to be just a man for once."

"What's that supposed to mean?"

Nik's eyes, still glittering with that wild look, burn and glow like molten lava. He leans closer to me until his forehead leans against mine. "As the *pakhan*, I have to think of others. I have to put their needs above mine. As a man, I could take what I want and need and tell the rest to go to hell."

Breathless, I ask, "What do you need and want so badly that you would risk a war for it?"

His eyes never leave mine, simmering with unrestrained emotion, as he says, "Right now, I need to take you away from this place and make you mine until there's no doubt to you or anyone else that you belong to me."

I stare at him, speechless.

Without another word, Nik kisses me.

3

KAT

Nik's touch isn't gentle or tender. No, his kiss is almost savagely overwhelming. With little preamble, his tongue enters my mouth, and he groans against my lips as he tastes me.

Next thing I know, Nik's left hand's fingers are tangled up in my hair as he pulls me even closer to him. With his right arm, he scoops me up against his body, lifting me.

I squeal in surprise as Nik walks with me tucked against his chest. My Russian climbs down a set of steps deep inside this darkened corner of the terrace.

"Where are you taking me?" I break our kiss to ask him, panting.

"Away from here," he says, grunting against my lips, annoyed that I dared to separate our mouths. "When I make you come, I don't want anyone else to hear you moaning in pleasure. That's for my ears only, *kiska*."

Nik carries me until we are standing under a tree. He leans my back against it, his body covering mine. I immediately pull him back to me by his hair and kiss him as hard as I can, wrapping my legs around his waist. His erection rests against the silk of my underwear, and I can't resist pressing against it. His fingertips sink into the flesh of my hips as he pulls me even closer, groaning into my mouth.

"I want you so bad," I say between erratic breaths as his mouth kisses its way down the column of my neck.

Nik's answering groan sounds almost pained as his lips suck hard on the spot where my neck meets my shoulder. Then he bites down hard there. I gasp, and his face returns to mine.

My maddening Russian looks into my eyes as he rasps, "I need you, Kat. You're mine."

As we kiss, I can't tell where I end and he starts. I breathe in the air he exhales, and yet, I need to be closer to him. Thoughts race through my mind—there's so much I need him to know. But right now, it's enough to feel his skin against mine, taste him on my tongue.

Time feels like an absurd concept as Nik's hand slips under my dress. I grow lightheaded, feeling like I can't get enough air even as his breath fills my lungs.

In one fluid movement, two of his fingers sink inside me. "*Kiska,* you're mine." His lips brush against mine.

I nod, grabbing a handful of his clothes and dragging him even closer. My tongue tangles with his and I push him to pick up the pace. I've waited too long. I want him now—all of him.

Almost surreally, I think for a second that I hear something. After a moment, I realize the sound is coming from behind Nik.

"Nikolai," the voice says again, interrupting us once more.

Vladmir.

"What?" Nik asks, furious anger vibrating through him. I

feel it all over my body, with my arms and legs still wrapped around him as he pins me against the tree.

"We have to go. *Now*," Vladmir says. He adds something in Russian, and Nik immediately straightens. His arms tighten around me and his expression changes into one of concern.

Nik glances over his shoulder at Vladmir before addressing him in Russian, his commanding tone familiar to me. Then he turns back to me.

"We have to get out of here. Erin is gone. McGuire thinks I'm behind it," Nik says, untangling my legs from around his waist. He gently lowers my feet to the ground, holding me steady as I process the news.

"What do you mean, she's gone? She said she'd meet me later tonight to tell me about her dad and Maxim," I say, trying to catch my breath.

"Well, she's missing. Vladmir says McGuire is out for blood. More specifically, mine. He's sure I only came to this party to abduct her in retaliation for Maxim." Nik takes my hand in his as he hurries away from the house with Vladmir by his side.

"Fuck," I say under my breath, doing my best to keep up with their long strides in my heels through the grass field. Me and impractical shoes in moments of danger. Name a more iconic duo.

"Fuck, indeed," Nik says, glancing over his shoulder before speaking to Vladmir in Russian. His urgency is unmistakable. Vlad speaks in the same tone.

"English, please," I say.

"I was just asking Vlad if he knows how many men McGuire has on the property tonight," Nik says, pulling me along. Clearly, I'm not moving fast enough for him.

"The answer is too many," Vladmir says. "We're vastly

outnumbered and outgunned. Plus, this is their home turf. We have to get the hell out of here now."

I'm surprised Vladmir has even deigned to address me after what happened earlier. "What's the plan?" I ask.

"The plan is to make it to the car, preferably without running into the Irish," Nik says as he and Vladmir frantically scan the area. "Come on, Kat. Less talking and more jogging. Maybe you should lose the shoes. I'll have to carry you if you don't start walking faster."

Nik's short tone startles me. I guess my expression shows it because he brings my hand to his lips and kisses it, still pulling me along the way.

"Sorry about putting you in danger," he says.

"No harm, no foul. Let's keep it that way," I say, still wary of his sharp command a second ago but slightly mollified by his tender gesture.

"I can't believe I thought it was a good idea to bring you here," he says under his breath. "Can't believe I dragged you into this situation."

"Don't beat yourself over it. It's not like you actually kidnapped the girl. I mean, you didn't, right?"

Nik looks at me, his lips curving into a smile. "Not this time."

"Well, good. For what it's worth, I was putting myself into danger every day and twice on Sundays well before you came into my life," I say, panting as I struggle to keep up with his pace.

"Kat, I'm getting you out of here safe. No matter what," he says, his tone allowing no doubts.

I sigh. "Nik, I know. But running away from an angry mob army is a little outside of my field of expertise. So, lead the way, and I'll follow."

The look he gives me is so scorching hot I'm mildly

concerned it will melt me in the spot. He pulls me suddenly against his chest, giving me a quick, rough kiss before releasing me, a smirk on his face.

"There's the garage," Vladmir says, pointing to a large building a few dozen yards away. We hurry towards it, trying to keep to the shadows, my hand still in Nik's. The three of us make our way to the back of the building, and I groan in frustration when I see a locked gate separating us from Nik's car. I can even spot it through the gate's mesh; its gleaming dark exterior is so close, and yet so far.

Vladmir slams his fist against the gate, and Nik curses under his breath. We look around, trying to find some way to lower the gate and clear our access to the vehicle, but nada. No keys, no electronic panels, no nothing.

McGuire and his men—whose voices grow closer and closer by the second—must have a remote key to lower the gate.

"We'll have to make a run for it," Nik says. "On foot. Kat, I really think you should lose the shoes. I can carry you, but it'll slow us down."

"If we're fast enough, we might lose them in the woods," Vladmir says.

"Wait," I say. "I think I see an access panel in the garage. It must lower the gate. I can climb it, get it to lower, and drive the car out. Give me the keys."

Nik glances at the panel as I point at it, hesitating. "I don't know if that's a good idea, Kat," he says. "What if it doesn't control the gate? What if you can't work it out? You'll be stuck in there."

"My plan will work. But even if it doesn't, I can always climb back out, and we'll make a run for it then."

"We'd waste too much time—time we don't have," Nik says, glancing over his shoulder. Even I can tell McGuire's men's voices are growing louder. They'll find us at any moment now.

"Nik—" I say with urgency. "I can do this. I know I can do it. You'll just have to trust me."

He studies me for an instant, and something I can't put my finger on flashes over his expression. He takes a deep breath. Then, to my surprise, he nods and tosses me the keys.

I smile at him, and it's my turn to steal a quick kiss. Before he can react, I step back and take a running start before leaping toward the gate. With a turn of my hips, I leverage my lower body until my legs swing over the top of the gate. Then, I jump from the top, landing gracefully on the ground, absorbing the fall's impact and straightening myself.

Vladmir lets out an impressed whistle, and I look over my shoulder to find an amazed expression on his face and Nik's.

With a smirk, I wink at them, hurrying toward the panel. "What did I tell you? Mad skills, baby," I brag as I run across the vast garage.

"Kat..." Nik says, exasperation and amusement warring in his expression and tone. But his eyes burn with warmth for me, and I melt completely, foolish as I am.

"I'd say this amazing display of breaking-and-entering mastery will cost you, but honestly, you can't afford me." I wink at him again.

Nik groans. "You can hustle me for all I'm worth later if we make it out of this alive. Hurry now."

"Don't worry, *miliy*. For you, this one is on the house."

Vladmir raises his eyebrows. I don't even care. When I finally reach the panel, I flip it open and study it. "Feeling lucky tonight?" I ask Nik with a throaty voice.

He half laughs and half chokes on a groan. He rubs a hand over his face before sighing. "Kat." His tone is as close as he's ever been to begging.

"Ok, here's the deal. I'll dumb it down for you two civilians," I say, as I work on the small keypad on the panel. "Usually, with this tech stuff, I get by with a little help from my friend A.J. But as it happens, I'm very familiar with this type of panel. It's very run-of-the-mill. Now, here's the catch —with this model, there are two things I can try. One will get the gate to open, but the other will sound an alarm. There's no way of knowing which one is each."

"You didn't tell me any of this before you pirouetted your way in there," Nik mutters through gritted teeth.

"Well, duh." I shrug. "You'd never have gone for it. It's a fifty-fifty situation. I'll take those odds. Here goes nothing."

My fingers work on the panel, and I hope for the best. Destiny laughs in my face as the garage's overhead lights start flashing red and an ear-splitting siren echoes through McGuire's property.

"Fuck," Vladmir groans as Nik shouts my name.

"My bad," I say. Then I run as fast as I can towards Nik's car. I unlock it and jump into the driver's seat of the shiny vehicle. After pressing the start button, I yell, "Step back."

Nik and Vladmir barely have enough time to react and follow my instructions because I slam my foot on the gas and ram the car into the gate. I waste no time before backing up and doing it again. This time, the metal partition falls over.

"Get in," I say to the two men as I drive through the garage's opening.

With a disapproving shake of his head, Nik yanks the door open before taking the passenger seat. Vladmir hurries to the back of the car, pistol in hand.

I stare at the gun in shock for some reason.

"Kat. Drive the fucking car," Nik grunts. His sharp tone snaps me out of my reverie.

I peel out of the area, racing through the property's driveway just as screams echo behind us and bullets zip past the car. Vladmir sticks his head out of the window and fires back.

I gasp, swerving, and Nik grabs the wheel. "It's all good, Kat," he says in a soothing tone. "Just keep your hands on the wheel and your eyes on the road. Don't worry about the shots."

"Don't worry about the shots?!" I yell, turning to face him. "Now, why didn't I think of that?"

The car swerves again as I speed away down the driveway and onto the main road. Nik tries to reassure me. "Shh. Just do your best. Please. Just worry about driving. Let's put some distance between us and them."

He's barely finished with his sentence when I spot headlights in the rearview mirror. Nik and Vladmir share a look that makes me feel cold to my bones.

"What is it?" I ask Nik anxiously.

"Can you drive with one hand?" Nik asks Vlad, making eye contact with him through the same mirror.

Vladmir hesitates for a moment before nodding.

"What are you talking about? Why would he have to drive with one hand?" I ask frantically, glancing at the headlights as they grow closer and closer.

Nik ignores my question, so I look at Vladmir, noticing his right hand wrapped in bandages. He even has a makeshift splint. It must be broken.

"What happened to your hand?" I ask. Vladmir shakes his head, glancing at Nik from the corner of his eye.

I look at Nik, too, but he doesn't make eye contact with

either of us. After a moment, I understand with a jolt that Nik must've broken Vladimir's hand. I'm even more shocked when it dawns on me that he must've done it to punish Vladmir for touching me earlier today.

"Are you fucking insane?" I yell, turning my head to look at Nik. "You broke his hand!"

Nik sighs. "Kat..." he says in a pacifying tone.

"What's wrong with you? With both of you!" I ask, yelling even louder.

"Kat, we can talk about this later. Now, for fuck's sake, will you please focus on driving?" Nik shouts right back at me while reaching over to keep the wheel straight.

"How can you expect me to focus on anything right now when I just learned you broke this man's hand as punishment for touching me?" I ask. My rising tone doesn't impress him. Nik makes eye contact with me, looking as angry as I've ever seen him.

"You're damn right I did," he says. "You're mine, Kat, and anyone who even thinks about laying a finger on you will have to answer to me. I'll kill the next one, too, if I think it'll drive my point home better."

4

KAT

I stare at Nik in shock.

"Eyes on the road," he says. I follow his command without thinking.

My mind races a mile per minute, and my heart might burst out of my chest.

This man—this crazy, absolutely out-of-this-world, scorchingly hot man will be the death of me. Even if I somehow survive him, once he's done with me, I'm not sure I'll even recognize myself. Because so help me God, I can't deny it. When Nik stared into my eyes and calmly threatened to kill anyone who dared to touch me, I was thrilled.

Not terrified or concerned.

Thrilled.

I'm nothing but thrilled that this impossibly dangerous man feels such a powerful urge to protect me.

Real life bullets are flying around our heads and angry Irish mobsters are racing to kill us as we run for our lives—yet, all I can think about is that I want to jump into Nik's arms and beg him to take me until I can't remember my own name.

"Kat, pull into that driveway over there," Nik says, pointing to a spot to our right. "Quickly, now. Before they come around the turn."

I rush to pull into the driveway he is indicating, slowing down before asking, "Why are we stopping?"

"Get out of the car," he says once the car comes to a full stop, opening his door.

I stare at him, confused, and he comes around the driver's side with a sigh. Wordlessly, he opens my door and drags me out of the car himself.

Vladmir rushes to take my place behind the steering wheel, closing the driver's side door shut.

Nik pulls me into his arms before addressing the other man. "You know what to do."

With a nod, Vladmir drives away.

I stare at the car as it leaves, dumbfounded again. I tilt my head back to look at Nik. "What are we doing here?" I ask.

"Hiding." He directs me towards the house. "Good. Nobody's home," he murmurs to himself while pulling me by my hand. He doesn't stop until we're standing behind the single-family home, completely hidden from the road.

"Now, what?" I ask impatiently.

"Now, we wait," Nik says.

"Why are we here, and where did Vladmir go?"

"It was the first place I spotted, and Vladmir's leading McGuire's men away from us."

"Why?"

"They were getting too close for comfort. I didn't want them to catch up to us with you in the car. And I wasn't sure how much longer you'd keep it together before you slammed the car into a tree."

With an insulted huff, I retort, "Well, I'm sorry I'm not as cool and collected as you when bullets are zipping past my head. This little adventure may be just another day in the office for you, but let me tell you—it's not commonplace in my life."

Nik sighs. "Kat, I didn't mean it like that. You did great—much better than most people would've managed in that situation. I'm just trying to get you to safety as soon as possible, as I promised you I would. You shouldn't even have been in danger in the first place. That's on me, and I'm so sorry—more than I can say."

"Oh, please. I'm a big girl. I can take care of myself."

"I know. You got us our getaway car, after all. Still..."

"You're damn right I did. And I'll have you know I had the entire driving thing under control. If you hadn't startled me with your neanderthal display of jealousy, I would've been completely fine."

"My what? Oh, you mean Vlad's hand. Kat, about that—"

"No, listen to me. I know you think I'm a helpless damsel in distress—"

Nik scoffs. "I most certainly do not."

"No, you do. Don't lie. But I'll have you know I've managed just fine for twenty-six years without your condescending, supercilious, overprotective ass."

He groans, rubbing a hand over his face. "Kat, just listen to me for a second—"

I do no such thing, of course, choosing to ignore his interruption instead. "If anyone saved anyone's ass tonight, it was me who saved yours, Nik. Your super tempting, looks-great-in-black-jeans ass."

Nik smiles. With a sigh, he pulls me closer. I try to resist him, but he's relentless.

"Come here, *milaya*."

Then I'm in his arms, and he's showering me with kisses. He tenderly nuzzles my hair, my eyes, my ears. Before I know it, his caress isn't as tender as it's scalding hot. I half expect things to pick up right where we left them against the tree in McGuire's property before Vladmir interrupted us, but Nik seems content to just lazily, languidly kiss my skin.

"Nik, please..." I say, sexually frustrated beyond measure.

He chuckles. "What do you need, *kiska*?"

"You. In me. Right now."

"Behind some random house while we're on the run from McGuire? I don't think so. Next time I have you, we're doing it properly. At last."

"But I want you. Right here, right now."

Nik's eyes glitter, turning the most devastating shade of golden brown as he softly laughs. "Ah, Kat..." he says, half-sighing, half-chuckling.

"What?"

"My world's crashing around us. We might not live to see tomorrow. All my plans for McGuire might be ruined. But you just made my day." He gives me his megawatt smile, the one I saw only once—when we stepped out of that little airplane.

Nik tucks me against his chest, and I sigh. After a moment, I ask, "What does *kiska* mean?"

"Don't even bother asking. I'm not telling you."

"Whatever. I'll just look it up online when I'm by myself." I shrug.

Nik shakes his head in disapproval, but his smile remains in place. "Maybe it was a mistake to give you that phone back."

"That bad, huh?" I say, teasing him. "*Kiska* must mean something super juicy."

The only reply I get from Nik is a kiss on my forehead.

Eventually, I pull away to look at his face. He gazes back at me, and he's so handsome—so dear and even familiar to me at this point—that it's hard for me to fully accept that because of me he's committed an act of such violence against a man sworn to him.

"You broke Vladmir's hand. For me," I say.

Nik studies me before saying, "I did." His eyes remain on me, observing my every reaction. Something he sees in my expression surprises him. Still looking at me, he raises his eyebrows, understanding washing over his expression before amazement takes over. While holding his breath, he stares at me, waiting, I realize, for me to say something.

With a slight nod, I pat his chest before telling him, "Good job."

Nik's amazed expression flickers into amusement, but then our eyes connect. His gaze turns darker—hotter. He sinks his fingers into my hair and pulls me closer, hard and fast. "Kat..." he says, my name nothing more than a sigh.

I wrap my arms around Nik's neck and close the distance between our mouths. I don't bother with a slow build-up before touching his tongue with mine. He holds me even tighter. In response, I push harder and faster, wanting all of him right now, but he paces me, clearly intending to keep his word from earlier.

I want to groan in frustration at the maddening man, but he's saved by the bell. Or close enough, as it is.

"We've got company," Nik whispers, breaking our kiss as headlights come up the driveway. With a sigh, he holds me against him for a moment longer before breaking our embrace completely. He holds my hand when we spot the approaching car.

5

NIK

"Relax," I tell Kat, who has gone rigid next to me. "It's just Dmitri."

She exhales in relief, and my chest tightens a little in response.

This is on me. I put her in danger.

Dmitri's silver car comes to a stop next to us in front of the serendipitously empty house. It's impossible to discern any of his features through the vehicle's blacked-out windows, but it doesn't matter. I recognize his car just the same. It means Vladmir survived long enough to follow my orders and send Dmitri my way. With any luck, Vlad has lost the Irish soldiers by now.

Wordlessly, I open the backseat door to Kat, gesturing for her to get inside the vehicle. She complies, sliding into the car with no complaints.

"Let's go," I say to Dmitri as I sit beside him. He does as he's told. Once he pulls out onto the main road, he glances at me, then at Kat.

"Are you guys doing fine?" he asks, eyes swerving from

the side mirrors to the rearview one, attentively surveying the road for any signs of McGuire's men.

I nod in reply, but Kat only shrugs, staring off into the distance through the window.

Dmitri exhales with a sigh. "Thank God. How do you want to do this, Nik?"

"Do what?" I ask, watching Kat through my side mirror. I can't really see her face as she watches our surroundings, lost in thought, which means I can't discern her emotions. Is she scared? As the adrenaline wears off, she's bound to feel exhausted. She's probably regretting the day she had the misfortune of crossing paths with me.

"Take out McGuire, of course," Dmitri says, exasperated.

With a frown, I glance at him, still studying Kat from the corner of my eye.

Dmitri is clearly in a heightened emotional state if the way his pale blue eyes frantically scan the sides and back of the road is any indication. His skin is tinted with a flush from exertion, and his dark blond hair is a mess. It's obvious that his usual composure is long gone.

I can't help but sigh, rubbing a hand over my closed eyelids. Suddenly, I feel exhausted, and I can't even blame it on the effects of the adrenaline rush wearing off. Is there anyone I haven't failed today? I didn't keep Kat safe. I couldn't even manage to protect the *bratva*'s interests. Now, I realize I also failed my most loyal friend.

Dmitri's always so calm, cool, and collected that I sometimes forget how young he is. For all his bravado, he's been fairly sheltered and protected since he started working for me—or at least as much as anyone working for the *bratva* could have been.

It was so easy for me to keep him relatively safe when

there were no significant threats. I just don't have the heart to make him grow up too fast, especially considering everything Maxim and I went through when we weren't much younger than he is now.

"Dmitri, McGuire is not your concern," I say.

Dmitri glares at me as if I've suddenly started speaking in tongues. "What do you mean, he's not my concern? He tried to kill you, Nik. You're my *pakhan*. It's my duty to take him out."

"I'll handle him myself. You'll stay out of this. You'll be needed elsewhere. Besides, I'm not ready to accept we're going to war with the Irish just yet."

Dmitri scoffs. "That ship has sailed, Nik."

"Maybe," I concede. "But I'm not ready to throw the towel just yet. If there's any way we can avoid unnecessary bloodshed, I'm duty-bound to try it."

Dmitri sighs. For a naively hopeful moment, I think he's dropping the matter. But that's just wishful thinking, of course.

"Here's an idea," he says. "Why don't I drop you and Kat off at home before circling back to take care of McGuire myself? I'll bet you dollars to donuts that it's pure chaos back at his fucking beach house. I can probably sneak in, off him, and get the fuck out of there before anyone even realizes what's going on."

I shut him down without a second thought. "That's the most brain-dead thing I've ever heard come out of your mouth. Absolutely not."

"Why the hell not? It's about time we give that fucker his due. And you could still avoid war with his men. You'll just tell everyone I acted on my own and exile me to Siberia like you did with Maxim. Or we'll fake my death or something of the sort."

Boys and their bravado...

"Over my dead body, Dmitri," I say, raising my voice at him as I start to lose my patience. "I'll be damned before I have you or anybody else doing my dirty work for me. Or taking the fall for me. And I won't sentence you to certain death or a life of misery in exile."

Dmitri has the nerve to roll his eyes at me. "Oh, come now, Nik. Be reasonable about this. Just think about it."

"No. I won't say it again, Dmitri. Don't test me on this," I warn him in a tone more assertive than I remember ever using with him.

The sight of him so deflated, especially when he means well, pains me. It's an idiotic idea, of course, but he's coming from a place of loyalty to me and the *bratva*.

"Yes, sir," he agrees as meekly as I have ever heard him.

I sigh again. In a gentler tone, I add, "I won't have McGuire killing anyone else I care about, Dmitri. I'll handle him myself."

"Just like you, I have a duty here, Nik. McGuire came after you. You can't expect me not to do anything about it. After everything you've done for me and my mom, you know I can't just let this go," he pleads, his voice rising an octave.

"Dmitri, my word on this is final. You'll do as you're told, or so help me God, I'll teach you a lesson I should've taught you a long time ago."

Dmitri stares at me in shock. I don't blame him. He's never heard me speak to him like this. Vladmir's right. I've been too soft on him. For the first time in the decade Dmitri and I have known each other, there's no rueful amusement or even tolerance in my tone as I respond to his challenge to my authority.

Suddenly, Kat's clear voice interrupts our tense back-

and-forth. "Hey, are you guys hungry? Because I'm starving. I think we should order some takeout when we get home. I don't know about you two, but I'm craving some Chinese."

It's obvious she's trying to lighten the mood and shield Dmitri from the worst of my temper. I scowl at her through the rearview mirror, and she smiles at me, wholly unconcerned.

"I'm fine with Chinese," Dmitri says through gritted teeth. "Didn't that cheap fuck have any food at his shitty party?"

"I'm sure he did," Kat says, shrugging. "But I was too busy to grab a bite. Our boss is an unreasonably demanding guy, as you know well."

I narrow my eyes at her through the mirror, and the little minx has the nerve to blow me a kiss.

Dmitri chuckles under his breath. Mostly for her benefit and out of politeness, I'm sure. "I'll plead the fifth on that one, Kat," he says.

Kat perks up at his amused tone, pleased at her success at lightening the mood and cheering him up. As I watch her, I can't help but smile a little.

"Oh, come on," Kat says. "You can tell us whatever's on your mind, Dmitri. Whatever you do, you probably won't piss him off as much as I have today. Trust me."

"Now I'm curious. What did you do this time?" he asks, eyeing her through the rearview mirror.

"Let's just say Nik was already feeling pretty on edge by the time I rammed his car against McGuire's gate. Twice. Or thrice. I wasn't keeping count." She sighs before smiling at me. "You should've seen his face, Dmitri."

He laughs, the tension in his shoulders slowly dissipating with each chuckle.

"All he would've seen was the expression of a man who's realized he's been hustled. I was promised a world-class burglar. All I got was a girl with too much sass for her own good and who can't even figure out how to open a garage door," I say, my eyes never leaving hers through the car's mirror.

Kat raises her eyebrows, but there's an amused glint in her eyes when she says, "Well, that says more about you than it does about me, *miliy*. If memory serves me, I was good enough to steal from the big, bad *pakhan* himself—right under his nose—and get away with nothing but a slap on the wrist."

I smirk at her. "Your recollection and mine vary wildly, Kat. I do recall a slap, but it certainly wasn't on your wrist."

Kat gasps, feigning outrage. But even as she pouts, acting incensed, her eyes sparkle with unmistakable humor.

Dmitri whistles before chuckling. Mid-laugh, his head snaps in Kat's direction like a whip. "Hang on, what did you just call him?" he asks her, his eyes as wide as saucers.

Kat shrugs in answer.

Dmitri turns to me, breathlessly and dramatically widening his eyes. "Did I just hear her call you *miliy*? Please say yes. I did, didn't I?"

My only response is a sigh as I roll my eyes because I know where this is going.

"Where did you learn that word?" he asks her.

"Online, of course," she says in a casual tone. "I learned the term is the male equivalent of the word *milaya* when I looked that one up. Nik wouldn't tell me what it meant even though he kept calling me that, so I had to figure it out myself, you know."

Somehow, Dmitri's eyes grow even wider. He's frozen in

place for a second before erupting in laughter. "Oh, man," he manages to say between howls of laughter, wiping at the corner of his eyes. "Thank you, Kat. Thank you so much. You just made my week. Oh, gosh. I can't believe my ears. Nikolai Stefanovich lets you call him *miliy* because he calls you *milaya*."

"Dmitri..." I say in warning, but my heart isn't in it, and he knows it. As usual, he disregards me completely.

"No one's going to believe me," he says with a groan, still chuckling. "I wouldn't believe it myself if I hadn't seen his expression just now."

"Since we are on this subject," Kat says, "I'd like to run some Russian words by you, Dmitri. For starters, what does *kiska* mean?"

Dmitri's jaw goes slack as his eyes widen again. "Does he call you *kiska*, too?" he asks her. "Please tell me he calls you *kiska*."

Kat nods. "Yes. Mostly when we're in the middle of—"

"Enough," I say with a grunt. "This conversation is over."

Of course, they both disregard my command entirely.

"Well, what does it mean, Dmitri?" Kat asks.

With a delighted smile, the jackass obliges her. "*Kiska*, my dear Kat, means kitten," Dmitry says. After sighing, he turns to me before quietly speaking in Russian under his breath.

"Hey!" Kat says "Not fair. English, please and thank you."

You've got it bad, my friend.

That's what the impertinent sod whispered to me.

He has no idea.

With a dangerous glint in her dark blue eyes, Kat scoots forward in her seat until her face is right next to mine. "Kitten, huh?" she says, teasing me with a smirk.

"Don't let it get to your head," I say, trying to play it cool. The moment she fully realizes her hold over me, I'm ruined.

Unimpressed by my dismissive tone, she rolls her eyes before turning to face Dmitri. "You know, Dmitri, Nik here talks a big game, but he was so mad at Vladmir for daring to touch me that he smashed the poor man's hand."

Dmitri glances between Kat and me in disbelief. "Holy shit," he says with a loud gasp. "She's serious. You did." He howls with laughter. Again.

I disapprovingly shake my head at her.

"What?" she asks. "You *did*."

"You're making me sound like a simpering idiot," I say, halfheartedly complaining.

With a cute pout, she shrugs. "Well, if the shoe fits, Nik... There's no shame about it." She winks at me before leaning forward and kissing my cheek.

Simpering idiot that I am, I'm instantly mollified, my reputation be damned.

Dmitri can't stop laughing, shaking his head. Somehow, he brings us back home.

He's still chuckling as he parks in my garage.

As the elevator doors open up at the penthouse, he breaks into a new laughing fit.

"Enough," I say. "We have work to do. If you can manage to curb this moronic giggling, I'll find you a way to make yourself useful."

"Yes, sir," he says, trying to contain his laughter.

"And you—" I say, turning to face Kat. "I'll deal with you later. Stay out of trouble until then."

"Aye, aye, captain." She winks at me, strolling towards the kitchen.

I don't miss the amused glance she and Dmitri exchange between themselves, but I let it go for now.

Soon, Dmitri's amusement dies, anyway. I'm relieved to learn Vladmir made it back safely, but as we set out to prepare for what's coming our way, Dmitri's uncontrollable giggling becomes a distant memory. We all know shit is about to hit the fan, and it might be a while before any of us has a reason to laugh again.

After hours of planning and preparation, I'm slightly less stressed out about our security situation. I won't make the mistake of underestimating McGuire again. With our plans and their orders in place, my men disband.

Not long after, I set out to find Kat. After wandering around the penthouse with no success, I call her name. She responds from inside the kitchen. I follow the sound of her voice and stop short at the sight that welcomes me.

I'm sure my astonishment is clear on my face as I take in the surprise. "You've waited to eat with me," I say, stupidly stating the obvious.

Kat shrugs, pouring me a glass of red wine. From the most expensive bottle in my collection, of course. "I figured you'd be just as hungry as me."

While I worked, Kat pulled out all the stops. She dimmed the kitchen lights and set out candles. She even ordered the Chinese food she mentioned she was craving.

"Did Vladmir make it back okay?" she asks, handing me the wine glass.

With a nod, I take the offered glass.

She sighs with relief. "Thank God. Now, let's sit down and eat, shall we? I'm famished."

I do as she asks, and we eat in comfortable silence. Except for the soft jazz music she has playing as background noise. Now and then, my hand brushes hers as I reach for one of the takeout containers, and her eyes meet mine, as deep and blue as the ocean. She smiles, and it takes almost all that I have in me not to have her over the fucking kitchen island.

But her day has been incredibly challenging, and I don't want her to be exhausted and emotionally drained if we take things in that direction again. Who am I fooling? *When* we do.

So I behave myself, even though it physically pains me to restrain myself at this point. I feel as if I've been mercilessly edging myself for days—constantly being brought to the brink of climax, just to be frustratingly brought back down to earth. Over and over again.

But as Kat smiles at me and plays with the fingers of my outstretched hand, I don't even feel frustration. Unexplainably, I feel almost content.

It's an unsettling thought, but Kat *soothes* me.

"Here," I say with a weary sigh, reaching for the handgun tucked in the back of my pants. "I want you to have this."

Curious, she glances at it, gasping in surprise when she identifies the object. She doesn't immediately reach for it, looking at me with confusion.

"It's untraceable," I say. "Go on, take it."

"Why?" she asks, still taken aback. Reluctantly, she grabs it, holding it carefully in her hands.

"I want you to have it. Do you know how to use it?"

Kat gives me an insulted look. "Of course I know how to use it. Just because I don't like guns, it doesn't mean that I don't know how to use them."

"Good," I reply with a nod. Then, before I can think better of it, I add, "I meant what I said before, Kat. I'll protect you with my life. My men will do the same. I'll do everything in my power to make sure you're never again in a position where a gun might be useful. But as you've pointed out, trouble seems to follow you disturbingly often. I don't want you to rely on others for protection. Whatever I can do to make sure you'll never feel helpless again, I'll do it."

Kat stares at me, her expression indecipherable. Then, without warning or preamble, her lips are on mine. Her kiss is hot and hard, and a groan escapes me as she wraps herself around me. As suddenly as it starts, it stops. The maddening woman untangles herself from me breathlessly.

"What was that for?" I ask her, confused and panting.

With a sigh, she says, "You have to stop doing stuff like that."

Even more puzzled, I ask, "Like what?"

"Like *that*. Stop saying things that make me want to kiss you. Do you know how hard it is to control myself all the time when I'm around you twenty-four-seven? I'm so tired of resisting you."

That shuts me up pretty quickly.

"Then, don't."

She scoffs, rolling her eyes. "Shut up."

"Come here and make me," I dare her. I beg her.

"That's probably a bad idea. Unless we're ready to go all the way..."

Kat and I stare at each other for a long while. She stretches her hand to trace the edges of my lips slowly. I'm careful not to move a muscle. Too soon, she drops her hands. She shakes her head, and I sigh.

Too bad.

"A goodnight kiss, then," I bargain.

After studying me for a second, Kat smiles, biting her bottom lip. This time, she nods, and I smile at her in triumph. She closes the distance between us and whispers, "I don't think I'll ever be able to resist you when you smile at me like that."

I give her a puzzled look, but she just shakes her head before softly pressing her lips to mine. The sweet torture of their velvety feel almost undoes me. While sinking my fingers into the silky luxury of her hair, I draw her closer. Again, too soon, she pulls away.

"Sweet dreams, Nik," Kat whispers as she leaves me, hard and wanting.

6

KAT

I'M SHOCKED to find the penthouse crawling with people at the crack of dawn.

After the previous day's excitement, I expect to wake up feeling completely drained and exhausted. Instead, to my astonishment, I rise with the sun, eager to learn what surprises today will offer. That's why I make quick work of getting ready for the day and exit my room less than half an hour after waking up.

To my surprise, the rest of the place is practically buzzing with Nik's men's restless energy. Most of them pay me no mind as they march up and down the hallways, off to do our master's bidding.

I go straight to Nik's office, not even bothering to search for him anywhere else. The room's paneled door is wide open, so I enter without knocking.

From behind his desk, Nik raises his eyes, surprised to see me. He smiles at me, and it's hard for me to suppress a sigh. He's exceptionally breathtaking this morning, dressed in a black cashmere sweater and jeans. His sleeves are rolled up, and his hair is an adorable mess.

"You're up early," Nik says.

"Clearly, not as early as everyone else. Did you even get any sleep?"

"Enough."

"What does that mean? How many hours are we talking about here?"

Nik picks up his steaming coffee mug before shrugging. "Definitely less than I wanted, but probably more than I could afford."

"Well, you obviously have a lot going on." I wave my hand around, pointing towards the activity outside his office. "So I don't want to bother you. Just give me my marching orders, boss, and I'll get out of your hair."

Nik's eyes soften, and he comes around his desk until we're mere inches apart. He pulls me into his arms. As soon as the comforting warmth of his body envelopes me, I sigh, melting against him.

"You could never bother me."

I scoff, burrowing myself deeper into his arms. "You and I both know that's not true."

Nik chuckles. "Speak for yourself," he says against my ear.

Dmitri's voice reaches us from the doorway. "Ah, love's in the air, I see."

"Good morning, Dmitri," I say in greeting. Nik's only acknowledgment of him is a disapproving grunt.

"Good morning, Kat. Nik. Am I interrupting something? Please tell me I am," Dmitri says. He sighs whimsically, and I can't help giggling.

"Stop encouraging him," Nik says, chiding me. "He'll grow even more annoying if he thinks he's amusing you."

I shrug. "Well, he *is* amusing me. Besides, I'd argue he's

doing it for your benefit. Your visible disapproval of his teasing remarks is all the motivation he needs."

"No comment. I won't confirm or deny anything," Dmitri says. Nik rolls his eyes.

"Since you're here, Dmitri, there's something you can do for me. You're taking Kat shopping. Or wherever she wants to go," Nik announces. He raises his voice an octave in warning, shooting Dmitri and me a serious look. "Within reason, of course."

I sigh, shaking my head. "I can't believe I'm about to say this, but what the hell are you talking about, Nik? We have work to do."

Nik wastes no time in correcting me. "No, *I* have work to do, which is why I need *you* to go for a ride with Dmitri. You're just too distracting. I can't think straight with you this close to me."

"Oh, come on, Nik," I protest, somehow resisting the urge to kiss him. "It's the bottom of the ninth and the bases are loaded... you can't just bench me now. Not when I'm about to hit a home run. I was so close to getting McGuire to brag about killing Maxim before you threw your little jealous tantrum."

Dmitri groans. "Come on, guys. You're killing me here," he says. "Do you have any idea how frustrating it is that nobody will believe me about this?"

Nik ignores him completely. "Kat, that's out of the question now. McGuire thinks I took his daughter. It's too dangerous. You're not getting within a mile of him."

I sigh. "Just because he's out for your blood doesn't mean he's out for mine. Maybe now he'll be even more motivated to steal me from you. He sure seemed pretty eager to do so last night."

"Thank you for the reminder, but it's unnecessary," Nik says through gritted teeth. "I assure you, I haven't forgotten."

I roll my eyes at him. "My point is that now's the time to strike. He's angry and desperate. Easy pickings."

"No. And that's my final word on this. The risk is too high."

"But the reward outweighs it by a metric ton."

Nik scoffs. He scowls at me, shaking his head with outrage. "It sure as hell doesn't. I won't put you in danger."

"Just think about it, Nik," I plead with him. "Maybe his rage is solely directed at you. For all we know, McGuire might think I'm completely innocent."

"It doesn't matter if you think he does. We're not taking the risk."

I groan in frustration. "Nik—"

He cuts me off before I have a chance to protest. "Save your breath. I won't change my mind about this. The only way you're getting within a mile of McGuire is over my dead body. And I'm a hard man to kill."

"It's true," Dmitri adds, amused. "Better men than you have tried, Kat."

"Maybe I'm the right *woman* for the job."

"I know you think I'm being unreasonable, but trust me, I could say the same thing about you right now," Nik says. He has the nerve to smirk at me. As I narrow my eyes at him, he adds, "Hey, if you want to make me pay, here's an idea—take my credit card and put it to work. Do your worst."

"Careful now, Nik. I think you're dangerously close to underestimating me."

Nik grins at me, and my anger dissipates a little. "Oh, I'm not making that mistake again. Trust me on that one." He winks at me.

Dmitri sighs, shaking his head in mock despair. "He just winked at you," he says. "I never thought I'd live to see the day Nikolai Stefanovich would playfully flirt with a woman."

I roll my eyes at Dmitri before grabbing his arm. "Come on, Ken," I say. "We're going for a ride."

"I think you just insulted me," Dmitri says with a laugh.

I turn to face Nik again. "No goodbye kiss for you this time," I inform him.

Nik sighs, shaking his head in mock disappointment. "Six figures really don't buy you as much today as they used to, do they?"

I scoff. "Six figures? Please. So much for you not underestimating me. For your information, I happen to know how much you're supposedly worth. I wouldn't bother getting out of the house for anything less than a cool million."

"Get something red, skimpy, and lacy, and I'll consider it money well spent," Nik says under his breath.

Dmitri chokes back his laughter as I level Nik with a no-nonsense look and stop by the office's door. "Feeling lucky, are you?" I ask with a raised eyebrow.

"Ask me later tonight," Nik says, winking at me again. He gives me a sexy, sexy smirk before grabbing his phone from his back pocket.

"Let's go, Dmitri. We aren't coming back until Nik gets a call from the bank. I won't stop swiping his card until he begs me for mercy."

Dmitri chuckles. "Yes, ma'am."

"Dmitri," Nik says before we have a chance to leave. "Keep her safe. If anything looks off, get her home immediately."

"Don't worry, Nik. I'll keep your little *kiska* safe and sound."

"Watch it." Nik halfheartedly throws a paperweight at him, but Dmitri easily dodges it with a laugh.

I roll my eyes and pull Dmitri out of Nik's office.

Dmitri and I drive mostly in silence. He hums to himself through most of the ride, tapping his fingers on the steering wheel to the beat of my playlist. For his benefit, I picked the most bubblegum pop soundtrack I could find, hoping to annoy him as payback for not taking my side with Nik earlier. Of course, it didn't work. Much to my chagrin, Dmitri took my girly music in stride.

While he dutifully and gleefully takes me from one designer shop to another, I cheer up. A content sigh escapes me as we enter one of my favorite high-end boutiques downtown. The crisp air-conditioned air blissfully welcomes us.

"See, this isn't so bad, is it?" Dmitri asks, with a teasing glint in his eyes. He smiles at me.

"I suppose not," I say with a slight shrug.

"I'll tell you something, Kat. If I had a multibillionaire man handing me his credit card and telling me to do my worst, I wouldn't waste my time pouting about it. Not a second, I tell you."

"Pouting, huh?" I ask, raising an eyebrow at him as we look around the store.

"Well, don't worry. It's a good look on you. You pull it off beautifully," he says diplomatically. "Which is why Nikolai Stefanovich, of all men, handed you his credit card in the first place."

"Are you saying I'm all beauty and no brains?"

Dmitri emphatically shakes his head. "Of course not. I know better than to underestimate you, believe me. Besides, you obviously have more brains than all of us together, if the way you have him wrapped around your little finger is any indication."

"Dmitri..."

He shrugs. "Well, it's true. You've managed what no one else has before. Congratulations, *milaya*."

"You're going to get yourself into trouble."

Dmitri scoffs. "Just like you, Kat, I'm very rarely actually in trouble. Especially when women are involved."

"Oh, I see. Silly me. All this time, I assumed you were clueless about your good looks. But clearly, I was wrong if you're bragging about exploiting the power of your boyish charms."

With a heart-stopping smile, he dramatically winces, clutching his chest. "Ouch. Boyish charms, huh? You wound me, Kat,"

I roll my eyes at him. "I really doubt that. Besides, as you know very well, I meant it as a compliment."

"All I know is that you're ignoring the fact that I'm obviously all man. I won't hear any of that boyish charm talk. I'm not that much younger than you."

"Oh, yeah, right. Refresh my memory... How do you know that, exactly? You mean from when you spied on me for Nik, right?" I playfully punch his arm.

Dmitri shrugs, smirking. "Hey, it's not much, but it's honest work."

I scoff. "Not even close."

"Well, maybe not. But the way I see it, I was doing God's work in a way."

"Is that how you refer to Nik now? Laying it on a bit thick, don't you think?"

It's Dmitri's turn to roll his eyes. With a grin, he playfully messes my hair. "No, smart-ass. I mean it was all part of the process of bringing the two of you together. If you think about it, I was basically playing Cupid."

"I don't think you realize how ridiculous that sounds."

"Well, what can I say? I'm a romantic, *milaya*."

"Watch it, Dmitri. I happen to know Nik has broken men's hands for less than that."

Dmitri sighs. "I still can't believe he did that. I was half sure you two were fucking with me until I saw Vladmir with his hand in a cast with my own eyes."

"All I'm saying is I wouldn't push Nik if I were you. He's under a lot of pressure right now."

"No kidding. And unlike some of us, I doubt I'd get his black AmEx as a reward for challenging him."

"Maybe not," I say with a smug smile. "But it's obvious he has a soft spot for you. And you know it."

"Perhaps. But who knows? It's a brave new world I'm living in right now, where my good friend Nik does wild things like breaking his soldier's hand over a woman. But don't worry, Kat. You're safe with me. When it comes to you, I'm no threat to Nik, and he knows it, too."

"Well, duh, Captain Obvious. You don't need to tell *me* that."

His grin grows wider. "Oh, I'm telling him you said that."

I roll my eyes at him for what feels like the millionth time today. Curious, I say, "I'm guessing you're referring to the mysterious woman you mentioned before."

Dmitri sighs. "You make it sound so dramatic."

"Am I wrong?"

"I guess not," he says noncommittally.

"Don't get shy now. You seemed eager enough to stick your nose in my business."

"Your business is my business."

"Is that right?"

"You bet. As long as my *pakhan* is your business, I'll always get up close and personal with you."

"Lucky me," I say sarcastically. "Well, turnabout is fair play. So, spill the beans. I'm dying to know all about your secret girlfriend."

"Girlfriend isn't the word I'd use," he says with a sigh, mindlessly fingering a necklace half hidden under his shirt.

I study him for a moment. The always ice-cold Dmitri is restless, his slender fingers—covered in a ton of minor cuts—anxiously fidgeting. It's so out of character for him that I don't immediately notice the gorgeous emerald hanging from his delicate gold chain.

Curiosity almost bursting out of my chest, I ask him, "Well, does your not-girlfriend have a name?"

Dmitri gives me a distant look, and I know he won't answer my question. Still, I'm eager to hear what he says instead, having a feeling that whatever comes out of his mouth will be another piece of the delicious puzzle that is his love life.

I never get to find out for sure, though, as an ear-splitting scream startles us.

7

KAT

The now-familiar sound of shots being fired reverberates through the store.

I gasp, looking around the shop to determine where the bone-chilling noise originated. Dmitri reaches inside his jacket for his gun before swiftly pulling me to the ground.

"It's just our luck," I groan. "Our day off, and these fuckers decide to rob this store of all places."

After frantically scanning our surroundings, Dmitri says, "No chance. It's the Irish."

I gasp. "What?! You don't know that!"

Dmitri's hand covers my mouth. "Shh. I'm sure of it."

And God damn him, his suspicions are immediately confirmed as a heavily accented voice shouts, "Where the hell is she? Find her now."

"I guess Nik was right," I say.

"You think?" Dmitri asks.

"How the hell did they find us, anyway?"

"They've probably been tailing us since we left the penthouse. I should've spotted that." He shakes his head, clenching his jaw.

"I'm sure there's a reason you didn't," I say in a poor attempt to reassure him.

"We have to get the fuck out of here now," he says in a hushed tone. "We're outnumbered and outgunned, and I can't get the cavalry here on time. If they find us, they'll kill me and take you. And if you die on my watch, Nik will find a way to resurrect me so that he can kill me himself."

"I'm so fucking done being kidnapped by fucking mafia men," I mutter through gritted teeth. "Let's get out of here, then. Lead the way."

After grabbing my hand, he does. Dmitri makes me crawl through the store as McGuire's men, in their search for us, unleash sheer terror on the poor salespeople. Somehow, we make it to the back of the store unnoticed. Luckily, we find an emergency exit.

"Wait! If you open the door, it might sound an alarm," I say to Dmitri in warning.

He shrugs. "We're out of options. Get ready. We're making a run for it. Whatever happens, run as fast as you can. Don't look back, don't wait for me. Just run. We have to get to the main road."

"But your car is parked out back."

"Forget about the car. Our best chance is to get to the main road. It's busier, and we can lose them there."

I open my mouth to question this flawed plan of his, but I change my mind after thinking better of it. He's right. We're out of options.

"Ready?" Dmitri asks. I nod. "On the count of three." He quietly counts down, and we run for our lives.

No alarm goes off once we shove the door open, but it doesn't matter. The mere act of pushing the heavy metal exit door makes enough noise to raise the dead, giving away our position. We hear the Irish excitedly yell behind us as we run through a back alley.

"Go, go, go," Dmitri yells.

For once, I listen.

Just as we get to the main road, I spot the beautiful, miraculous sight of a cab driving down the street. We frantically wave at the driver, and—thank our lucky stars—the man pulls over.

Dmitri pushes me into the vehicle before I can even react to the car slowing down before me. He barks the penthouse's address at the taxi driver, promising him a small fortune if he can get us to Nik's place without stopping for any reason.

The man eagerly puts the pedal to the metal, and I turn to Dmitri. "Shouldn't we try to lose McGuire's men before returning to the penthouse?"

He shakes his head. "There's no point. It's not like they don't know where Nik lives. We'll be safe at the penthouse. Trust me—if they had the manpower or firepower to hit it, they would have by now."

I'm no mafia affairs expert, but I think Dmitri's probably right. He pulls out his phone, and, after glancing at the screen, he exhales loudly, cursing.

"Fuck. That motherfucker hit Nik hard," Dmitri says under his breath.

"What do you mean?" I ask, alarmed.

"I didn't feel my phone vibrate, so I had no idea until just now. Right after we left home, McGuire torched half a dozen of Nik's properties without warning. Nik must be so fucking mad."

"Is he okay?" I ask, holding my breath. My voice breaks slightly, and my vision gets blurry.

"I'm sure he's fine. Like I said, they wouldn't dare hit the penthouse, and Nik knows it. Even McGuire isn't that bold or stupid. He's trying to flush Nik out. I guess that explains the courtesy visit his goons just paid us."

"Are you saying they were trying to take us to use us as bait to lure Nik out of the penthouse?" Blood-red anger washes over me. I feel it overtake me almost to a physical level, with every inch of my skin growing warmer and tingly as the feeling takes hold inside of me. I've had it with being a pawn in these ludicrous mafia schemes...

"That'd be my guess," Dmitri says with a shrug. "Damn it, Nik. Pick up the fucking phone."

"He isn't picking up the phone? Oh, god, Dmitri—what if something happened to him?"

"Nothing's happened to him, Kat. I'd have heard it by now. He's probably just busy or trying to get a hold of us."

"Well, let's keep trying to get him on the phone. I need to hear his voice to know he's okay." I fish inside my purse for my phone. Hands shaking, I manage to pull it out and ring his number.

Dmitri and I have no luck getting a hold of Nik before we reach the penthouse. Dmitri pulls out a thick wad of cash out of his pocket and hands it to the taxi driver, while almost simultaneously dragging me out of the car.

After frantically searching the area, Dmitri quickly leads us inside the building, completely ignoring the people in the lobby. Less than a full minute after the cab stopped out front, he has us in the elevator. He exhales loudly with relief.

"I'm sure Nik's waiting for us," he says with a smile. I can't tell if his reassurance is for my benefit or his.

As soon as the elevator comes to a stop, Dmitri completely leaves my mind as I desperately search for Nik. Inside the penthouse, it's complete pandemonium. The commotion that greets us on the other side of the elevator doors takes me by surprise, but I probably should've expected it. After all, all hell has broken loose for the *bratva* since we left.

More guns than I've ever seen in my life are being passed around. For a second, I think I see a handful of grenades, too, but I must be mistaken.

Over two dozen men move with military efficiency, donning bulletproof vests while talking among themselves in Russian.

My legs almost give out under me, and I stagger sideways when I spot Nik tucking a pistol in his waistband. I exhale a breath I didn't realize I was holding in until now, urging my shaky limbs to get me close to him.

"Oh, thank God you're fine," I say.

Nik's eyes find me right away as his head whips in my direction at the sound of my voice. "Kat." His voice is more than a little rough as he shoves his men out of his way. Before he even has a chance to do anything else, I leap into his arms, knowing without any shadow of a doubt that he will catch me. He clutches me almost painfully tight to his chest. I bury my head in his neck, and he kisses my hair over and over again.

"Are you okay?" Nik asks.

"Yeah, I'm completely fine now. Are you hurt?" I ask, turning to inspect him.

Nik glares at me as if I just asked him the most ridiculous question ever. "Why would I be hurt?" he asks with a slight frown.

"Dmitri told me McGuire attacked the *bratva*."

"A bunch of unoccupied warehouses. No one's hurt. He's trying to bait me." Nik kisses my forehead. While glancing at Dmitri, he acidly asks, "Why didn't either of you answer your phones? Once I got word McGuire openly hit us, I tried calling you to tell you to come home. I was crazy out of my mind, worrying they would track you down. But thank God he didn't. You're both home safe now, and that's all that matters. But for fuck's sake, pick up your fucking phones next time."

I stare at Nik with confusion. "You don't know," I say.

"Don't know what?" he asks, turning to look at Dmitri.

"Connor and a few others came after us in a shop downtown less than twenty minutes ago. Bold as fuck, Nik. Guns blazing in broad daylight, in the heart of the tourist district of all places," Dmitri says.

Around us, all *bratva* soldiers freeze in place after hearing Dmitri's news.

"They did *what*?" Nik yells. His fingertips painfully sink into my arms as he grips me too tightly.

"I'm not fucking with you. They were looking for Kat. We barely made it out."

Thankfully, Nik lets go of my arms. Gently, he lifts my chin, scanning me from head to toe. Then he glances at Dmitri, checking for any visible wounds.

"Did they hurt you?" Nik asks me softly.

I shake my head. "No, I'm fine, Nik. Dmitri, my knight in shining armor, was excellent thinking on his feet. This damsel in distress has no complaints."

Dmitri's stunning pale blue eyes glint with humor as he turns on his heels to face me, an appropriately inappropriate comment undoubtedly on the tip of his tongue.

"Don't even think about cracking a joke about this," Nik says in warning to Dmitri. Uncharacteristically wisely, Dmitri shuts his mouth.

"And you—" Nik says to me, holding my face with both

hands. "You're never leaving my sight ever again. At least not until that motherfucker is dead and gone."

I laugh, although not unkindly. I rise on my toes to press a kiss on Nik's cheek. "I appreciate the concern, but we'll talk about this later. You're not thinking clearly right now."

Nik's eyes darken, and I'm sure he fully intends to put me in my place, but I'm saved by the bell.

"We got him," Vladmir says, marching into the room. "Lucien sent us word of McGuire's location, and I've confirmed it myself. Just saw the fucker with my own eyes, Nikolai. As you suspected, he's hiding near the port. A studio a block south of the docks, to be exact."

With no hint of hesitation, Nik cooly says, "Let's go."

Not needing to hear it twice, his men snap into action. Shortly after, the room is practically empty.

To my surprise, Nik seems intent on following them. I watch with horror as he slips a knife in his pocket. Another one follows the first, cleverly hidden inside his boot.

"Where do you think you are going?" I ask.

Nik gives me a confused look. "You heard Vladmir. We've tracked McGuire down."

"Yeah, and I saw your little death squad arm themselves to their teeth. They can handle it. Let them."

Nik laughs. "Come on, Kat. I can't just sit here and let McGuire's direct attack on me and my men—and worst of all, on you—slide."

"If you retaliate, you'll start a war. I thought the entire point of my involvement in this scheme of yours was to avoid that."

His eyes soften. "Things change, *milaya*. If he wants war this badly, then I'll give it to him."

"You don't mean that."

"I do, Kat. Enough is enough. It's time. And frankly, I'm glad. I'll be done with this nightmare at last. I'll do my duty to Maxim, and I'll never have to endure the sight of another man flirting with you ever again." His eyes smolder, and he sinks his fingers between my hair, sighing with unconcealed pleasure.

"Nik, no," I say, shaking my head with horror. "This is a mistake. He's dangerous. You've said it yourself so many times. You're rushing into this without thinking about it rationally."

He shakes his head, smiling at me. "It'll be okay, Kat. You'll see."

"You don't know that," I say, my voice shaking. "If you absolutely won't listen to reason, then at least don't be stupid enough to go after him yourself. What's the point of having your own personal army if you can't send them to kill your enemies for you?"

Nik chuckles, kissing my forehead. "I'd never do that. I could never have another man do my dirty work for me, Kat. I can't ask my men to put their lives on the line for the *bratva* if I won't do the same."

I scoff. "That's the stupidest thing you've ever said."

"Besides," Nik adds, ignoring my interruption, "this is too personal. He took my best friend from me and dared to try to harm my woman. After plotting to steal you from me, too. It'll be my pleasure to take him out myself."

"Nik—" I say, not too proud to beg. But I see in his eyes that it's pointless. He's not changing his mind.

After glancing at Dmitri, Nik says, "I need you to stay here."

Dmitri groans. "You can't be serious."

"You'll stay and protect Kat."

"Kat will be fine here, Nik. She doesn't need me. My place is with you."

Nik shakes his head. "I can't go after McGuire if I don't know with absolute certainty that she's safe."

Dmitri beseechingly glares at Nik, echoing my frustrated plea from earlier. "Nik, come on. Don't do this to me."

"You're the closest thing I have to my own blood now, Dmitri," Nik says, pointing out what's clear to anyone with eyes and ears.

Dmitri hesitates, and I realize I have to intervene. "Nik, Dmitri's right. I'll be fine here. You should let him go with you."

Nik scowls at me and Dmitri. "You two seem confused about what kind of operation I'm running here. This is not a democracy," he says, raising his voice.

"Nik, please. Let him go with you. Please. For me. I'll feel so much better if I know he's looking out for you." My voice embarrassingly cracks, and my vision gets blurry as tears threaten to run down my face.

With a sigh, Nik rolls his eyes before pulling me into his arms again. He presses a tender kiss against my forehead, failing to hide his amused grin. "Come now, *milaya*. I'm flattered, but there's no need to cry for me. I'll be fine. I don't need my *bratishka* taking care of me."

Dmitri's touched expression—plus his sharp intake of breath—tells me that Nik called him something sentimental and special. His unusual silence confirms it.

I grab handfuls of Nik's sweater and pull him closer to me. "Please," I say with a sniff, pressing a kiss to his bare throat. "For me. For my peace of mind."

I expect Nik to shut me down immediately, but he hesitates. After a moment, he sighs. "I have one condition," he says. "You'll promise me you won't step out of the penthouse. You *will* listen to my men guarding the place."

I promptly agree, nodding my head. "Okay. I promise."

"Actually—" Nik says. "I have a better idea. You'll lock yourself in my bedroom with the gun I gave you. If anyone who isn't me tries to come through the door, shoot them."

"No problem," I say. If he's going to be somewhat reasonable, then I will, too.

Nik kisses the top of my head. "Good girl. Now get to it." He playfully slaps my butt. Still teary-eyed, I don't even protest.

I turn to face Dmitri. "Please be careful," I say. "And make him be careful, too. Look out for him and yourself."

Dmitri nods, and I take a deep breath, bracing myself to say goodbye to Nik. But one look at his beautiful face—his warm brown eyes and his glossy dark hair—and I break down. My tears come rushing, and I launch myself into his arms, hugging his neck as hard as I can. Just thinking that I might never get to do it again makes me sob even harder.

Nik hugs me back, wrapping his arms around my waist. "*Milaya*," he says with a sigh, chuckling. "I'm flattered, but there's no need for tears. I'll be fine. You're not getting rid of me so easily."

"I can't believe you're laughing," I say between sobs.

He chuckles again. "I don't mean to. How about this—why don't you wait to eat dinner with me again? I'll bring a pizza home. Or whatever you want."

I sniff. "Bring yourself home."

Nik smirks. "I already told you I will. Now, be a good girl and go to my room. I'll see you soon."

"Promise."

"I pinky swear." He laughs, his eyes melting.

With a final kiss on my forehead, Nik untangles my arms from around his neck.

I watch, cold inside, as he and Dmitri leave me. Hopefully, not for good.

I'm not sure how long I stand there, but eventually, my tears dry, and I walk to Nik's room. On any other day, I'd be excited to snoop around such prime real estate. Right now, I couldn't care less. I barely even see the room's furnishings and decorations. I can't muster any other emotion besides worry and despair as I sit on Nik's bed.

I sniff again, trying to keep my tears at bay, and I'm assaulted by his familiar scent. It's a painful reminder of the warmth of his skin against mine, the softness of his hair against my fingertips...

If I never get to feel him again, to taste him...

I close my eyes, searching for a reprieve from this unbearable emotional and sensorial avalanche, but all I see is him—the glimmer in his eyes as we bicker or as I tease him relentlessly.

There's nowhere to go, nowhere to hide—no way to avoid the reality that I might never be with him again. And I never got to kiss him goodbye...

Before I even understand what I'm doing, I'm on my feet at the bedroom door. In an instant, I'm running towards the elevator.

Some unfamiliar men try to stop me, but I pay them no mind. I lose them with little effort. What they have in size, I make up for in speed.

The elevator ride takes years off my life, but at last, its doors open up, and I'm at the garage.

I locate Nik in a heartbeat. Thank God he hasn't left yet. His back is turned to me, and he's talking to someone I don't recognize.

A couple of his men exchange worried glances when they see me, uncomfortably murmuring between themselves. Their eyes dart towards me, and it's clear they aren't sure of what to do.

As I make my way to Nik, his back and shoulders tense up. Slowly, he turns in my direction. When his eyes land on me, his expression belies his complete shock and disbelief. Then, pure, unadulterated fury takes over his handsome face.

"What the hell are you doing here?" he shouts. "I'm pretty sure I told you to stay inside. I thought you promised me you would."

His rage burns brighter once he spots the guards he left at the penthouse struggling to catch up with me. He narrows his eyes at me with undisguised anger while yelling at me, rambling and ranting.

I don't hear a word of it, and I don't pretend to. I don't even pretend to care. Instead, I run up to him. Then I leap into his arms. Reflexively, he catches me. Before he has a chance to process this recent development, I'm already kissing his mouth—hard.

I tug him closer by his sweater and hair, pouring all of my longing and troubled emotions into this kiss.

Stunned, Nik just stands there for a moment, letting me kiss him with all that I have. His surprise, however, quickly gives way to passion. With a pained groan against my mouth, he kisses me even harder.

Too soon, Dmitri clears his throat next to us.

Against my better judgment, I let Nik break our kiss. He gently sets me down on my feet. He leans forward and whispers, "This isn't over. We'll continue this. Later."

I agree, nodding.

"Now, go back inside and do as I've told you," Nik says. "I better see your ass on my bed when I get back."

Still speechless, I nod again.

With a final warning glance, Nik starts getting into a black SUV.

Finally finding my voice, I say, "Come back to me, Nik."

Wordlessly, he turns back to face me. Quick and hard, he kisses me again. It's a brief, fierce caress. It's over in a second. He rests his forehead against mine before murmuring against my lips, "Wild horses couldn't keep me away."

Without another word, he gets into the car.

Helpless to do anything else, I watch him drive away.

8

NIK

As it has become the norm for me since that fateful night when I first met Kat, my temper gets the best of me. Again. In what I would like to think is an uncharacteristically childish display of frustration, I practically kick my bedroom door open. It slams against the wall with a satisfying bang.

With a startled gasp, Kat almost jumps out of her skin at the sudden noise. "Thank God. You're alive," she says seconds later, rising from where she sat on my bed. Without warning, she jumps into my arms. It sure seems like it is going to become a habit for her. I have to bite back a sigh. I could get used to this.

Her body is shaking as she wraps her legs around my waist while her arms clutch my neck tightly. I hug her back just as hard, holding her firmly against me. With an almost imperceptible groan, Kat buries her face against my neck, inhaling deeply.

"Did you just... smell me?" I ask.

Unabashedly, she says, "Oh, yeah. And I'm about to taste you, too."

Diamond Dream

And God help me, true to her word, she does.

Kat slants her head, kissing my mouth like she does everything else—with her own brand of passionate intensity and effortless expertise. As her tongue curls around mine, I struggle to catch my breath. I pull her even closer, resigning myself to the idea that closer will never be near enough when it comes to her.

Just as tempestuously as the embrace started, it ends. Kat breaks our kiss with little warning, pushing me away almost forcefully.

"Hang on a second, Nik," she says, her breath as erratic as mine. "Are you hurt? Let me take a good look at you."

With a shake of my head, I say, "Looking is overrated. I think you should go back to tasting me instead."

Unfortunately, Kat doesn't oblige me. Instead, she scans every inch of me with her watchful eyes.

"I'm fine," I say, scoffing as she fusses over me. It's an unfamiliar feeling. I can't remember the last time a woman worried about whether I made it back home in one piece. It's entirely possible one never has.

"I'll be the judge of that," she says, scolding me while still assessing me for damage.

I roll my eyes and spin on my heels, lifting my arms and giving her a full, three-hundred-and-sixty-degree view. "See? Like I said, I'm fine."

Kat raises an eyebrow, clearly unimpressed at my surly tone. "Hmm. I'm not so sure about that, Nik. Why don't you take your clothes off so I can be certain?"

Her eyes glint mischievously and I play along. "As your boss, I must say I'm very impressed by your dedication. Something tells me you just might earn yourself a raise."

"I see that," she pointedly says with a smirk, deliberately

glancing at my jeans just below my waist. "What can I say? I'm nothing but thorough."

"Ah, I wouldn't say that. It's been my absolute pleasure to learn your many other things beyond that, *milaya*."

The smile she gives me makes my knees feel weak. It reaches all the way to her eyes, turning them a deep midnight blue.

"Only good things, I hope," she says.

"The best, Kat. The very best."

After this frustrating emotional roller-coaster of a day, I can't wait a second longer to have her in my arms again. Especially not when her beautiful eyes glow with warmth and pleasure whenever they meet mine.

While holding her hand, I slowly draw her into my arms. "Come here," I say against her lips.

Kat wraps her arms around my neck, placing a quick, almost dismissive kiss against my mouth before pulling away again. "So, how did it go?" she asks with a smile as I sigh with frustration.

"Can we talk about this later?" I ask, even though I already know the answer. Like a dog with a bone, Kat isn't likely to let this go.

"No way," she says, looking at me as if I might be out of my mind for even asking. "I've been sitting here for hours, biting my nails and wondering what had happened to you. I can't wait any longer."

With a shake of my head, I lean forward until my mouth reaches the sweet-smelling column of her neck. I kiss it languidly. "Then, *kiska*, I believe we're at what they call an impasse. Because after dreaming about having you back in my arms all afternoon, I can't fucking wait, either."

Kat groans in frustration. "Nikolai Stefanovich—be serious."

I nip her ear lobe. "Katherine Devereaux—I assure you, I've never been more serious in my life. I warned you we would continue this later."

Kat rolls her eyes before pushing against my chest. "The sooner you tell me everything that happened with McGuire, the sooner we get to do just that."

After cursing under my breath, I give her the most disapproving look I can manage. "You're a piece of work, did you know that?"

She shrugs. "Duh. And we both know you wouldn't have me any other way. Now, spill the beans. How did it go?"

I resist the urge to grind my teeth and grimace. "Well, how should I put this, Kat? Let's just say that coming home to find your pretty ass in my bedroom—on my bed, no less—is the only good thing that came from this whole pointless afternoon."

"No luck finding McGuire, then?" she asks with a slight frown.

I shake my head. "No, there's no trace of him. Lucien's intel was bad—or outdated, at least. McGuire was gone."

With a deep exhale, Kat hugs me, and it almost unmans me. To my absolute dismay, my cheeks grow warm and I find myself blushing, embarrassed that she's witnessing my failure at taking down the Irish family's boss. I'm glad Kat's head is pressed against my chest and she doesn't see it. A bit awkwardly, I wrap my arms around her shoulders.

"Oh, well," she says. "Nobody's hurt, right?"

"No, but—"

"Well, then today's still a win in my book."

I scoff at that ridiculous statement. McGuire got away with directly attacking me—and worst of all, Kat—unpunished. Under no circumstances would I ever count that as a win.

"Kat—" I say, but she interrupts me.

"I mean it. We're all going to live to fight another day."

"Including McGuire."

She dismisses that fact as insignificant with a decisive wave of her hand. "It's just a matter of time before you track him down. All will be well when it ends well, Nik. And it will. I have no doubts about that. Trust me."

"I'm trying, believe me. But you have to understand, Kat—I won't be able to rest until he's dead. It was one thing for him to murder Maxim. For better or for worse, Maxim made his bed. Don't get me wrong, I'll have McGuire's head for it. But Maxim knew the consequences of fucking around with the man's daughter. But for him to come after you…"

She sighs. "Nik—"

"I'll make him pay for what he did to Maxim—and me, to an extent. But Kat, for what he did to you, I'll make sure he suffers."

Wide-eyed, Kat shakes her head. "I don't need you to fight my battles for me."

I shrug. "I know. It doesn't matter."

She shakes her head frantically. "I don't want the weight of an all-out mafia war on my head. I can't even bear the idea."

"It isn't on you, *milaya*. It's on him. He knew what he was doing when he came after you. He forced my hand, and I can't hold back any longer."

"Nik—" She grabs handfuls of my sweater and shakes me, undoubtedly attempting to force some sense into me. She doesn't realize it's far too late for that. "This is madness. You don't want this."

I laugh humorlessly. "I don't?"

"No. Think of your men. Think of Dmitri. I know you don't want their blood on our hands any more than I do."

"Kat, I know it's hard for you to understand this, but they don't expect or want me to show McGuire mercy. He openly challenged me. It would be a show of weakness. That's not our way."

"If something were to happen to you, it'd destroy me." I silence her with a quick kiss as my heart painfully tightens inside my chest. Her heartfelt cries and pleas out of concern for me—of all things—are dangerously close to destroying *me*.

"Kat, listen—I can't hold back any longer." I'll lose my mind if she isn't mine at last before the night ends.

Tears threaten to stream down her face as she glares at me, her hopelessness unmistakable in her expression. She must think my confession is about McGuire. "Nik, please..."

With a shake my head, I lift Kat's chin until she's looking into my eyes. I lean forward, resting my forehead against hers before repeating myself unfalteringly. "Kat. I can't hold back any longer."

Her frown deepens, and I close the distance between us, kissing her. I try to pour everything I don't know how to express into that kiss. I need to make her understand how much I crave her... how much I need her.

"Nik—" Kat says with a gasp, breaking our kiss.

Unyielding, I grasp the back of her neck, sinking my fingers into the soft, luscious mass of her dark hair. "I won't hold back any longer, Kat. Not when it comes to you."

9

NIK

Kat's eyes widen.

For a timeless moment, I hold my breath as she stares at me wordlessly. Then, with the same heart-wrenching, resolute decisiveness she does everything else, she eagerly presses her warm, soft lips against mine.

God have mercy.

In the same heartbeat, Kat throws her arms around my neck. She clings to me as if her life depends on it, and her lush curves slowly slide down my frame as she hangs from my neck. Still, she doesn't pull her mouth away from mine.

I step back, staggering until I lean back against the wall as my legs wobble. The scent of her skin—a mouthwatering blend of bitter oranges and freesias—drives me wild. I sink deeper into our kiss and under her spell as her kips devours mine unabashedly. My mouth craves the sweet taste of her, and I melt under her ardent kiss.

Kat runs her fingers through my hair and sighs into my mouth, clinging to me even harder. "Nik, I need you so much."

My chest tightens and aches, and I groan into her mouth. "I need you more," I say against her velvety lips.

Kat shakes her head, but I sink back into her, taking her mouth again. Her lips yield to me, and her tongue welcomes mine. Unable to wait any longer, I scoop her into my arms. She wraps her legs around my waist, and, on unsteady legs, I manage to carry her to my bed.

Almost reverently, I place her on top of the deep blue covers, then I step back in an attempt to savor the moment. At last, after all those nights spent by myself here yearning for her, I have her right where I've dreamed of her...

Her silky hair fans out around her face, and she breathlessly stretches her hands in my direction. I wrap my fingers around hers and let her pull me towards her.

A small smile curves her mesmerizing lips as my body covers hers. Her mouth immediately finds mine again, and she impatiently tugs at my sweater after hooking her right leg around my hips.

Breaking our kiss as briefly as possible, I hurry to oblige her, quickly pulling my sweater over my head.

Kat whimpers, and her dark blue eyes turn almost black as she stares at me. She wraps her hands around my wrists before pulling me back towards her. Before I can react, she flips me over, reversing our positions.

Next thing I know, I'm on my back with Kat sitting on my hips.

She bites her bottom lip while slowly running her hands down my torso until they rest on my belt buckle. With no hint of hesitation, she bends over at the waist, raining soft kisses on my neck.

"*Kiska...*" I say.

"You're so gorgeous it hurts me," Kat says as her delicate caress descends upon my chest. It makes me want to weep.

This beautiful, bewitching creature wants to lavish me, of all men, with her tender kisses.

Helpless to do anything but let her do as she will, I sigh. My exhale swiftly morphs into a groan as her kisses turn hungrier once she reaches my stomach. Her tongue mercilessly lashes against my skin. I can't manage to catch my breath for the life of me.

Hastily, her fingers make quick work of my belt. Before I know it, my pants are unzipped. Eager to help her, I kick my jeans out of the way as gracefully as I can manage at the moment, which isn't graceful at all.

Kat wastes no time as her fingers wrap around the waistband of my boxers.

If she keeps at this pace, it will be over before it starts.

"*Kiska...*" I halfheartedly protest. "Slow down."

With a shake of her head, she retorts, "Sorry, *miliy*—no can do. You've known what I look like naked this entire time, while I've done nothing but daydream about learning the same about you. Fair's fair."

She *daydreamed* about me? About what I look like naked?

With a choked laugh, I somehow say, "It can't be fair, *kiska*, because I can't ever compare to you. No one can."

I grab her waist and reverse our positions so her back is against the mattress, and I'm finally nestled between the maddening warmth of her thighs.

Kat sighs with a smile. "Sweet-talker."

I shake my head. "It's true. One look at you and I was done for. You've had me wrapped around your little finger since day one."

Tired of wasting time talking, I rush to match her level of undress to mine. With another sigh, she lets me, languidly smiling as I peel one article of clothing after the other from her body.

Soon, her body is bared to me, and I bask in her unequaled beauty. While kissing her lips, I reverently brush my trembling fingers down her neck, against her breasts, coming to a stop against her stomach. It quivers a little, and I draw small circles on her soft skin with my palm.

Unable to restrain myself, I rub my cheek against hers, marveling at the softness of her face.

I half sigh, half groan against her neck. "You're more beautiful and precious to me than all the diamonds in the world—more than all the stars in the sky. *Ya skhozhu po tebe s uma.*"

She pulls my hair until my eyes meet hers, waiting. An unspoken question hangs in the air between us. With another sigh, I comply, unable to deny her anything. "I'm crazy about you. That's what it means."

"Nik—" she says, then her mouth is on mine again. I'm more than eager to return her kiss. "I need you and want you more than I've ever thought was possible."

As if to prove her point, Kat's lips press against mine almost painfully before traveling down my throat. She wraps both her legs around my waist before pulling my boxers down. This time, I don't stop her. Her hand envelopes my cock, and the warmth and softness of her palm almost undo me. I groan. "Kat..."

"I always want you closer and closer. But it's never close enough," she says against my neck. Against my mouth this time, she says, "If you aren't inside me soon, I think I might die."

Roughly, I kiss her, moaning her name into her mouth. I grab her wrists to pin them above her head with one of my hands. I lose myself in the deep blue of her eyes for good. "*Kiska*, you'll be the death of me."

I wish I could be tender and patient. I wish I could slow down and pace myself, enjoying this moment to its fullest. But I'm just a man. It's beyond my abilities. Her soft confession unleashes something wild deep inside me—a desperate, insatiable hunger that has been hibernating for too long.

As my mouth closes around the hard tip of her breast and she cries out my name, I close my eyes, feeling my chest tighten. I never knew it was possible to need someone like I need her. No woman has ever wanted me like this. No woman has ever wanted me for me—not for my money or power. But because of who I am. For one to want me this badly, even after seeing firsthand the worst of me... Even more incredibly, for Kat to be this woman...Try as I have, I can't for the life of me get her out of my head or my heart.

Kat arches her back, running her fingers through my hair. While clasping my head against her chest, she pants my name over and over again. It's enough to bring even a better man than me to his knees.

Her hand slips my hold, and she wraps it around my painfully hard cock again. I groan against her chest. Almost too forcefully, I grab her wrist again and restrain her once more with one of my hands.

"Nik, please," she says, protesting. I shake my head, panting hard.

Understanding that by some miracle, my beautiful, irresistible Kat feels just as impatient as I do, I waste no time bringing my other hand between her thighs to part her lips.

"Yes, yes, Nik..."

As my fingers slip inside her to find her warm and wet, I can't hold back my groan. After tracing the edge of her opening, I press my tongue against the peaks of her breasts. I circle them with my tongue just as my fingers do the same around her clitoris.

"Please, please, please," Kat says, thrashing around.

I press my thumb against the little nub while sucking the tip of her breast. As my hand rubs her flesh, my mouth attempts to match the same rhythm.

Kat stops trying to escape my hold, spreading her legs wide instead. When my movements speed up, her breathing grows shallow while her cries grow more urgent.

She sighs. "Fuck. Nik, I'm close. Please..."

Desperate to watch her unravel before my eyes, I increase my pace.

Kat, however, shakes her head weakly. "Please, Nik, I'm close. Come with me. I want to do it with you. I need you inside me now."

With a hoarse cry against her skin, I relent, giving in.

I let go of her hands to position myself against her entrance, and she wraps her legs around my waist.

Her eyes hold mine as I slowly enter her.

All the air in my lungs rushes out of me as her warm, wet pussy embraces me. I groan, cursing in Russian and English, as she grips me tightly. She quivers around me, sending shivers down my spine. With one swift, deep movement, I plunge deep into her.

Kat gasps, and I freeze in place. Fuck.

While holding her head, I sink my fingers into her hair before brushing my lips against her eyes and cheeks. "I'm sorry, *kiska*. So sorry. I'm an idiot. I didn't mean to hurt you. Tell me I didn't hurt you."

Kat sighs, seeking my mouth with hers. "You didn't. It's just an... adjustment. But I'm fine now. I've been dying to feel you again. Don't stop, please."

With a horse groan, I don't even bother resisting her. Still, I begin moving inside her hesitantly, fighting the undeniable urge to lose myself in her. But when Kat moans my name—raising her hips to meet mine, matching my slow pace—I lose any semblance of self-control. At last, I let go, allowing the need, the hunger and the yearning I've been feeling since that last time to take over.

I wish I could say I made gentle love to her—the woman I've grown to care for in such a profound way since that first fateful night.

I wish I could say I took the time to savor this moment, to experience everything I've craved my entire life.

All I can say instead is that I'll make sure we have plenty of time for sweet, tender lovemaking, even if it kills me.

But it won't be this time.

Kat tugs hard at my hair—while her other hand claws my back so hard I suspect she might've drawn some blood—and I completely give up on even trying to take it easy.

As her heels press against the back of my thighs, urging me to go harder and faster, I'm lost.

Her hips ground against mine, and we find our rhythm. With every thrust, she sighs my name.

When she sinks her fingernails into the flesh of my ass and kisses me, her tongue deep inside my mouth, I become her slave.

And then, somehow, something even more extraordinary happens.

As our foreheads press together and we get closer and closer to the point of no return, Kat opens her eyes. They are, of course, as gorgeous and hypnotizing as ever. But their beauty isn't what strikes me. And even though I recognize in them the same unsatisfied hunger I know she sees in mine, the evidence of her passion isn't what gives me pause, either.

No—as I frantically and inexorably sink into her repeatedly, my heart beats out the truth. And like a broken dam, it can't be stopped.

"*Ya ne mogu bet tebya zhit, dusha moya,*" I say with a whisper against her lips.

Kat cries out in pleasure, closing her eyes. Her erratic breathing tells me she's irrevocably close to the edge, and I can't wait to follow her.

Because I know she'll find out anyway, I repeat, "I can't live without you, *dusha moya.*"

She moans against my lips. "Nik..."

I sink into her, faster and harder and deeper. With a cry, she arches her back, holding me tightly. As she pulsates around me, I come undone. With a roar, I plunge deeper into her, taking her lips at the same time.

When Kat brings me over the edge, I drag my mouth to the sweet spot where her neck intersects with her shoulder. I bite it hard as my release erupts out of me, perpetually claiming her as mine.

10

KAT

I wake up in a dream.

In my dream, a ravishing angel watches over me, his warm brown eyes aglow in the morning light. His full, velvety lips rain feathery kisses on my cheekbones, throat and stomach. My belly flutters at the caress, and he smiles against my skin.

Then, wickedly, his mouth languidly descends on my sex, drawing a rapt, impassioned sigh out of me.

As the pale sunlight softly filters through the thick drapes, haloing his dark-haired head between my thighs, I realize my lover is a fallen angel, after all.

His gaze seeks mine as he lazily kisses me. After a moment, I can't admire him any longer. My hands grab fistfuls of the crisp white sheets, and I struggle to keep my eyes open as his devilish mouth brings me closer and closer to heaven.

Mercilessly, he teases me with his tongue, flicking and circling me where I crave him the most. His warm finger soon joins his tempting mouth in its delicious caress, gently entering me. His lips close around me. Gently, they suck and tease, making me gasp. He kisses me over and over again, not even pretending to be in any rush to end my torment.

When his finger and tongue reach an unholy pace, I can't hold it back any longer. I moan his name, and he rewards me by quickening his tempo.

"Nik..." I say, begging him for mercy. I finally manage to open my eyes again. His gaze is still unwaveringly trained on me. The carnal look in his eyes reflects the hunger he must see in mine.

As he lavishes wet, open-mouthed kisses on the inside of my thighs, I'm left with no choice but to groan in frustration.

"No, no. Don't you dare. Don't stop," I say in protest, shaking my head.

With his lips curved in an amused smirk, he looks sinfully gorgeous as he nips the delicate skin on the inside of my left leg.

"Tsk, tsk. Ask me nicely, *kiska*," he says, his eyes glittering with mischief as he chides me.

I exhale, almost trembling with frustration. "Please, Nik." I roll my eyes, and he chuckles before reaching up with his left hand. His long fingers pinch my nipple almost painfully, and I gasp. The feel of his lips against the sensitive spot behind my knee as he laughs in response makes me want to scream with unsatisfied hunger.

"Let's try this again, shall we?" he asks, his mouth vibrating just below my navel.

I grab handfuls of his hair, pushing his head lower. He grins, resisting me. It's his boyish, sunny smile—the one he first showed me that day in the airfield.

I have no defenses or weapons against this grin. My tight grip softens, and I brush his hair off his forehead. "Please, Nik. Kiss me again," I softly ask him.

"Good girl, *kiska*," he says before giving me what I want. "*My* good girl."

"Yes," I moan, throwing my head back as his lips close around my clitoris. Finally. "Yours."

Nik groans against my flesh, and the vibration brings me to the brink of the abyss. I cry out, almost there, but he pulls away from me without warning.

I raise my head from the plush pillows, glaring at him with outrage. His smug, amused face is too much, even though he looks as handsome as he the devil himself.

With an indignant huff, I sit up, still panting. Nik's expression turns curious. I move quickly, pushing my palm against his chest. I catch him by surprise and have him on his back before he can process the change in our positions.

In the same heartbeat, I straddle his hips. Nik's eyebrows raise at that, but his answering smile is one of delight.

He chuckles with a smirk. "All right. You have my attention."

I roll my eyes at his condescending tone, even though I barely manage to stifle my smile. Then I grab his hard cock with my right hand, positioning him just outside the entrance to my sex.

"Oh, please. We both know I have way more than your attention, *miliy*. I have *you*." With one swift movement, I bring him inside me.

Nik throws his head back, groaning loud enough to wake the dead. "Yes, *kiska*. You do. You fucking have me." His words are practically a growl.

He grips my hips as his hands reverently caress me before guiding me to match his rhythm as he drives into me. His right hand lingers there as his left one reaches my chest. He grasps me tightly, squeezing the tip of my breast between his thumb and his finger.

Nik's touch rekindles the fire of my desire. I dig my fingernails into his broad chest, crying out his name. He gasps, then groans, grabbing a handful of my hair. He forcefully drags my face down to meet his, and his mouth ravenously devours mine.

It drives me crazy, and I can't restrain myself any longer. I ride him faster and harder, wildly bucking against his hard body. By the grace of God, Nik doesn't fight me. Instead, he meets me at every thrust, plunging into me deeper, harder, and faster each time.

Sweet, ecstatic bliss begins to pool in my lower abdomen. It won't be long now. Nik's grip on me grows more powerful and unyielding, and I know he will follow me.

I force my eyes to open so I can take a good look at him.

His shiny black hair is so soft against my fingertips. His dear brown eyes are tightly shut in rapture, but a thousand years couldn't make me forget even the most minute details of what they look like.

I brush my fingers down the column of his neck, and he shivers.

My hopelessly infatuated gaze strokes his broad shoulders, his muscular chest, his flat abdomen glistening with sweat.

I bend forward at the waist to kiss every inch my eyes lovingly caressed.

"Mine," I say against his chest. "You're mine."

Nik chokes back his groan. "Kat..." he says with a sigh, holding me tightly against him.

My breath catches as I fall over the edge of the precipice he had me teetering over this entire time. I moan and gasp, throwing my head back.

Nik hoarsely cries out before following me. "Kat..."

As my limbs become weightless, I open my eyes to find

him watching me. He can't catch his breath, either. Wordlessly, I fall into his chest with him still inside me, and his strong arms protectively surround me.

Minutes or hours—I couldn't determine to save my life—pass before either of us moves or makes a sound.

Eventually, Nik sighs.

"I swear, woman—I had every intention of slowly making love to you this morning, but you just had to push my buttons, didn't you? It's almost like you aren't happy until you have me in some maddened frenzy," he says, grumbling with mock exasperation.

With an unladylike snort, I lift my head to glare at him. "Oh, so it's my fault?"

Nik's eyes glitter with undisguised amusement. "All I'm saying is you bring out the worst in me."

"I beg to differ. I think I bring out the best in you. Take this morning, for example. Exhibit fucking A, I'd say."

He chuckles. "I'll defer to you on this, I guess."

"That'd be a first." I laugh, and he playfully nips at my earlobe.

"Well, there's always tomorrow, I suppose." Nik sighs.

"Tomorrow?" I ask with feigned horror. "Screw tomorrow. What about tonight?"

Nik's answering grin would have turned my knees into rubber if it wasn't for the fact that I'm still flat on my stomach on top of him.

"God have mercy on me," he says against my lips, tenderly kissing me.

The mood, however, is completely ruined when my stomach loudly growls, denouncing a hunger of a different kind.

Still chuckling, Nik says, "Shame on me. Here I am,

practically devouring you while you're starving. What are you in the mood for? I'll have it brought to you."

"Well, one thing comes to mind," I say against his lips lasciviously.

Nik's delighted laughter adorably wrinkles the corner of his eyes, leaving my chest aching. Sweet, wonderful, gorgeous man. He's so devastatingly handsome sometimes. And now he's all mine.

"I'll most definitely hold you to that," he says. "Later."

I sigh dramatically. "Later? You're no fun."

"You know very well that's just not true. But I won't be able to forgive myself if you die of malnourishment under my watch." He mockingly shudders.

"Again, I know just the thing to keep my hunger at bay," I say with a shrug.

With a shake of his head, Nik drags me out of bed. "You're going to be the death of me."

I roll my eyes. "Fine. Feed me, then. I'll have some freshly baked croissants. And some orange juice, too. Please and thank you."

"How about some protein?" he asks, and I can't resist it.

I smile slowly, while suggestively staring at him. "You know what I want."

Half groaning, half laughing, Nik kisses my lips. "*Kiska*. Mercy, please."

"Very well. Since you asked me so nicely."

Nik's eyes heat dangerously, and he pulls me into his arms again. But behind me, the familiar sound of my ringtone echoes almost simultaneously.

"I think that's for you," he says, looking over my shoulder.

With a frustrated sigh, I walk to the nightstand where I placed my inconvenient phone at some point the day before.

"It's A.J.," I say.

"You should take it. I'll take care of breakfast," Nik says, kissing the top of my head. "Come and join me in the kitchen when you're ready."

I nod before answering the call.

"Thank God you picked up. I've been out of my mind with worry," my friend says, sighing dramatically.

I laugh, sitting on the edge of the bed. "Hello to you, too, A.J."

"Oh, yeah, hi," she says. "I've been thinking about you all night."

"Sorry, girl," I say with a sigh, raptly watching as Nik gets dressed. He chooses a pair of light blue jeans and a light gray sweater, and I smile in approval. "Can't say the same."

"Well, you should have, considering I've been busting my ass for the two of us," she says acidly. "But I guess this ungrateful disregard of yours truly would be understandable if what I've heard through the grapevine is true. Did the Irish and the Russians really attack each other last night?"

I exhale wearily. "Yes."

Nik approaches me then. He's heartbreakingly handsome in his light-colored outfit, and I want to drag him back to bed immediately. He presses another quick kiss on my forehead before exiting the room.

"Well," A.J. says with a sigh. "Fuck."

"Fuck, indeed," I say.

"Are you okay?"

"I'm fine. We're all fine, thankfully."

"*We*? Since when there's a *we*? Who the fuck is *we*?"

"It's a long story."

"How can it be? You haven't been gone for *that* long."

"I guess. But things have progressed...exponentially."

"Okay," A.J. says cautiously after a moment. "I'm listening."

With a sigh, I fill her in on everything that has transpired since we last spoke. I tell her what I've recently learned about McGuire and Maxim's involvement with each other and what happened leading up to the Russians and Irish flagrant attacks on each other yesterday.

"That motherfucker came after you?" A.J. screams in outrage. "Oh, we're taking him down, Kat. As soon as we're done with the *stronzo*."

I share with her Nik's promises about McGuire's days being numbered, letting her know that the Irish mobster will probably be dead and gone before she even gets a chance to take a shot at him.

That line of thought leads to me trying my best to explain to her how things have changed between me and Nik since she and I last chatted.

My best friend quietly listens as I gush about my Russian, doing my best to convey how wonderful everything between us feels now.

"Wow," she says, once I'm done with my recap. "Just... wow. I have no words, honestly."

I scoff. "Now, *that* would shock me."

"Don't get cute with me now," she says acidly. "I won't be distracted by your shenanigans. I can't believe you didn't tell me what's been truly going on between the two of you until now."

"Well, I've been busy," I sheepishly say.

"I know, Kat. But, I mean... wow."

"You've said that already."

A.J. huffs indignantly. "Well, it bears repeating."

Impatient, I ask, "A.J., please stop talking circles around me and tell me what you're really thinking."

"Look, honey. Don't get me wrong—if you like him, then I love him. Really. But it's a lot to take in. Just the other day, you told me he had you kidnapped and was blackmailing you into fucking with a gangster. Mind you, this is not a figure of speech. You did tell me all that just the other day—quite literally. And now you're saying you're willingly *fucking a gangster.*"

I sigh. "I know. But honestly, Nik isn't who I initially thought he was. Well, except the drop-dead gorgeous and great in the sack part. He's *exactly* like that. But he's so much more. He's so reliable, so attentive. He's caring, too. And protective, sweet, and wonderful."

"You've got it bad," she says pointedly.

I admit it without hesitation. "I do. I really do. You have no idea. I just never imagined everything could ever feel so right with him. But it does. It feels perfect."

"I'm sure that the fact that he's indeed drop-dead gorgeous and great in bed doesn't hurt, either."

I exhale dreamily. "It really, really doesn't."

"Oh, Kat... Then I'm happy for you. Really. Just please be careful, for fuck's sake."

"Always. Now tell me—anything new with the *stronzo*? What about that favor I asked you? I don't suppose you managed to work your magic on the museum's security footages? I'd love you forever if you did."

A.J. scoffs. "Bitch, please. We both know you worship the ground I walk on."

Glad to revert to the more familiar subjects of work and business, A.J. tells me how things are going in her pursuit of the *stronzo*. She mentions again that the wretched man has been blessedly—although strangely—quiet since I handed him the Flame of Mir. She hopes to have all she needs to free us from him soon.

In other news, even though A.J. tried her best, the gala's surveillance footage is unsalvageable, except for the small snippet of the metal detectors' surveillance feeds she sent us days ago.

I can't deny it's not the outcome I wanted, even though I knew it was a long shot. I've been secretly hoping that the footage could provide us with indisputable proof of McGuire's involvement in Maxim's demise, or exonerate him entirely. One way or the other, it could have been a priceless tool to deescalate things between Nik and McGuire.

Since A.J.'s attempts to recover the footage didn't pan out, Nik's quest for McGuire's head will go on. And if something were to happen to my Russian because of it, I don't know what I'd do...

I thank A.J. for her efforts and promise to keep her informed about everything going on with me, Nik, and McGuire. After we hang up, however, she remains in my thoughts, even as I hurry to get dressed for the day, eager to be back with Nik.

There simply must be something I can do. There has to be a way for me to kill two nasty birds with one stone—namely, the *stronzo* and McGuire.

11

NIK

Dmitri's voice greets me as I enter my dark office. "Look what the cat dragged in."

After flipping the light switch on, I glare at him. Dmitri lazily lounges on my chair, his handmade Italian shoes boldly propped up on my desk.

"Hiya, Nik. So good of you to join us, hardworking men, on this fine morning. Or is it afternoon yet? Did you sleep well?" The impudent fool smirks at me.

I sigh. "It's clear to me now that your saint of a mother—God rest her soul—must've dropped you on your head a few times when you were a child. That's the only explanation I can come up with for your complete lack of self-preservation," I say as I walk towards my desk.

"Where's your better half, Romeo?" Dmitri asks, still comfortably occupying my seat.

"If you don't remove yourself from my chair in the next five seconds, you'll never get to know."

With an unconcerned smile, Dmitri complies, slowly standing up. "I expected you to be in a much better mood today after spending the entire night—and the better part of the morning—in your little *kiska*'s arms," he says impishly, unhurriedly taking a seat on one of the chairs in front of my desk. Not a care in this world.

"Dmitri..." I say with a sigh, finally dropping my weight on my own fucking chair. "One of these days, you *will* push me too far. And you won't like what'll happen then."

He shrugs, completely unrepentant. "Maybe I like to live dangerously."

With a shake of my head, I tell him, "For your own sake, I sincerely hope you haven't been twiddling your thumbs all morning. I trust you have something new to report."

"Of course. Once we're done talking about the actual important stuff. Come on, Nik. I've been waiting all day. Don't leave me hanging now. I'm too invested in your romantic life. Are you going to make me beg?"

"Not that it's any of your business, but if you must know, I spent the night with Kat, yes. Now that we got that out of the way, about McGuire—"

Dmitri chuckles incredulously. "Hang on. Come on, Nik. You can't just leave it at that."

I sigh again, accepting I won't get anywhere with him until I give him what he wants. I suppose I might as well indulge him. "What can I say, Dmitri? It was great. Everything... clicked into place, I guess."

"And...?" he asks, staring at me, avidly waiting for more.

I take a deep breath. "And I've never met anyone like her. Obviously, she's exceedingly charming and attractive. And it's no secret to you or anyone else that she often drives me to distraction. I can't pretend to understand it, but she has this mind-boggling way of getting under my skin like no one else. Half the time I'm with her, I don't know if I should throttle or kiss her. But there's just something about her—

no matter what I do, I can't seem to shake her. Honestly, I'm not sure I ever really wanted to."

After an unprecedented amount of blissful silence, Dmitri whistles. "Wow," he says, slowly shaking his head. "Damn. I knew it. She *is* the one, isn't she? I called it from the start, remember? I'm sure you do. I just know you too well. I knew there was something different about the way you were obsessing over her."

"Well, to be fair, she had stolen the Flame of Mir. And I don't know about your choice of words, Dmitri. Obsessing sounds a little melodramatic—"

"I call it like I see it, Nik. I could tell your *obsession* wasn't about the diamond. You were just so *emotional* about it," he says apologetically, as if the term is a curse word.

Exasperated, I can't help laughing a little. "Regardless," I say, "I see your point. You aren't wrong. She certainly made an impression on me from the beginning. And she does affect me like no one has before. I guess last night was just us finally being on the same page at the right place and time."

"I'll say," Dmitri pointedly remarks. I shoot him a warning glance, but it's pointless. We both know he'll never learn to behave appropriately.

"The timing could be better, with everything coming to a head with McGuire," I say with a slight shrug. "But hey, I'll take it. Gladly."

Dmitri grins at me, almost beatifically. Then, with a slight shake of his head, he sighs theatrically. "I can't believe my eyes and ears. I never thought this day would come. Nikolai Stefanovich is *taken*."

"Okay, okay," I say, lightly reprimanding him. "Don't push it, Dmitri. Now that our little heart-to-heart is over, I can't wait to hear how productively you've spent this morning, certainly chasing after McGuire."

Still smiling, Dmitri is finally persuaded to change the subject. I listen to his report about last night's and this morning's recent developments in our search for the Irish family boss until we're interrupted by a knock on the door.

"Come in," I say.

Kat enters the room. Naturally, just seeing her face is enough to make all rational thoughts vacate my mind. She smiles, and my heart practically somersaults in my chest.

She's dressed in a black silk dress that hugs every delicious curve of her body. Her long, dark hair is down, flowing around her shoulders.

She narrows her eyes at me in mock accusation. "You promised me food. Croissants, I was told. And orange juice."

"My word is my bond," I say, rising from my chair. "Whatever my Kat wants, she gets."

"Empty promises. Do you know what else is empty, *miliy*? My stomach." She sighs. "Oh, hello, Dmitri. Nice to see you in one piece, too."

"Hiya, Kat. I told you I'm a big boy. I can take care of myself," Dmitri says, winking at her. I can't bring myself to care about his unabashed flirting too much right now, not after everything that happened last night.

I find myself grinning at Kat's new pet name for me instead. I come around the desk to grab her hand.

"Let's go," I say to her. "I have a reputation to protect. I can't have you thinking I'm not a man of my word, can I?"

"Chop-chop, then, mister. Lead the way."

In the kitchen, Kat's over-the-top reaction to the baked goods she demanded makes me laugh, even as the strangest warm feeling spreads inside me.

She sighs, effusively kissing my cheek. "You're a prince among men. A king, even."

"I need you to do me a favor and bring this same energy tonight," I say, pouring some coffee for myself and her.

Kat rolls her eyes at me, laughing. "Well, it *is* true that good food and drink are often the way to my heart."

"I'll make sure you have nothing but lobster and champagne, then. If only I'd known it was that easy this entire time..."

"Cute," she says with a chuckle. "As far as you're concerned, I've been pretty easy—"

I scoff. "You can't be serious."

She shrugs. "It's true. But I'll have you know, I'm not *that* easy. You're going to have to work for it, *miliy*."

I brush a quick kiss on her lush lips. "Of that, I have no doubts."

While smiling so beautifully it almost physically pains me, Kat shrugs. "It's not like you didn't know what you were getting yourself into."

I wrap my hand around her neck and pull her closer until her face is a couple of inches away from mine. "You're damn right, Kat. I knew exactly what I was getting myself into. Every step of the way." Unable to restrain myself for a second longer, I kiss her hard, clasping her against me. "Now eat your food. You're going to want your energy later."

Kat's lips curve in a dangerously tempting smile that has me straining against the zipper of my pants, not even a full hour after spilling myself inside her.

"Well, Nik, you certainly talk the talk. But will you walk the walk? I wonder..."

I lean forward towards her, narrowing my eyes at the little minx. "That sounds a lot like a challenge," I say in a low voice. "Make my day, *kiska*, and call my bluff. You seem to have forgotten who you're speaking to, so maybe it's time I remind you."

With a smirk, she asks, "Is that a threat or a promise?"

"Keep fucking around, and you'll find out."

Openly giggling now, she wraps her finger over the collar of my sweater, drawing me close enough for her to place a quick kiss on my lips.

The sound of her carefree, cheerful laugh warms me all the way to the pit of my stomach.

"I'll never finish this meal if you keep shamelessly teasing me," she says, playfully chiding me with a shake of her head. "And trust me, you don't want to see me hangry. Now, please try not to be so irresistible for a moment, will you? Just so I can manage to take more than two bites of my flaky croissants before having to fight the urge to steal a kiss from you."

"I don't know why you'd feel the need to steal something I'm dying to give you."

She sighs, pointedly glaring at me. "Nik, please! This is exactly what I'm talking about."

I laugh. "Fine. My lips are sealed. I won't say anything else until you're done eating."

"Thank you," she says, spreading even more butter on the already pretty buttery croissant. "You're a doll."

"Is that supposed to be a compliment?" I say with a scoff, and she holds up one finger as she chews.

A moment later, Kat shuts her eyes, her face shifting into an expression of pure bliss. "Mmm," she moans, and I have to adjust myself as my jeans grow increasingly uncomfortable in the crotch area. "I swear, there's nothing better than a fresh croissant. Certainly better than drugs. Maybe even better than sex."

"Is that right?" I ask.

Kat's eyes glow with amusement. "I said 'maybe.' And obviously, I was referring to inferior, underwhelming sex. As in, with anyone else but you."

"If you think that talking about sex with other men will appease me, you're going to be really disappointed."

With a sigh, she presses a quick kiss on my cheek. "I just love it when you get all jealous. I think I could watch you throw tantrums in a fit of jealousy all day long."

"Oh, no, you don't. Don't even think about it. I won't put up with you going out of your way to make me jealous on purpose."

Kat winks at me, but before I can put the fear of God into her, she takes another bite of the flaky pastry. After closing her eyes again, she throws her head back, moaning once more.

"For fuck's sake, Kat," I say with a groan. "Mercy."

Bewildered, she glances at me. Then she smiles. "Am I getting you all hot and bothered?"

"Always," I say through gritted teeth.

Kat laughs with delight. After setting her plate aside, she rises from her seat, strolling towards me. A second later, she plops her plump ass down on my lap, wrapping her legs and arms around me.

Unfortunately, I don't have time to react to this fortuitous turn of events appropriately since Vladmir walks in with an envelope in hand. "Nikolai," he says, expressionless, handing me the item. "A courier just delivered this. He didn't know who hired him. It was all arranged via phone, and he was paid in cash."

Curious, I forget about chewing him off for interrupting Kat and me again. With a nod to me, he leaves without even acknowledging Kat's presence. I'll have to speak to him about it. I won't tolerate him touching or upsetting her again, but that doesn't mean he gets to ignore her or be rude to her.

"What is it?" Kat asks.

I flip the white paper envelope, surprised when I see it's addressed to her. "No clue," I say, offering it to her. "Why don't you tell me? It's for you."

With a frown, Kat picks it up. She doesn't waste any time before prying it open with her index finger. Her frown deepens as she reads the letter contained inside the mysterious envelope.

"Well?" I ask, unable to contain my curiosity.

"It's from Erin," she says as her eyes scan the message.

"Erin McGuire?" I ask, shocked.

Kat nods. "Yeah. It's bizarre. Erin says she can't tell me all the details right now, but she wanted to share something with me. She's now certain her dad didn't kill Maxim. She claims it's just not possible that McGuire murdered your friend. But she can't explain how she knows that yet."

"Convenient," I say dryly. "Why would she tell you any of this?"

"She and I had a moment at McGuire's party. We sort of connected. She was a little hesitant, but I believe she meant to tell me everything she knew about Maxim's death before she disappeared. And she hinted at knowing a good bit. I'm not shocked to learn she feels compelled to share her feelings with me. I'm surprised, considering everything else—but not shocked."

"Well, I wouldn't trust her so easily. She's her father's daughter, after all. Besides, we can't know for sure she's even the actual author of this letter."

"There's more," Kat says, still reading the note. "Erin warns me not to trust your men. She specifically says I should trust no one but you, actually."

I laugh humorlessly. "See? This sure looks like some plot from McGuire himself. I wouldn't pay it any mind. This message isn't worth the paper it's written on."

Kat doesn't seem convinced. "Maybe. But maybe not. We can't know for sure. I've been meaning to talk to you about this, actually. I feel like perhaps we shouldn't have been so set on McGuire from the start. I'm not completely sold on the idea that he's the only one who would have—or could have—killed your friend. Maybe we should step back and rethink our approach to this whole thing."

I scoff. "You can't be serious."

"Why not?" she asks, raising her eyebrows at me.

I don't want to upset her and start an argument, especially not about something so pointless. But now is not the time to get sidetracked by irrelevant musings. Not when McGuire sent his men after Kat not even a day ago.

"Look," I say in my best diplomatic tone. "It means a lot to me that you care about finding Maxim's killer. And I value your input. I appreciate the fact that you've given this matter so much thought. But you'll have to trust me on this one, Kat. McGuire is our guy."

"How can you be so sure?"

"I just am. I know him better than you do."

Kat frowns at me. "Sure, but that doesn't mean you shouldn't consider all the options."

"I have," I say. "How can you suggest I haven't?"

"I don't mean to insult you," she says cautiously. "But we both know you haven't. Not really. You've been set on McGuire from day one."

I sigh wearily. "Because he did it. No one else had means, motive, and opportunity. Or the fucking balls to take my best friend from me just when I got him back. Besides, it doesn't even fucking matter—not after he attacked you and me. I have to kill him for that alone. Anything else would be a waste of our time and resources. Look, I understand you disagree with my judgment. I respect that. But we won't waste time on any Hail Marys or wild goose chases while McGuire is out for our blood. I need you to go with me on this one and stay out of trouble while I deal with him. After I handle him, we can discuss this again."

"Nik..." she says, shaking her head in disbelief. "You wanted to avoid a war, remember? That's why you asked my for my help in the first place. Just give this some thought."

"No, Kat. I won't. And I'd greatly appreciate it if you didn't, either. As a matter of fact, I don't want to have this conversation again. Not while McGuire's still breathing. I want to focus on getting rid of the man so we can move on with our lives. And I want *you* to focus on staying safe while I do just that."

Kat scowls at me indignantly. "You can't tell me what to believe. And you don't get to just lay down the law and tell me a subject is off-limits. I'm not a child."

Suddenly exhausted, I ask, "Can't you just trust me on this one?"

"I trust you, Nik, but you're not being reasonable."

"I'm not being unreasonable just because I disagree with you. I value your insight, but I understand this game and the players better than you do. Think about it—you've just entered my world. I've been living in it my whole life. I've known McGuire for over a decade. In a perfect universe, we'd have all the time and resources to pursue every lead and make peace with him. But my world is far from perfect. All I can do is make the best decision available to me with the information at hand. Right now, that's focusing on ending the man who's actively trying to kill you and me. I can't have you undermining me or distracting me from this by putting yourself in danger chasing this far-fetched idea of yours."

She glares at me in disbelief. "All I'm doing is trying to save *you*. These mafia disputes have a way of getting deadly and bloody fast. I don't want to lose you. And I know you don't want to lose your men. You're also being so unfair. You want me to disregard my thoughts in favor of yours when you didn't consider my opinions even for a second. You say you appreciate my insight, but that's just not true. It's clearly worthless to you."

"That's absolutely not true," I say. "I think you're brilliant. The way you see the world fascinates me. But I don't have the luxury of getting sidetracked. Not about this and not now. Not when I'm in open conflict with one of the heads of the Seven Families. I really don't want to upset you, but being the *pakhan* means I have to make tough decisions sometimes."

Kat sighs exasperatedly, shaking her head. "I just think you're making a mistake. I don't want it to cost us your life—or Dmitri's or your men's."

"Kat, you've come to know me better than most. You know I wouldn't make a decision that I wasn't sure was the best one. Not with this. After everything we've been through, can't you just trust me? Can't you blindly follow my lead this one time? Just this once, can't you let it go and drop this topic until McGuire is gone?"

"You've come to know me, too, Nik," she says, her eyes sparkling with unconcealed anger. "After everything we've been through, I thought I earned a little more respect than this from you. If Dmitri or Vladmir suggested you take a second to think this through, I'm sure you'd hear them out. I'm sure you wouldn't tell them to just drop it."

"If Dmitri or Vladmir even thought about questioning

my authority so openly and brazenly, I assure you I wouldn't be half as tolerant with them as I am with you when you do it on a daily basis."

Kat narrows her eyes at me while crossing her arms. "Why don't you just give me a comprehensive list of all topics that are off-limits? For my personal edification, of course. God forbid I insult you by disagreeing with you ever again."

I laugh humorlessly. "If you're so eager to talk about things one of us doesn't want to discuss, why don't we begin by discussing whatever happened to my diamond? I've been dying to know. You might've noticed I've been gracious enough not to press you about it, but if we're tackling uncomfortable topics, maybe we should start with that."

Kat's eyes widen, and she gasps, staring at me as if I had struck her. Her incredulous and wounded expression gives me pause, making me wish I could take my hurtful words back, especially considering what she shared with me about her motives for stealing it. She told me it wasn't greed or any other frivolous reason that motivated her to steal the damned thing. She did it for love—to protect herself and someone she loved.

Stupidly, at the first opportunity, I betrayed her confidence and trust. I made a mess of things. It was a spiteful thing to say, a mistake made out of anger. Even worse, it was uncalled for and unfair. After all, she's just trying to help.

Kat blinks at me, swallowing deeply. Utterly ashamed of myself, I watch with horror as her big blue eyes fill up with unshed tears.

"Kat, I'm so sorry. No, don't cry. I'm an idiot, *dusha moya*. I didn't mean any of it. Tell me how to fix this."

Without meeting my eyes, she stands up. Losing the feel

of her body against mine makes everything a hundred times worse.

"Kat—" I say, pleading. I grab her hand as I rise from my seat. "Come on. Give me a chance to apologize."

She shakes her head, refusing to make eye contact with me. "There's nothing to apologize for, Nik. You've made a good point. Will you excuse me for a second? I could use a moment for myself."

Wordlessly, Kat untangles her hand from mine. After shaking me off, she exits the kitchen without looking back at me.

Helpless, I watch her leave, terrified I just might have fucked things up.

12

KAT

THE MUFFLED sound of a hesitant knock echoes through the cavernous bedroom, interrupting my dark thoughts.

After a moment of indecisiveness, I answer, not bothering to rise from the bed. "Yeah?" I say guardedly, glancing at the closed door from my comfortable observation point. Slowly, it opens.

To my surprise, it's Dmitri. He glances at me, clearly unsure of his welcome.

"Can I come in?" he asks from the doorway, his pale blue eyes cautious.

I nod, sitting up. "Yeah, of course."

He comes in carrying almost a dozen shopping bags. Wordlessly, he looks around the sparsely furnished room before asking, "I'm not sure where you want these. The boutique clerk sent them over today."

After noticing my puzzled expression, Dmitri says, "It's the stuff we had with us when the Irish rudely interrupted your little shopping spree and we had to run for our lives."

"Oh." I rise from the bed. "I guess we'll put it all in the

closet. I can't believe the store kept it for us. And then had it delivered here, too. That was nice of them."

"I'm sure they were more than happy to go out of their way to please Nikolai Stefanovich's new girlfriend," Dmitri says, following me into the walk-in closet.

As I take the bags from him, I laugh humorlessly. "Girlfriend? Yeah, I don't know about that."

"Soul mate it is, then," Dmitri says, teasing me. He impassively watches me empty the bags. "I heard you two had a lovers' quarrel."

I roll my eyes at him. "Nik's right. You don't know how to mind your business, do you?"

Dmitri sighs wearily. "Come on, Kat. We've already discussed this. Nik *is* my business. Stick around long enough, and I'll make you my business, too." He winks at me.

I scoff, ruefully shaking my head at him. "We'll see about that."

He smirks. "Oh, you bet we will. Now, let's hear about this little trouble in paradise."

I hesitate to say more, but if anyone can offer me valuable insight on what to do with that impossible man, it's Dmitri. "What can I say? As you're undoubtedly aware, Nik can be a very challenging man. He's also a stubborn ass. Sometimes, it's hard to curb the urge to force some sense into his thick skull."

"You're preaching to the choir, sister."

"I guess you could say I'm struggling to figure out where I stand with him. Am I still his underling, or are we past that now? I know he and I started off on the wrong foot—and, truth be told, he's not entirely to blame for that. But I thought that was water under the bridge by now."

Dmitri raises his eyebrows. "It isn't? That's news to me."

I shrug. "Not if what he said to me earlier is any indication. And I'm not sure I can fully trust him when I don't know if we'll ever move past our rough start. This whole Jekyll and Hide song-and-dance is giving me whiplash."

Dmitri sighs, leaning his broad shoulders against the closet's door frame. "Look, Kat—I've known Nik for most of my life. For what it's worth, I've never seen him so taken by someone as he is with you. If anybody had described his recent behavior to me, I'd have called it bullshit. But I've seen it with my eyes. This lovesick, infatuated way he acts around you probably seems like the norm for you, because that's all you've known from him. But let me tell you, that couldn't be farther from the truth."

"What are you trying to say?"

He shrugs. "Just give him time. It's all new to him. He's adjusting to you—to all these new responses you evoke in him—just as you are to him. He's many things, but a disappointment isn't one of them. I'm sure you know that by now. If you're patient with him and give him a chance, he'll come through. He always does."

I sigh. "Oh, Dmitri... If only it could be this simple. There's just no way of knowing—"

"Listen—" he interjects. "I get it. This shit's scary. And it's hard as hell, too. But take it from someone who knows—you don't want to lose your once-in-a-lifetime opportunity to have something as life-changing and special as this kind of love. Not over something fixable, workable."

His heartfelt statement gives me pause. It's a welcome distraction from my emotional conundrum and another piece of the intriguing puzzle of his mysterious love life. I decide to prod a little. "It sure sounds like you're speaking from experience, Dmitri."

As always, he remains noncommittal. "We all have our romantic disappointments here and there, don't we?"

I scoff. "Oh, cut the crap. Don't give me that. I've opened my heart to you. It's only fair that you do the same."

Dmitri shakes his head, a sad look lingering in his beautiful eyes. "I can't. And trust me, it isn't a story worth telling."

"I'll be the judge of that."

He bites on the side of his cheek, seemingly deep in thought. As I start thinking he won't give me an answer, he sighs again. Then, he mumbles, "I guess I could tell you some of it. There's this girl."

"No shit, Sherlock."

He goes on as if I haven't spoken, rolling his eyes. "She's always been special to me, but it took me a while to realize the nature of my feelings for her. By the time I was able to admit to myself that I was in love with her, it was too late for us. I had lost her. And now, not a minute goes by without me wishing I could turn back the clock and do things differently. There's absolutely nothing I won't do to get her back."

"What happened between you and her?"

"That's a tale for another time. If we make it that far," he says with a sad chuckle. "The moral of the story is that finding someone who makes life worth living is fucking hard. And rare. So don't throw it away if it happens to you. Don't take it for granted, or you might regret it for the rest of your miserable existence. I know this now. So does Nik. He knows what it's like to lose someone you love forever."

One way or the other, everything seems to go back to Maxim eventually.

"Nik has had little practice at loving or being loved, Kat," Dmitri says quietly. "He hasn't been that fortunate. But I know he'll bend over backwards to give you anything you want or need if you ask him for it. And I think you know it, too."

I sigh again. "Dmitri—"

But whatever I meant to say is quickly forgotten when we hear the bedroom door open and shut quietly.

Immediately straightening, Dmitri raises an eyebrow at me before glancing at the newcomer over his shoulder. He turns back to me. "Just think about what I told you," he whispers. "And try to be patient. Please."

Without waiting for a response, Dmitri leaves.

I don't need to sneak a peek to know who my visitor is. That's why I turn my back to the doorway and resume sorting through the shopping bags.

Dmitri's story and advice still echo in my mind when Nik stops by the closet's entrance.

I have no intention of making his groveling any easier for him—and, frankly, I also have no clue what to say—so I remain silent, waiting for him to take the first step.

He watches me in silence for an impossibly long moment. Or maybe it just seems like that because I can't stand this uncomfortable silence between us.

Just as I'm about to cave in and blurt out something outrageous, he sighs. "Kat, I'm sorry."

His willingness to offer an olive branch promptly renews my resolve to remain silent. After all, if he's ready to admit he can be a supercilious bastard when the mood strikes him, then I won't to be the one to stop him.

"Kat, look at me. I shouldn't have spoken to you like that. I regretted it the moment the words left my mouth. I can't tell you how sorry I am for upsetting you. I just hope I haven't completely ruined things between us. If there's anything I can do to make you forget I was a complete jackass, then you have to tell me. Whatever it is, I'll do it. Just name it."

I can't remember ever hearing his voice sound so unsettled. There's no point in denying it—his obvious discomposure at the prospect of having irrevocably damaged our relationship mollifies me a little. I glance at him over my shoulder. It's a mistake, because one look at him and my steely resolve is gone. The troubled look in his eyes warms my heart. To make matters worse, he still looks as devastatingly handsome as he did this morning in his light blue jeans and gray sweater. The only noteworthy difference is the state of his hair. It's now an invitingly glossy mess. My guess is that he's been repeatedly running his fingers through it.

The pale colors of his outfit bring out his dark coloring in the most stunning way. His dark hair and deep brown eyes are strikingly alluring, and I bite back a titillated sigh.

"Did you send Dmitri to sweet-talk me into forgiving you?" I ask accusingly.

Nik wordlessly glares at me for a second before sighing. He shakes his head, looking slightly insulted. "I'm not ashamed to admit that I would happily stoop very low to get you to forgive me. Truth be told, there isn't much I wouldn't do to get back in your good graces. But honestly, Kat, at this point, if you seriously think even for a second that I'd ever send another man into a bedroom with you, then I don't know what to tell you."

I struggle to hide my captivated smile, completely charmed by his earnest disgust at the mere idea. Still, I compose my face into a dispassionate mask before speaking. "Be that as it may, your seemingly sincere apology doesn't impress me much. To be perfectly candid with you, even the most heartfelt words can only go so far after a person shows you how they truly feel inside. Talk's cheap, Nik."

"I know," he says with a grunt, approaching me. "That's why I'm going to show you with my *actions* that the idiotic things I said earlier do not reflect how I truly feel about you. Not in any way, shape or form. I'm not afraid to grovel. Repeatedly and indefinitely, if that's what it takes. It's also why I come bearing gifts."

Nik's long fingers reach inside the front pocket of his jeans, pulling out a glittering bauble. He steps behind me wordlessly before brushing my hair aside, away from my nape. A moment later, the cold feel of metal against the skin of my throat makes me shiver. His competent fingers make quick work of the clasp before he softly asks, "Well? Do you like it?"

I move towards the closet's full-body length mirror to glance at my reflection. Mesmerized, I turn my head left and right, my gaze fixated on the sparkling choker necklace around my neck. My discerning eyes lose count of how many cushion-cut diamonds make up the breathtaking piece. Over two inches wide, the necklace is striking and understated at the same time. The light-colored gems beautifully contrast against my tan skin and dark hair. It's precisely what I'd have purchased for myself if I happened to be a multibillionaire, like the man standing behind me.

With a slight shrug, I meet Nik's eyes through the mirror. "It'll do, I suppose," I say.

My own eyes, however, give away my delight. Nik smiles, pleased with himself. "Am I forgiven, then?" he asks, raising his eyebrows.

"Yes, *miliy*. But not because of the necklace. It's beautiful, but don't think for a second that it's a get-out-of-jail-free card."

"Damn it, there goes my plan, I guess. I can't use diamonds to buy my way into your heart. Noted."

"Well, I certainly wouldn't be terribly put off if you tried it anyway."

Nik laughs. "I'll keep that in mind. Will you be terribly put off if I kiss you now? I need to know we're okay, but I don't want to incur your wrath again. Not if it can be avoided. Although, truthfully, I'm craving you so much right now that I might risk it, anyway."

"That depends. You don't happen to have any more diamonds on you, do you?"

A slow smirk curves his lips. "Come here and frisk me. Find out for yourself."

I tug him closer by his sweater to answer his request with a kiss of my own. Long, languidly delectable moments pass before I pull away from his mouth when a question pops into my head. Nik grunts in protest when I push him away, but I ignore his objections. "I have to ask—do you always keep a few pieces of jewelry at hand just in case some disgruntled woman in your life needs appeasing?"

"For your information, there's only one disgruntled woman in my life that I'd bother to appease."

"Meaning there are other disgruntled women in your life that you wouldn't bother to appease?"

Nik laughs, eyes glowing with amusement, before stealing a quick kiss. "Let's stay on topic. No, I don't have jewelry lying around the house, just in case I need it. I'm sorry to disappoint you. But if you were considering going on a little treasure hunt, don't let my words discourage you. By all means, knock yourself out looking around. It'll entertain me immensely."

"Your entertainment is always my main priority," I say

with a smirk. "So, where did my gift come from? Did you run out to get it or something?"

He laughs again. "No. I'm a collector of sorts, I guess. Not necessarily of diamonds, but of anything particularly beautiful. Art, jewels... It doesn't matter to me what it is. If it catches my eye, then I'll own it."

I sigh. "Oh, to be *that* rich. It must be nice to be able to purchase anything that strikes your fancy on an impulse—money be damned."

Nik smirks. His finger traces the borders of the choker around my neck. "I've had this particular piece for a while. I bought it years ago at an auction in London. I was fascinated by it from the start. It seemed fitting that you should have it."

"Sweet-talker," I say against his lips, and he parts them with a sigh. "It sure is a bit funny that you're gifting me a diamond necklace now when another diamond got us in this situation in the first place."

"The irony isn't lost on me," he says, raising his eyebrows with amusement.

"Well, the first one started us off on the wrong foot, so who knows? Maybe these will mark a change in our course or the beginning of a new era. Maybe it's a good luck charm."

Nik's eyes soften. "The Flame of Mir brought you into my life. That's as lucky as it gets if you ask me."

"I'll remind you of that next time."

After kissing the top of my head, he asks, "Did you know that the ancient Romans believed that Cupid's arrow tips were made of diamonds? Do you think that's why I can't get you out of my head since that first night?"

Heartily laughing, I say, "Who knows? Perhaps. Or maybe I'm just that good in bed. Or on a desk, I guess, as it was."

"Oh, you most certainly are, *kiska*."

I press a kiss against his chest. "You're not so bad yourself."

"I'm glad you think so. Because you're stuck with me now. As a matter of fact, don't bother unpacking these shopping bags. I'm having them moved to our bedroom as soon as we're done here. The rest of your stuff, too, of course."

He announces his decision with such an aggravatingly imperiously tone that I can't help teasing him a little. "*Our* bedroom, is it? Do I get a say in that?"

"Sure. If you don't like it, I'll move my things here instead—or wherever you prefer to be. Hell, if you can't find a single room in this penthouse that you like, we'll just buy a place that suits you. It doesn't matter to me one bit, as long as I'm where you'll spend your nights."

"Is this your way of asking me to move in with you? Because I believe that ship has sailed a long time ago. Namely, when you had me kidnapped and chained to that bed out there."

"You have such a flair for the dramatic, Kat. No, this is my way of telling you I don't want to be apart from you from now on. You're out of your mind if you think you'll sleep anywhere but in my bed. Try it, and I'll actually chain you to my bed. For real this time. Without hesitation."

I can't tell if he's joking or serious. Likely the second, knowing him. Regardless, the point is moot since there's no place I'd rather be than in his arms.

That's when it dawns on me that I don't have to let the Flame of Mir come between us. The diamond and the heist don't have to be this horrible memory, a taboo subject in our relationship. A.J. told me just today that she's closer than ever to delivering the final blow to the *stronzo,* and I have no reason to doubt her. Once we no longer have to worry about the Italian mobster, there won't be a reason not to retrieve the Flame of Mir from his possession. If he still has it, of course. It may be long gone by now.

This whole idea could go nowhere, so I must be careful and keep expectations in check. Especially after our fight from earlier. I'd hate to disappoint Nik by promising him something I'm not sure I can deliver. It's wise not to mention this idea to him until something comes of it. It'll be a pleasant surprise. My gift to him.

Besides, sharing my idea would lead to him asking too many questions, the type I can't afford to answer just yet. The odds are that the *stronzo* has long fenced the diamond, anyway. But if he hasn't, then I could easily rectify this blemish in my history with Nik so it can no longer affect our future. I could clear the slate between us. For the first time in our relationship, we'd be on even ground—equals, at last.

Best of all, I would return Nik's prized possession to him. I would give it back to the man who gifted me this beautiful diamond necklace—as an apology for bringing up the one I've stolen from him.

"Chain me to your bed, huh?" I ask with a laugh before kissing this gorgeous man's mouth. *My* gorgeous man. All mine. A priceless, unequaled gift from Cupid himself. "You'd have to catch me first."

13

KAT

"You have completely lost your mind," the familiar voice says with unconcealed astonishment.

I stifle a sigh, making sure to employ my sanest, most reasonable tone. "If you'd just listen to me for a second instead of yelling at me over the phone—"

"Oh, you think this is yelling, Kat? Uh-uh, honey. Keep this idiotic, suicidal idea in your head, and I'll show you yelling."

I exhale loudly, fighting the urge to groan with frustration. "Come on, A.J. Just give me a chance to explain my plan to you."

"Why? What difference would that make?" A.J. shouts over the line at the top of her lungs. "I just can't imagine what you could say that would matter to me. And that's because no ridiculous plan can change the fact that you want to steal from the head of the freaking Italian mafia, Kat."

"Will you please hear me out?" I ask, exasperatedly. But my pleas don't move her. I'm not sure she even hears them. I lost her the moment I asked her to help me find out where the *stronzo* has stashed the Flame of Mir.

"Snooping around this man's business got us into this mess in the first place," A.J. says.

I feel compelled to correct her. "No. *Getting caught* snooping around his business got us into trouble. All we have to do is not get caught this time."

"That simple, huh? Now, why the fuck didn't I think of that in the first place?"

"It might not even matter in the end, anyway. You said it yourself—you're so close to finishing him, A.J. By the time I have all my ducks in a row and feel ready to make my move, he might have no option but to let us do whatever we want —and that includes taking back the diamond."

"If you are willing to bet your life on something so uncertain, then you might be too stupid to live, Kat."

"Hey, you know what they say—faint heart never won fair lady. Luck favors the bold. And the prepared. Which is why I've come to you, my best and most resourceful friend. You know, because that's what friends do. They help each other out. Just like I helped you when the *stronzo* caught you in the first place. Remember that, A.J.?"

My indignant tone doesn't concern her in the slightest. After a decade of friendship, I suppose her reaction—or lack of one—is to be expected. "I *am* trying to help you by talking some sense into you. You've made some questionable decisions in your time, Kat—but this? This one takes the cake."

"You don't approve of it. I get it. Loud and clear. But I'm doing this anyway, A.J., whether or not you help me. So what's it going to be? Do I have to figure this one out by myself?"

"As if you'd have any idea where to even start," she says

scornfully. "It's probably pointless, anyway. I strongly doubt the son of a bitch has been sitting on that diamond this entire time. It was just too hot, and you know it. There's no way that thing isn't long gone by now."

"Maybe," I say, conceding that she has a point. "But maybe not. Before calling you, I reached out to every fence on the East Coast that could've possibly pulled off a job of this size. No one's heard a beep. *Nada*. I don't see how the *stronzo* could've gotten rid of it without someone I know hearing about it."

"He's a freaking mob boss, Kat. One of the old school ones, too. Do you think that maybe he just might have more contacts than you do?"

"When it comes to most of his extracurricular activities, sure. Absolutely. But there's no feasible way for someone to fence the largest red diamond in the world in my corner of the planet without someone I know hearing about it."

A.J. sighs wearily. "You don't know that for sure. You can't know what you don't know."

"Perhaps you're right, and I'm just wasting my time. But there's a chance I'm onto something here. I'm not asking you to get yourself into more trouble, of course. I just called to check if you think you can learn the Flame of Mir's location without getting caught. If you don't think you can, that's completely fine. I don't want you to do anything even remotely risky. Especially not when this nightmare is so close to an end. But you're a freaking genius, so I thought I should ask—just in case it's something you could easily pull off."

"You're talking about it as if it's a simple errand. You're asking me to spy on one of the heads of the Seven Families. One who's had his eye on me for a while now. It's a little more complex than picking up your dry-cleaning for you."

"I know. And there'll be no hard feelings if you tell me you can't do it. I mean it, A.J. Cross my heart and hope to die."

A.J. remains silent on the other side of the line for so long that I start to worry the call has dropped. But then, she sighs. "I'm not making you any promises, understand me? Let's make that very clear," she finally says under her breath.

"Got it. No promises."

"I'll see what I can find out. Again, I can't guarantee anything. But I don't want to have to save your ass if you decide to do this by yourself, so I'll try to get you some intel. But no promises, Kat."

"Of course not. And thank you so much. I owe you big time."

"Yes, but I owe you, too. So don't get killed over a freaking rock, and we'll be even, okay?"

I laugh, trying to lighten the mood. "After all these years, who's keeping track, A.J.? Not me."

She chuckles halfheartedly. "Fair enough. I'll call you once I have an update. Stay out of trouble until then."

A.J. and I say our goodbyes, and, too soon, I'm left alone with my conflicting emotions.

On one hand, I'm a little closer to making amends to Nik for taking the Flame of Mir. I'm closer to leveling the playing field between us and putting this problem behind us. On the other hand, A.J. has a point. My plan could backfire horribly.

Still, I can't very well sit down and expect all my problems to be miraculously fixed. I can't just accept things as they are, either.

Dmitri *is* right. This magical thing Nik and I were lucky enough to stumble upon is too precious and rare to be thrown away. Unfortunately, there are some issues the two of us have to overcome. I have no intention of letting any easily fixable problems from our tumultuous past stand in the way of our future.

Just thinking about everything we have already faced together and all we must still overcome makes me crave Nik's presence even more than usual. I need his strong arms around me, his raspy voice against my ear... My Russian is just what I need right now to chase the blues away.

After setting my phone down, I leave *our* bedroom to search for him. Unsurprisingly, I locate Nik in his office. Funny enough, he's on the phone, too. He paces behind his desk, grunting indiscernible Russian words while running his fingers through his hair in frustration.

While standing just outside the room, I sigh, inadvertently announcing my presence to Nik. His dark brown eyes land on me, and his entire countenance changes in an instant. I smile at him, and his frantic pacing comes to a stop.

Nik quietly mutters something before ending the call, never breaking eye contact with me. The next thing I know, his arms are around me, pulling me close to him as his mouth lands on mine. Nik's kiss is unabashedly needy and hungry. The frantic way his lips devour mine leaves no doubts—his usual cool, calm, and collected act isn't coming to him as naturally today. Just as abruptly as it started, it ends. Without warning, he breaks the kiss, leaning his forehead against mine as his eyes remain closed.

"Tough day, huh?" I ask, rising on my toes to brush my lips against his gorgeous face.

"You have no idea," he says, his voice barely more than a murmur.

"I warned you this morning that getting out of bed was a mistake."

Nik laughs, opening his eyes to glance at me. "You did. And you were right."

"I usually am. A lesson you'd do well to learn, *miliy*."

"I'd be crazy not to, even as it pains me to deprive you of the satisfaction of reminding me of it whenever you can. But enough about me. Tell me—to what do I owe the pleasure of this impromptu visit?"

I shrug. "I just missed you."

Nik groans against the top of my head, tightening his hold on me. "*Kiska*... I swear, you'll be the death of me."

I laugh against his chest. "Unlikely. But your line of work just might. You're always a bundle of nerves, Nik. What's stressing you out today?"

Nik raises a dark eyebrow at me, even as his eyes glint mischievously. "Believe it or not, my life usually isn't this exciting. Most days, the only real danger I face is possibly dying of boredom. But then you come along, and now I don't have a moment of peace."

"And you love every second of it. Don't bother denying it." Nik chuckles and I nip his earlobe. "But for the record, I don't believe that for a second. I can't be that exciting—or dangerous—to the *pakhan* of the freaking *bratva*. And don't avoid my question. Will you tell me what's going on, or do I have to make you?"

Nik's brown eyes burn hot, and his hands drop to my hips, pulling me closer. "I'd love to see you try. Believe *that*." The bulging pressure I feel against my stomach doesn't leave room for any doubts.

Still struggling to keep my poker face on, I fake an exasperated sigh, trying not to let him distract me. "Come on, Nik. Talk to me."

It's Nik's turn to sigh, amusement still twisting the corners of his tempting mouth. "There's nothing you need to worry about, Kat. I'm handling it. It's just frustrating that no one seems to know where McGuire is hiding. We've searched every single place even remotely connected to him —anywhere we could think of—and nothing." Exasperation drips from his every word, and his body tenses against mine.

"Well, I'm sure it's just a matter of time. You'll find him soon enough. He can't run from you forever."

"You'd think," he says bitterly. "I'd feel better if there was anything I could do besides wait for him to come out of wherever he's hiding."

"You are doing all you can. You've been busy. It's not like you're sitting around doing nothing."

Nik clenches his jaw. "I might as well be at this point. The man killed my best friend and tried to take you. No words can describe or emphasize how much I wish I could get my hands on him right now to put this whole nightmare behind me."

I rise on my toes, kissing his lips. "You will, Nik. You will. But you must take care of yourself in the meantime. You have to find a way to keep your stress levels down. You don't want to give yourself a heart attack."

Nik scoffs, rolling his eyes. "Your concern's appreciated. Truly. But I'm fine."

"You shouldn't dismiss me so carelessly. Constantly being on the edge of a major temper tantrum can't be good for you. And you're no spring chicken, *miliy*."

Nik scowls, outraged. "Temper tantrum? For your information, I've never thrown a tantrum in my entire life. Never, you hear me? And I'm only in my thirties—not my eighties!"

I smile, keeping my expression a perfect picture of placidity. "Whatever you say, Nik. But my point stands. You want to be at your best when McGuire pops up. That means taking it easy right now. I know you're trying to do right by me and Maxim—and I love that about you. But I want to see you well, and I'm sure Maxim would want the same."

I expect Nik to admit I have a point, but what he does instead surprises me. His face falls, and a frown forms between his eyebrows. With a small kiss to the top of my head, Nik untangles himself from me, walking towards the floor-to-ceiling windows behind his desk. For the first time since I can remember, the thick velvet drapes have been pulled back to let some sunshine into the usually dark room. Nik stares blankly ahead, unseeing, shoving his hands inside the pockets of his jeans.

Confused, I study him, perplexed about his reaction to my seemingly harmless words.

Before I figure out what to say, Nik breaks the silence between us. "I wish I could say I share your beliefs."

"What do you mean?" I ask, puzzled.

"You said you believe Maxim would want to see me well. I'm not so sure of that."

I approach him, my steps silent on the plush rug. "Nik—" I say, tentatively touching his shoulder. "You don't mean that. How can you say something like that?"

He sighs wearily. "I knew Maxim better than anyone, Kat. I'm not sure he'd want to see me well after everything I put him through. And I never got to make amends for any of it. Maxim never got to rebuild his life. McGuire made sure of that."

"We all make mistakes. You were just trying to do the right thing. And you loved him. I'm sure he knew that. He was your best friend. How could he not want to see you happy and well?"

Nik laughs humorlessly. "There's just so much you don't know."

14

KAT

"Well, why don't you tell me, then?" I softly ask.

Nik remains silent for a long while, seemingly lost in thought. Eventually, he sighs. "It's a long story. One that I wish you never had to learn. It doesn't paint me in a good light, Kat. But I guess you should hear it if we're going to do this." He pauses, and I wait for him to go on, barely daring to breathe, fearing that any disruption might make him change his mind about sharing this chapter of his life with me.

"I don't remember exactly how old I was when I met Maxim, but I'm sure I was barely ten," Nik says. "Maxim was around the same age but much more experienced. My parents had just kicked me out, but he had been by himself for most of his life by then. We were fast friends, always looking out for each other. Even before the *bratva* came along. But eventually, it did come along, as it usually does for boys in our circumstances. I suppose things could've changed then, but luckily, our friendship remained the same. There was so much backstabbing and internal violence within the *bratva* ranks back then, before I became the *pakhan*. Things were very different for a young *shestyorka* back in those days. I'd like to think I changed that for the better." He shrugs.

Still staring ahead, Nik adds, "Maxim and I—we were so young and hungry, so desperate to improve our circumstances. We also had nothing to lose but each other. A man with nothing to lose is a very dangerous man, Kat. That's how Maxim and I survived early on. It's how we rose through the ranks. It's how I became the *pakhan*. But I'm rambling."

He laughs under his breath humorlessly, and I take the opportunity to interject. "Nik—"

I press a tender kiss on his back, but he shakes his head, cutting me off. "No, Kat. Don't pity me. I don't deserve or want your pity."

"Nik, I've told you I don't pity you."

He resumes his tale, disregarding my interruption. "We were still pretty young when I found the Flame of Mir. Maxim was so happy for me. He saw it as a good omen, as a sign of great things to come. Of course, he wanted me to sell it for capital so we could gather the resources to take over the *bratva* right then. I couldn't do it, though. I suppose part of me bought into his sentimental nonsense, and I couldn't bring myself to part with it. I guess it was also the beginning of my collection. Over time, I started to think of it as a symbol of all the good, admirable things about me and my journey. I'd look at it, and it would remind me of how far I've come, of how proud of myself I was for overcoming the shit hand I'd been dealt. It also reminded me of Maxim and the bond we shared. After all, he was there through it all. I couldn't have done any of it without him."

Nik's words almost tear me in half. A sharp, burning sensation rips through my chest as it fully sinks in—I took the diamond from him and gave it to the *stronzo*. It was bad enough when I thought I had stolen something of inestimable monetary value. But to know it meant so much for him on a personal level...

And just like that, my determination and resolve to return the Flame of Mir to Nik are renewed. I will get it back for him no matter what. The only way the *stronzo* gets to keep it is over my dead body.

Completely unaware of the havoc his words wreaked in me, Nik says, "I was very young when I became the *pakhan*. At least if compared to my predecessor and my peers in the other six families. My position wasn't so secure back then. I was desperate not to return to where I started, so I did everything I could to solidify my hold over the *bratva*. Most of the heads of the other families stayed neutral towards me at first, waiting to see what I was made of before supporting me or not. I don't blame them. McGuire, however, reached out to me. He offered to mentor me and was even open to publicly supporting me. That would have been a huge coup for me back then, Kat. The Irish have always controlled the port; if I could get him on my side, the sky was the limit for me. We became friendly and even a little close. He told me he had been struggling to subdue some unrest among his men. He seemed genuinely concerned, mentioning his worry over his daughter's safety over and over again. Eager as I was to consolidate our alliance, I offered him the perfect solution—the only way to make sure his daughter was safe from his men was to bring an outsider to protect her. Someone whose loyalties weren't in question."

Maxim.

Breathlessly, I wait for Nik to continue, wrapping my arms around his waist so he won't see my hands shaking.

Nik mindlessly caresses my hands before continuing, his

voice as emotionless as ever. "I'm sure you can guess what happened next. I volunteered the services of my best man. I sang all of Maxim's praises to McGuire, raving about how there was no better man for the job. I assured him there was no one I trusted more, and McGuire was more than happy to accept my offer. By then, tales of my takeover of the *bratva* had spread, and Maxim's reputation had grown exponentially with them. I was very proud of myself for arranging all that, Kat. I thought nothing could go wrong, and McGuire would soon fall to his knees to thank me. But not long after, I realized my mistake once I learned Maxim was involved with Erin McGuire. Unfortunately for Maxim, it could never be. Not only was the princess of the Irish family completely out of his league, but she had been promised to Lorenzo Salvatore, the heir of the Italian *famiglia,* since they were kids."

Upon hearing the familiar last name, I freeze. I never had the pleasure of meeting Lorenzo in person, but his uncle—also known as the *stronzo*—was, unfortunately, an acquaintance of mine. Immediately, I force my body to relax. I don't want to alarm Nik and cause him to stop his story. I also can't afford to have him question my sudden, visceral response to the Italian name.

Thankfully, Nik is too immersed in his memories to notice my reaction. Tensing, he says, "When it came out that Erin was cheating on Lorenzo with Maxim, the engagement was broken. It was a huge scandal. McGuire was furious that his alliance with the Italians would never come to be and that his daughter's virginity had been taken by someone he saw as unworthy of her. The Italians weren't thrilled, either. Giuseppe Salvatore, the reigning boss, was livid that his nephew and heir had been publicly humiliated. If I could go back in time, Kat, I would do things differently, but you have to understand—I was new at this job, and I struggled to find a way to protect both Maxim and the *bratva*. My back was against the wall, so I took the path of least resistance. I couldn't have possibly withstood a war against both the Italians and the Irish back then, so I did what I could to appease them. I made massive concessions to them, and I exiled Maxim. I sent him back to Siberia, even when he told me how much he cared for Erin."

I sigh, holding him even tighter. "Oh, Nik. I'm so sorry."

Nik grasps one of my hands wrapped around his waist, bringing it to his lips. Mindlessly, he brushes a kiss against it before returning it to where it rested against his stomach.

"Eventually, I got to a point where I felt like I didn't have much to fear from McGuire or Salvatore. That's when I brought Maxim back home, hoping I could fix things between us. Of course, thanks to McGuire, we'll never know. Now all I have left of Maxim is the unresolved issues between us, all the things we left unsaid..." Nik's pained tone and poignant words make my chest ache.

"Oh, Nik, no," I say, coming around to face him. After wrapping my arms around his neck, I kiss his mouth. "That's not true. I didn't have the pleasure of knowing Maxim, but I know that just can't be true. In everything you do, I see how much he meant to you. Whenever you speak of him, I see the love between the lines. He left you with much more than your regrets and your need to avenge him. The bond you shared and your love for each other will always be with you. No one—not McGuire, Maxim, or even you—can change that."

Nik groans as his mouth oppressively crushes mine. He grabs the back of my neck with one hand, pulling me into his kiss as his fingers sink into my hair. His other arm tightens around me just below my hips, lifting me. He turns around, setting me down on the edge of his desk before stepping between my legs. I wrap them around his waist, drawing him closer.

Between the feverish, open-mouthed kisses Nik rains on my face, my neck and my shoulders, he says, "I don't know what the fuck I did to deserve you, Kat, but whatever it was, thank God I did. Thank God."

With a pained moan, I pull Nik's face back towards mine. I kiss him long and hard, urging him to realize what I can't put into words—hoping he'll understand how much I need him.

Somehow, he does. Somehow, I understand he feels the same.

Soon, my fingers are undoing his zipper as his hand pulls my underwear aside. I wrap my hand around his thick length, and he curses under his breath. His fingers sink into me, and I gasp, biting his shoulder to curb my scream of pleasure.

Impatiently, I draw him closer, guiding him inside me. The now-familiar, focused look on his face tells me he intends to torture me, slowly entering me inch by inch. But I have no intention of cooperating with this ridiculous plan of his.

As I press my ankles against Nik's superbly formed ass, I slide my hips forward at once, and his cock enters me in one deep plunge.

Our groans echo in synchronized bliss, and I smirk at him, leaning back over his desk.

With a shake of his head, Nik bends over until his mouth touches my neck. He playfully nips at my ear before ruefully whispering, "Bad girl."

While tracing his way down my neck with languid, wet kisses, Nik reaches the area where my neck meets my shoulder.

He takes his time there, lavishly worshiping my skin with his mouth and tongue. Then, without warning, he bites me almost too hard, beginning to move his hips in a punishing rhythm.

"Nik..." I say in a breathless moan.

"You're mine, Kat," he groans, his lips trembling against my skin as he brings us closer and closer to the edge. "I can't lose you. I'll never, ever let you go, *kiska*. Never, you hear me?"

I nod, dragging my nails down his back. "Yeah, Nik. Yours. I'm yours, and you're mine."

The responding sound that leaves Nik's throat comes from deep inside his chest, and I feel it to my core. It's more growl than groan, and I know he's past the point of no return by the way his hips grind against mine.

Nik bends low to kiss me again while his hand between my legs searches for the spot he knows will make me yield everything to him. I cry out into his mouth when he finds it. His fingers expertly work it until it drives me wild.

"Say it again," he rasps between thrusts. "I want you to look into my eyes and tell me who you belong to as you come around my dick."

"Fuck," I moan, throwing my head back.

His hand reaches my breast, mercilessly pinching my nipple until I cry out in a mix of pain and pleasure.

"Look at me and say it." He slows down the movements of his hips, tightening his hold on the tip of my breast.

"*You*," I say with a gasp, gazing into his crazed eyes. "I belong to you."

"Good girl," he groans, resuming his thrusting.

His fingers find my clitoris again, as he frantically fucks me hard enough to make my teeth clatter. In a few heartbeats, I lose it, diving head-first into the abyss. Nik rushes to join me. With one final deep thrust, he buries himself deep inside me, and we climax together.

Time seems to stand still as I lie in his arms, savoring the feel of him on me, in me. I sigh, relaxed from the top of my head to the tip of my toes. He nuzzles me, his face against mine.

Nik and I wordlessly stare into each other's eyes for countless moments until his eyes start glimmering with amusement. "What's it?" he asks, his voice deliciously hoarse and raspy.

I shrug. "Nothing. I was going to comment that your mood seems to have vastly and miraculously improved. That's good for your health, you know. *I'm* good for you health."

Nik smiles, all gorgeous. He glances over my head, and his grin turns into a frown. He groans.

"What's the matter now?" I ask with a chuckle.

"The door. We never shut it. It's wide open."

Nik quickly zips up his pants before hurrying towards it. I can't help but laugh as I watch him.

He returns to me just as I'm done straightening my clothes. Tenderly, he helps me get down from his desk.

"I take it there's no chance we're home alone?" I ask, ruefully amused.

Nik shakes his head. "No. But my men know better than to invade our privacy. Still..." He grimaces.

I shrug, still laughing. "Well, they sure got an earful. We weren't particularly quiet."

"I know. I'm sorry, Kat," he says, scowling.

I pat his hand reassuringly, trying to make light of it. "It's okay, Nik. I'll survive. At least word will spread around that you're taken now."

Nik's eyes melt as he smiles. His arms wrap around me. "You're going to unman me, I swear."

I scoff against his chest. "I sure hope not. I have a healthy appreciation for how much of a man you are, trust me."

Laughing, he kisses me slowly.

Eventually, I pull away. While looking into his eyes, I say, "I meant what I said earlier, Nik. I want you to take it easy. You're way too hard on yourself. You must take a page from my book and *carpe diem* a little. Tell me, is there anything I can do to help? There has to be."

With a dismissive shake of his head, Nik shuts me down. "The last thing I want is to burden you with my problems."

"You're not. I'm offering you my help—willingly and free of charge. It's a rare, rare occasion. You shouldn't waste it."

Nik teases me with a dramatic, over-the-top sigh. "My charitable beauty. A veritable Mother Theresa."

I roll my eyes. "I'm serious."

"I know. But you already help me so much by just being around me. More than you know."

"Yeah, yeah. I'm great in the sack. Tell me something I don't know. But surely you realize that I have more to offer than earthshaking orgasms."

Nik howls with laughter. "Oh, Kat—"

"What if I called some of my contacts to see what they know? Maybe some of my people have heard something about where McGuire's hiding."

Nik hesitates. "I don't want you to get even more involved in this mess than you already are."

"It would just be a couple of phone calls, Nik. There's no risk at all. What's the worst that could happen to me? Carpal tunnel syndrome?"

Eventually, he agrees. "All right. A couple of phone calls

should be fine, but don't go out of your way to go the extra mile or something like that. I mean it, Kat."

"I won't, I swear. Is there anything else I can do? I'd love to get stuff off your plate so you can relax a little."

With a smile, Nik kisses my forehead. "Just be safe. Stay out of trouble."

"Your wish is my command. Consider it done. Well, I'll do my best, at least. I can promise you that much."

"I'd greatly appreciate it if you could stay at the penthouse until we catch McGuire. Knowing where you are—and that you are safe—at all times will put me at ease."

"I'll keep that in mind. Now, why don't you sit down and have a drink while I call some people? I don't have my phone on me. I'll be back in two shakes."

Nik ruefully shakes his head at me, scoffing with outraged amusement. Nonetheless, he does what I ask him to do.

I glance at him before exiting the room, and something about the shadows under his eyes and the tension already returning to his shoulders give me pause. Nik's story about how the Flame of Mir came into his life returns to the forefront of my mind. It pains me to know that I took something so special from him and handed it to someone so undeserving. It must've been an immense blow to lose the diamond, just as he learned his best friend was gone forever.

Even worse, I'm forced to face an uncomfortable possibility—once Nik is no longer burdened by his quest to avenge his friend, will he realize he's not over me stealing the diamond? Will he resent me forever? Will he ever forget that our relationship started with betrayal?

I know better than to waste my time wondering about what might or might not happen. My energy is better spent controlling the controllable, so I must focus on retrieving the jewel. After all, it'll be a cold day in hell before I let the *stronzo* ruin my future.

Nik smiles at me quizzically, puzzled by my intense stare. For a moment, I hesitate. Maybe I should tell him the truth about my plans and my involvement with the *stronzo*. Deceitfulness and subterfuge come much more naturally to me than unrestricted honesty. I'm many things—an open book isn't one of them. But keeping these secrets from Nik has started to not sit right with me, especially now that he's shared with me these painful stories about his past. Still, it's hard to speak of a secret I've kept for so long openly. A secret that isn't just my own.

I also can't help but worry that his instinct to protect me could become a problem. I have no doubts I'm capable of safely retrieving the Flame of Mir once I know where the damned thing is. But I have a feeling Nik would disagree with me. I suspect he'd try to stop me.

Still, my heart wins, and I find myself saying, "Nik, about the Flame of Mir. I've been thinking—"

Nik's distracted gaze raptly focuses on me. Now that I know how much the diamond means to him, I'm not exactly shocked by his eagerness to learn more about its fate. And, to be fair, it must frustrate him I've kept this secret from him for so long. It's the one part of me I've denied him, and I know he is dying to have me yield all of myself to him at last.

But, more than ever, I understand how vital it is that I make amends for taking the Flame of Mir. I know for a fact that I won't be able to move on if Nik decides he can't get over the fact that I stole it from him.

Because I know how protective he is of me—and how stubborn he can be—I decide against telling him my secret just yet. I'll gladly tell him everything eventually. But I just can't lose him. If I tell Nik what Giuseppe Salvatore, the *stronzo*, put me through, he'll set out to destroy the man without a second thought.

The idea of Nik and the *bratva* facing the Italians *and* the Irish at the same time makes me shudder. I can't bear the thought of him succumbing to his foe or mine because his resources are stretched thin between a war on two fronts.

The old Nikolai Stefanovich might have been able to cooly assess the situation before rushing into any ill-advised actions. But my Nik will undoubtedly just storm out in a fit of righteous rage to punish the man who hurt me, consequences be damned.

Above all else, I can't allow that outcome. It's my duty and my right to protect him from himself.

"You were saying? About the Flame of Mir?" Nik says, disrupting my reverie, and I realize I've been staring at him in silence.

I smile at him, my heart aching. I don't bother hiding my sadness as I tell him what I can for now. "There are no words to express how sorry I am for taking it. I never knew it meant so much to you. I hate that you lost it just as you lost your best friend, too. I'm sorry that's how our relationship started. I wish I could go back in time and change what I did, but I can't, and I'm so sorry, Nik."

He is next to me in a heartbeat, embracing me with no hint of hesitation or resentment. "It's okay, Kat," he says against my hair. "Please don't get upset over this. I can't bear to see you sad—least of all because of me. And the diamond doesn't even matter to me anymore. I mean it. I appreciate the sentiment, but it doesn't matter to me anymore. I couldn't give less of a fuck about it. You said you'd go back in time and do things differently if you could, but I'd beg you not to. I wouldn't dare change a single thing that happened in the past. Not if there's any chance it would keep you from coming into my life."

I gasp against his chest. "You don't mean that."

"I do, Kat. I really do. I'd give up every cent I have, the blood in my veins, the skin off my back, anything—if it meant I'd end up right here, right now, with you in my arms."

I drag Nik's mouth to mine, praying I can show him all I feel, even when my words fall short. He returns my kiss with his usual abandon, and I lose myself in his embrace.

15

NIK

Before I know it, it's dark outside, and I'm mildly surprised to realize I've been working for hours.

I rub my tired, bleary eyes and force myself to stretch my back, my tight muscles groaning in protest. Even those too-brief, heart-arresting moments spent making love to Kat earlier were not enough to erase the stress I've been carrying in my shoulders and neck.

It has become clear to me that the only way out of this nightmare is through. I'll rest and relax once McGuire is dead. There'll be no lasting reprieve for me until then.

Of course, it goes without saying that I hope Kat won't stop trying to change my mind. Especially if what we did earlier today is how she plans to go about it.

After rising from my chair, I decide I've spent enough time without her for today. It's been too long already, and I miss her too much to stay away from her a moment longer. Quietly, I set out to find her, walking through the penthouse.

Just thinking about finding her in our bed—comfortably tucked under the blankets—makes my heart ache. Eager to hold her, I open the bedroom door to look for her inside. To my surprise, Kat isn't in bed. In fact, the covers are completely undisturbed.

So I make my way to the kitchen. It's possible, perhaps even likely, that Kat made her way there for a late-night snack. I'm a little hungry myself—for food and for her. But after switching the kitchen lights on, I frown—Kat's nowhere to be seen.

With an exhausted sigh, I rub my tired eyes again. She's probably back in the guest room, the bedroom she first occupied. Whether she went there to fetch something she left behind or to provoke me, I don't know. I'd bet my money on the latter, knowing her.

If that's the game she wants to play with me, I'm more than happy to oblige her. It's not a problem. Nothing will delight me more than meeting her challenge.

So I shove the guest room's door open. My amusement promptly dies away when I find the room empty.

I quickly step into the adjoining walk-in closet, but Kat's nowhere to be found.

Frantically, I search every room in my home, practically kicking doors open and impatiently turning on the lights. But it's all for nothing—Kat's whereabouts remain a mystery to me.

A horrible, icy feeling settles in the pit of my stomach when I realize I have no idea where she is or if she's safe.

Enraged, I make my way to the penthouse's east wing. Without knocking, I push the door of the room next to my office open. A young *shestyorka* whose name has completely evaded me chokes on his coffee as Vladmir inquisitively glances at me. The only indication of his surprise at seeing me is the slight rise of his eyebrows.

Before they can say anything, I ask, "Where is she?"

I don't miss the look the two men exchange between

themselves before Vladmir says, "Ms. Devereaux left a few hours ago, Nikolai. She told me you let her go out on her own."

"Did she now?"

Vladmir nods. "She said she had a few errands to run."

"And did that sound like something I'd realistically allow her to do by herself in our current circumstances?"

Vladmir visibly swallows. "I didn't think—"

I cut him off. "Oh, we can agree on that. You most certainly didn't think. Did she mention where she was going?"

Vladmir shakes his head, and I leave him, cursing. This is a waste of my time, and I have a feeling I won't be able to keep my temper in check if he keeps looking at me like that —as if I'm a besotted fool who can't control a woman who's clearly playing him.

I can't believe Kat did this. A few hours ago, she promised to stay in the penthouse until I finished dealing with McGuire. But now, she's gone without so much as a by-your-leave. God only knows where she is or if she's safe.

I tried to explain these things to her, but she refuses to understand that while I can guarantee her safety while she's under my roof, it all goes out the window once she's out there. As long as McGuire is on the loose, Kat isn't safe out in the streets by herself. There's nothing he would love more than to punish me by harming her.

If there was an important matter that required her immediate attention, why not just tell me? I would handle it for her. Or, at the very least, I would have escorted her while she was out and about.

Kat promised me she would stay at the penthouse, and I thought I could trust her to keep her word. I thought I could expect her to trust my judgment.

Dmitri's excited voice interrupts my thoughts. "Nik, there you are. You're not going to believe what I have for you."

I pivot in his direction. Could it be? Did he run into Kat? Did he bring her back home? But no luck. Instead, Dmitri is by himself, looking a little out of breath.

One look at my face and his expression turns into a frown. "What's wrong? Did something happen?"

"Kat's gone. She went out a few hours ago and isn't back yet. I don't know where she is or if she's all right."

Dmitri's frown deepens, but he tries to reassure me. "I'm sure it's nothing you need to worry about, Nik. I'm sure Kat's fine. Maybe she wanted to get some fresh air or something like that."

I shake my head, grimacing. "Then why wouldn't she say something to me before leaving? Just a few hours ago, I asked her to stay here until I have a chance to take care of McGuire. She promised me she would."

"Well, you know how Kat is. Maybe she forgot to tell you she was going out. I'm sure she just needed a break from the tension around this place, so she stepped out for a moment. You were hard at work, and she probably didn't want to disturb you. I'm sure that's all. I have no doubts she'll turn up safe and sound any minute now."

A terrible, ominous feeling festers inside me. "I hope you're right, Dmitri. But I'm not sure I buy this idea that she just forgot to tell me she was going out. She knew I wanted her to stay here for the time being. She promised me she would. You can't tell me she didn't know what she was doing when she left without speaking to me."

Dmitri interjects with a sigh. "Did it occur to you that Kat might feel a little claustrophobic if you try to keep her in this expensively decorated gilded cage? I'll bet you dollars to donuts that's what happened. I'm positive she needed a moment to herself. But she'll be back any minute now. If you want my advice, you should probably reevaluate this super controlling approach of yours."

"The only thing I'm reevaluating right now is the idea that I can trust her blindly. I can't believe I'm letting myself be fooled by my own wishful thinking."

Dmitri places his hand on my shoulder. "You're only saying that in the heat of the moment. You're out of your mind with worry for her, and it's driving you a little crazy. I don't think for a second that you actually mean that."

I shake my head. "I'm not so sure about that, Dmitri. Why would Kat do this? Why does she always have to go behind my back? This little stunt makes me wonder what else she's been hiding from me."

"May I suggest you take a deep breath before making any impulsive decisions you might regret later?"

On the brink of losing control, I snap at him. "Watch it. I'm very tolerant with you, Dmitri. More than any other man in my position would be. But don't mistake my tolerance for weakness."

"I would never, Nik," he says in a slightly pacifying tone that is a bit insulting.

"If McGuire gets his hands on her—" I choke. "If something happens to her, Dmitri, I don't know what I'll do."

"Nik, nothing will happen to her. Kat's a big girl. I'm sure she's completely fine. Don't start thinking of worst-case scenarios just yet. Besides, I have some good news. It might cheer you up."

I scowl. "Not now, Dmitri. I'm not in the mood."

"You will be once you learn who I ran into just a few blocks from here. Guess who it is."

I impassively stare at him for a moment, waiting for him

to go on. When he doesn't, I say, "I honestly hope for your sake that it was a rhetorical question and you aren't actually expecting me to try to guess."

With a sigh, Dmitri says, "Connor Daniels. I caught him scouting us. Now, I'll admit I wasn't sure if I should bring him back here, but I figured you'd like the opportunity to talk to him yourself."

Even though it's terrific news, I almost can't focus on what Dmitri's telling me. Connor is McGuire's right-hand man, and this could be a game-changing development for us. Still, it's hard to let go of the urge to set out to find Kat right now, tracking down wherever she's hiding from me.

In the end, Dmitri's advice sticks with me. Maybe Kat does need some space from me and this whole mess with McGuire. For all her faults, she isn't careless. She is brave and bold to a dangerous degree, but never needlessly reckless.

It goes against my every instinct not to hunt her down and drag her back home, but I can't afford to lose her. She knows I'm only one call away if she needs me. Besides, there's no better way to ensure her safety than to find out where McGuire is hiding and kill him at last.

"Bring him up," I say. "But tell Vladmir I want him to find Kat. I don't want him to let her spot him or try to bring her home just yet. I just need him to keep an eye on her." If nothing else, Vlad will be glad to have a chance to fix his mistake.

"No problem," Dmitri says.

My mind is elsewhere, and my heart isn't in it—but Dmitri and I mercilessly question Connor. We quickly learn the reason he ventured so close to my home. He was searching for Kat. His orders were to take her at all costs.

My blood runs cold upon hearing the man's bold confession. I don't even realize I'm choking the life out of him until Dmitri physically stops me from prematurely killing him.

Connor tries to put up a show of loyalty to his boss, but McGuire isn't the type to inspire self-sacrifice in his men. In the end, bloody and beaten, Connor tells us what he knows. "You know the story as well as I do," he says, sputtering while struggling to catch his breath. "Your pal Maxim came to be in Patrick McGuire's service because there was a rebellion within our ranks. My predecessor was their leader. He was a cunning bastard. Good ole Jack."

Connor pauses for a second, coughing up some blood.

"What you don't know is that, close to the end, Jack had a feeling that old man McGuire was onto him. But Jack was a clever man. He wrote down everything he knew about Patrick in this small black book—and he knew a lot. Every dirty secret or minor detail about the man's operations or assets Jack could think of went on the little notebook. Not satisfied, Jack stole millions of McGuire's money. Legend has it that he buried it, noting the location in the same book. And then he hid it. It was supposed to be his insurance against McGuire, you see. Unfortunately for Jack, he was taken out in that nasty car accident. Or maybe it was for the best. At least he died before Patrick got his hands on him."

"And why is it again that we should care about any of this?" Dmitri asks.

As he struggles against a hacking cough, Connor says, "Because Jack's little black book was presumed to be lost forever since his unexpected demise. But then we learned he kept a lady on the side. Someone he kept a secret from all of us. This woman had no lost love for Jack, so she was more than happy to tell McGuire all she knew in exchange for some coin. And what she told him drove the old man up a wall. You see, according to her, before dying, Jack had only trusted one person with the location of the book. Imagine our surprise when we learned that person was one and the same with your good friend Maxim Petrovski."

Connor's fantastic story surprises me, and it takes me a moment to process his words. Dmitri, however, promptly scoffs. "Do you honestly think we believe in this fairy tale of yours? You'd say anything to save McGuire and yourself."

Connor shrugs. "Believe what you want, pup. It makes no difference to me. It's the truth, though. I have no reason to lie. Whether it's by Nikolai's hands or McGuire's, I knew my life was forfeited the moment you managed to drag me back here. Why do you think Patrick didn't throw a fit when your boss brought Maxim back from Siberia? The old man saw it as his chance to get his hands on that book and retrieve his money. It was going to be tough to get a chance to interrogate Maxim when he was all the way across the ocean in your territory. Now, if he was here... Unfortunately for us, though, we never got a chance to get our hands on Maxim. That's why we went to that museum party, you know. McGuire meant to grab Maxim once he had a few drinks in him. But someone else got to him before we could make our move."

"You expect me to believe your boss had nothing to do with Maxim's murder?" I ask, barely managing to keep my temper in check.

Connor shrugs, grimacing in pain. "Like I said, it doesn't matter to me if you do or not. I know I'm as good as dead. All I can hope for now is that it's quick and painless. The way I see it, maybe if I tell you what you want to know, you'll grant me that mercy."

"Nik, you don't believe this crap, right? Connor's obviously full of shit," Dmitri says with a scoff. "I say we kill him to send a message to McGuire."

I stare at Connor, debating my next steps. A heartbeat later, I completely lose my train of thought once Kat's familiar voice echoes outside my office, just before an angry baritone voice responds.

I'm making my way to her before my brain even fully registers that she's back. I yank the door open, and the sight of her turns my limbs to rubber.

She's safe. She's back.

Indescribable relief washes over me, and I take a moment to look at her, quickly scanning her from head to toe. My eyes assess her for any signs of injuries while my brain tries to commit every detail to memory.

Kat seems completely fine. More than fine, actually, if the outraged way she's giving Vladmir a piece of her mind is any indication.

Vlad is visibly upset as he chastises her for lying to him about having my permission to leave by herself. Normally, I'd lash out at him for talking to her in such a disrespectful manner. Right now, however, I'm more than inclined to let him give her a piece of *his* mind.

"Dmitri," I say over my shoulder. "You and Vladmir. Get Connor out of here now. Stash him somewhere safe for the time being."

My voice startles Kat, who hadn't noticed me standing a few feet away from her as she faces Vladmir.

With a gasp, she turns in my direction, having the audacity to ask, "Connor? As in Connor Daniels? McGuire's right-hand man?"

"You must be kidding me," I say, somehow managing to address her without yelling. "That's what you have to say to me? After breaking your promise to me and leaving home without warning?"

With a beatific smile, Kat pats my cheek. "Nik, I'm sorry I

upset you. I thought I'd be back before you even noticed I was gone. I know I should've said something, but there was something I had to do and I didn't want to interrupt your work. But I'm back now—safe and sound. We don't need to argue about this, right? No harm, no foul. Now, tell me about Connor. Exciting news, huh?"

And then, Kat smiles at me. She fucking *smiles* at me.

"Have you lost your mind?" I ask, for all intents and purposes yelling at her at the tops of my lungs. "You could've died! Do you have any idea what kind of horrible scenarios were going through my mind once I realized you were gone? Not to mention—you made me a promise, and then, almost with the same breath, you broke it."

With an exasperated sigh, Kat says, "I understand how you would see it that way, but Nik—I was fine. I can take care of myself. I knew I was going to be completely fine, and I didn't want to disturb or worry you unnecessarily. You already have a lot on your plate right now. I'm sorry I upset you. I truly am. I was hoping I'd be back before you were done with work."

"That doesn't make it okay! I trusted you to keep your word to me, but you disregarded it a few hours later. And for what? Some stupid errand? Do you seriously expect me to believe that?"

Kat's eyes narrow slightly. "If you must know, it was for something a little more serious and urgent than a simple errand. Like I said, I'm sorry you feel like I broke my promise to you, and I'm sorry for upsetting you. I don't want to add another worry to your already gigantic pile of problems. But I hope I don't have to remind you I don't need your permission to come and go as I see necessary. I appreciate your concern for my safety. I'll certainly take your advice under consideration when assessing the risks of going out, but you must understand that I'll do that out of care, concern and affection for you. I trust I don't have to point out that you, as a matter of fact, do not own me."

I practically shout in her face. "You did not just say that to me. You promised me, Kat! You promised me. You said you wouldn't leave the penthouse."

Kat shakes her head, raising an eyebrow at me. "Actually, no. I did not promise that at all. I said I'd keep your request in mind. I promised I'd do my best to stay out of trouble and be safe. Which I was, whether or not you choose to believe it. Now, Dmitri—since it's clear Nik's too far gone with his temper tantrum to tell me anything, can you please let me know what Connor had to say?"

"Dmitri—" I say in warning. "Don't you dare answer her. Get Connor out of here. *Now*."

Kat rolls her eyes. "Come on, Nik. Don't be like this. Dmitri, you know I'm a part of this now, too. I deserve to know. What did Connor have to say?"

Dmitri's head swivels back and forth between us, but I expect his loyalty to ultimately lie with me, his *pakhan*—the man who signs his paychecks and the man who helped raise him. I expect him to follow my orders and leave immediately. As it turns out, that was foolish of me.

Still, I can't say I'm too surprised when the insubordinate fool obliges Kat instead, relating every tidbit of information we just learned from McGuire's right-hand man. Once he finishes reporting to her, he turns to me. He has the nerve to shrug, apologetically. "Sorry, Nik. I'll get Connor out of here now. Let's go, Vlad."

"Get the fuck out of my sight," I say under my breath.

"Nik, this changes everything, right?" Kat asks, breathless with unbridled excitement once we are alone. "You have to see my point now. You have proof that it's entirely possible McGuire isn't behind this. No need to go to war against him just yet."

"This changes nothing," I say, angrily refuting her suggestion. "Of course Connor would say that McGuire didn't kill Maxim. He'd say anything to try to save his boss. I don't know how many times I have to tell you he's the one who killed Maxim. An incredibly fantastical story from an untrustworthy source changes absolutely nothing. Besides, as I've already fucking told you, it doesn't matter anymore. Patrick McGuire attacked you in broad daylight. *That* was an act of war."

Disappointment shadows Kat's features. "How can you say that? Think of all the horrible things that could happen to all of us if you insist on heading down this path," she says.

"You aren't listening to me," I say, grabbing her shoulders and shaking her. "And it doesn't fucking matter to me right now, anyway. You lied to me, Kat. I trusted you, and you went behind my back when I let my guard down. You could've gotten yourself killed. Connor just told us his orders were to capture you. Do you have any idea what it would do to me if McGuire got to you? If I lost you, Kat, I don't know what I'd do. I wouldn't have been able to go on."

Kat's eyes soften as she touches my face. "Nik, I'm sorry. I didn't mean to cause you this much pain."

"You even made me look like a fool in front of my men. You undermined me and endangered our plan to catch McGuire. You left me. You endangered yourself. You betrayed my trust and you disobeyed me. You did it just to prove you could."

Kat's tender expression hardens. "You have no idea what you're talking about. You don't own me, Nik. I don't owe you obedience. I thought we saw eye-to-eye on this, but it seems I was wrong. You tell me I've broken your trust, but the way I see it, you're breaking mine right now. You're trying to control me. I'm setting very clear boundaries, and you insist on kicking them aside. I thought you respected me more than that. After everything we've been through, I expect you to know that you can't shackle me to you. Believe it or not, I'm not just being a brat. I have a really good reason for doing what I did today. Believe it or not, I did it for you and me. I'll tell you all about it soon. Right now, you need to trust me to come back to you. You need to trust me—period."

The hurt and seriousness in her tone give me pause and make me second-guess myself. The very last thing I wish to do is hurt her. But I just can't agree with her. Unlike her, I'm not making the mistake of underestimating McGuire again. I know better than she does that he is a genuine threat to her safety. Everything I've done has been for the right reasons. Can Kat say the same? If she had such a good, legitimate reason for breaking her promise to me, then why be so secretive about it?

"I guess I never realized my trust would be put to the test so soon or so often," I say, still reeling with anger. I should've realized that if I let myself need her—if I let myself trust her—then I'd be powerless to stop her from thoroughly ruining me if she decides to leave me.

Like my parents did. Like Maxim did. Their loss nearly broke me in half. It took all that I had to pull myself back together and fix the mess their absence created in me. If Kat leaves me, it will destroy me. There'll be nothing left to fix.

She sighs wearily. "I hate to break it to you, Nik, but that's exactly why it's called trust. There's always going to be an element of uncertainty. You'll just have to chance on me. On us."

The coldness and disappointment in her dark blue eyes

almost rip me in half. With a sharp pain in my chest, I wonder how it's possible that we're looking at each other like this right now when I was lost inside her mere hours ago. I don't want to lose that Kat, the one who sighed in my arms, showering me with kisses while playfully calling me *miliy*.

"*Dusha moya*," I say, reaching for her hand. *My soul*. Kat's ice-cold blue eyes melt slightly at the endearment, and I allow myself to hope. "I don't want to lose you. I *can't* lose you. Believe me, I want nothing more than to see you happy and content, and I'll do my best to make you feel satisfied with your life. With me. But make no mistake—my priority will always be to keep you safe. Whether you like it or not, I'll do what it takes to ensure that. Even if it displeases you. I won't let McGuire, the threat of war among the Seven Families, or the devil himself stand in my way."

Kat's face falls, and her disappointed expression gives way to fury. Without another word, she shoots me a disenchanted look before storming away.

16

KAT

The nerve of that man...

Hours after our unfortunate disagreement, the sun rises, announcing the beginning of a new day. But I'm not ready to move on and let go of yesterday's resentments just yet.

After reliving our argument all night, I'm struggling to forgive Nik for having the audacity to threaten to "do whatever it takes" to keep me safe. As if his judgment of what is good for me is superior to mine. As if I can't be trusted to take care of myself.

It's one thing for Nik to be protective and caring. I've come to accept that's an endearing, albeit at times aggravating, part of his personality. Last night, however, was something else entirely. Nik turned into a possessive and controlling jerk right before my eyes. I can't even begin to imagine what gave him the illusion that I'd ever be this meek and subservient creature he wants me to be. Me, his little submissive girlfriend? I don't think so. I may have given him a chance to be a part of my life, but I pity the man if he seriously believes I'll become nothing more than his other half.

Yesterday, I hesitated before leaving the penthouse without giving him a heads-up. Now, I feel validated that I ultimately decided to do so. His overbearing reaction proves that I was right to sneak out.

Truth be told, I hate to put Nik in a position where he will inevitably struggle to subdue his trust issues. But, at some point, a woman must stop making excuses for grown men and their emotional baggage. At some point, Nik has to take responsibility for his personal shortcomings. He must accept that I'm not something he can own—a prize to be added to his collection. Sooner or later, he has to decide if he trusts me or not. He'll have to choose between keeping his misgivings about who I am or keeping *me*. I can't make that decision for him.

Besides, everything I'm doing is to ensure our relationship has a future. I know with every fiber of my being that Nik and I have no shot unless I wipe the slate clean. It's why I haven't told him everything yet. Someone has to save Nik from himself. Who else's going to protect him when he's busy protecting me? The ridiculous man is ready to start a war to avenge me, even though I'm completely unharmed.

So when A.J. shared with me a promising lead on the Flame of Mir's location, I jumped at the opportunity to check it out. At least some good news came out of the ordeal. As usual, my friend's intel was worth its weight in gold. Or, in this case, in diamonds. I know now for a fact that the *stronzo* was stupid enough to keep the Flame of Mir. Even better—I know where he's been hiding it.

After my little surveillance session, I rushed home to Nik, giddy and excited to get started on my plan to rescue his diamond. Of course, once I arrived at the penthouse, I was unpleasantly surprised by his temper tantrum. I retired to the guest room after our fight, feeling like I was falling from cloud nine. I even locked the door. I knew it wouldn't stop Nik if he wanted to come inside, but with any luck, it would at least infuriate him a good deal.

To my great disappointment, it was all for nothing. Nik never even tried to open the door. I would know if he had, since I stayed up most of the night working on my plan for my daring rescue of the Flame of Mir. Truthfully, I also had a feeling that trying to sleep would be a waste of time. My mind couldn't stop replaying all the horrible things Nik and I said to each other. At least I put my restlessness to good use, letting it fuel me to power through my project.

As the first hints of dawn begin to populate the sky, I finally feel satisfied with my plans. I force myself to lie on the massive bed that occupies the guest room and at least try to get some sleep. God knows I'll need all my energy to deal with Nik and the *stronzo* today.

Just as I start to succumb to exhaustion, my phone rings. With a groan, I pick it up, deliriously thinking for a second that maybe it's Nik, ready to beg me for forgiveness. Why he would call me instead of bursting through the door, I couldn't say. Instead, A.J.'s voice greets me when I hoarsely croak hello.

"Hey, girl! How did it go yesterday?" she asks. In my exhausted state, her cheerful tone sounds like nails against a chalkboard.

"It went great. Thanks again."

"Are you okay? You don't sound like yourself."

"Yeah. Sorry. I'm still half-asleep."

"Did your new boyfriend keep you up all night with his reportedly amazing lovemaking skills?" she asks in a teasing tone.

I scoff. "As if. No, I stayed up working. By myself. Trust me—if I hadn't, the only thing Nik and I would've been busy doing is driving each other crazy. Probably through the break of dawn. And not in a good way."

"Uh-oh. Trouble in paradise? What happened? You were so into him last time we talked."

I sigh. "I still am. God help me. It's just...We had a major fight last night. Long story short, I guess you were right after all. I can't completely let my guard down around him just yet. I need to look out for myself. Don't get me wrong—I'm still hoping for the best. But after last night, I'm a little concerned. Let's just say that his overprotectiveness and his need to be in control of all things—including yours truly—cannot be overstated."

A.J. whistles. "Wow. Damn, Kat. I wish I could say I'm surprised, but knowing his background, how could I be? Still, you know I'm here for you, right? If you need me to come to your rescue, all you have to do is say the word, and I'll be there."

"I know, honey. I know. And I appreciate that—and you—so much. But I'm fine. Really. I think I can handle him. Or at least I hope so. I'm not ready to give up just yet."

"Well, if you change your mind, you know where to find me. In the meantime, maybe I can cheer you up with some good news?"

"Please do," I say, not too proud to beg.

Almost giddy with excitement, A.J. tells me how well her plan to take down the *stronzo* is going. As his former secretary, Camilla, mentioned, there's hard evidence of his secret. A.J. is close to tracking down the paper trail Camilla reported seeing during her time as his employee. A.J. believes that soon we'll have indisputable proof that the man's been cheating on his wife, even though the poor woman is the reason he became boss of the Italians in the first place.

When A.J. hangs up, I feel cautiously hopeful. Maybe our luck is finally turning around. If that's the case, then there's no better time than the present for me to strike.

I grant myself the luxury of a daydream for a brief moment, mentally visualizing how terribly furious the *stronzo* will be once he realizes the diamond is gone and there's nothing he can do about it—not anymore. I even picture Nik's astonished expression when I finally present him with the Flame of Mir.

Nik and I will finally be equals. And hopefully, this will allow us to move on and forward. Who knows? Maybe he'll finally realize he can trust me. It might even give us the morale boost we need to power through this ordeal with McGuire—preferably without starting a war among the Seven Families.

It's all wonderful to think about. But until I make it happen—until I actually have the Flame of Mir in my hands—it's just wishful thinking, nothing more. As always, it's up to me to make this dream a reality, and I know I'm up to the task. Unfortunately, I know Nik won't share this belief. After last night, I'd have to be a fool to tell him my plan. Once all is said and done, I'm sure I'll be able to look back at last night and think of Nik's overprotectiveness as cute—and even kind of sexy. But right now, it makes him a liability to my plans to save us all. So telling him about them is out of the question. He is a risk I can't afford.

Above all else, I can't lose him. If he learns what the *stronzo* has put me through, he'll go after the man without a second thought. I can't allow that to happen under any circumstances. Not while his conflict with McGuire isn't resolved. Besides, this isn't Nik's fight. It's mine and A.J.'s. It's a matter of pride for me that the *stronzo*'s downfall is brought on by my hand or hers. I'm not a damsel in distress, and I don't want Nik to come to my rescue—especially not at great personal cost to himself.

There is no doubt in my mind that Nik will be livid once he learns what I've been keeping from him—let alone the lengths I went to make amends for the harm I caused him. But all will be well once it ends well. Once I'm safely back with the Flame of Mir as an olive branch, I'm positive he'll forgive me. Eventually. Once I give him some sugar. But until then, dealing with him will be no picnic.

Just thinking about how worried and upset he will be until then makes my heart ache. He might be a controlling, possessive jerk at times, but he is *my* controlling, possessive jerk—and I'll have no other. Despite all his faults, he's also impossibly wonderful and caring—much more often than he's a pain in the ass. The mere idea of bringing him pain and stress makes me sick to my stomach. Still, as always, I know that a girl's gotta do what a girl's gotta do.

All this thinking of Nik and pining for him makes it impossible for me to keep my distance for much longer. After our awful fight—and an entire night spent away from him—I suddenly feel an unbearable need to see him again. So, I exit the room to look for him, bracing myself for what I'm sure will be a very non warm welcome.

Surprisingly, he isn't at his office. I walk around the penthouse somewhat aimlessly until I hear signs of life coming from the kitchen. Cautiously, I make my way there. I find Nik leaning against the counter, nursing a steaming coffee mug while not looking any more rested than I do.

"Hi," I quietly say in greeting. Nik nods in reply, and I

realize, after a long moment of uncomfortable silence, that's all the answer I'm getting. With a forceful smile plastered on my face, I add, "I've been looking for you."

"Well, here I am," Nik says, moodily. His hair is a mess, and there are dark circles under his eyes. His black cashmere sweater is a wrinkled disaster, and he's never looked scruffier.

"Any news about McGuire?" I ask.

Nik shakes his head no.

I sigh. "I don't suppose you're ready to consider that maybe—just maybe—he is not behind Maxim's murder. And that maybe—just maybe—you should let cooler heads prevail and try to mend fences with him before it's too late."

He shoots me an exasperated and angry look as if he can't believe I'm still thinking about this entirely reasonable and logical possibility. Men—I swear.

"I'll take that as a no," I say under my breath once it's clear Nik won't say anything. I'm aware I've hurt his feelings. But he's hurt mine, too. Once again, I sigh. "Well, don't let it ever be said that I don't know how to take a hint. You don't want me around, and this is, after all, your place. So I'm going out to take care of something important. Don't say I didn't warn you this time."

Nik's impassive, disinterested demeanor is gone in a flash. Directly looking at me for the first time since I entered the kitchen, he narrows his eyes at me. "Where?are you going?" he asks through gritted teeth.

"Out," I say with a smile. "That's all I can say for now."

While taking a deep breath, Nik squeezes his eyes shut before rubbing a hand over his face, clearly struggling to keep his temper in check. His tone is deceptively calm when he speaks to me again. "Kat, unless you need to attend to some sort of life-and-death matter of the utmost importance and urgency, I must insist that you stay here for the time being. At least until McGuire is found."

"As it happens, that's my exact situation, Nik. There's something I need to handle immediately. I'm doing this for us. *Trust me.*"

My emphatic reference to his inability to trust me doesn't go unnoticed. He clenches his jaw so hard I worry for a second that he might crack one of his teeth. "What could be more important or urgent than staying out of danger?" he asks.

I shrug. "I can't tell you. At least not yet. In due time, though, I will. Until then, you'll just have to *trust* my judgment."

Nik's breathing grows shallow, and his complexion becomes remarkably flushed. Still, he takes a deep breath, seemingly trying to keep his temper under control. "Work with me here. Please," he finally says.

"I'm only telling you I'm going out to avoid another argument, Nik. I don't want you to worry. Once again, please don't mistake what's simply a courtesy on my part with me asking—or needing—your consent to come and go as I please. Which, may I remind you, you told me I didn't need in the first place, back when we first started working together."

I half expect him to lose his cool completely, but he surprises me. "Will you let me come with you at least?" he asks.

"Sorry, no," I say, more gently than he deserves.

With a long-suffering sigh, Nik asks, "Can Dmitri come with you, then?"

I scoff. "Absolutely not. Who's going to babysit him while he's babysitting me?"

"Will you take *any* of my men with you?" he asks through gritted teeth.

I shake my head no.

"Fine," Nik says loudly, throwing his half-full coffee mug in the sink. I jump at the sound of it breaking against the stainless steel surface. "Have it your way, then."

Before I have time to react, Nik wraps his hands around my waist. The next thing I know, he throws me over his shoulder. I struggle against his hold, but it's pointless. I might as well be trying to bend metal.

"Let me go," I ask, kicking my legs and hitting his back with my closed fists.

Easily subduing my attempts to free myself, Nik marches out of the kitchen, ignoring my protests.

He laughs humorlessly. "Not a chance. If you want to behave like a reckless, unreasonable child, I'll treat you like one. If you insist on showing me I can't afford to trust you, then I have no choice but to respond accordingly."

Nik's long strides make quick work of the penthouse's vast corridors and halls. Before I know what's happening, he drops me on a soft surface. Slightly disoriented, I'm slow to recognize it's his bed.

"Once I've dealt with McGuire, we'll talk," he says, walking towards the door. "You'll stay here until then." He inserts a key into the bedroom door's outside keyhole, and I gasp, horrified.

"Nik, no. Please don't do this. I'm begging you."

My pleas do nothing to move him. Relentless, he isn't dissuaded from locking me away in his bedroom, making me his true prisoner at last.

"I wish I didn't have to," Nik dispassionately says under his breath. "But I just can't trust you not to put yourself in danger. I can't trust you not to leave me. And I can't lose you."

I sob, shaking my head frantically. "If you do this, Nik, there's no turning back. I won't forgive you for this. I can't."

Nik's dark brown eyes—once so dear and familiar—look utterly alien to me as he takes his time studying me. Without another word, he steps outside the room and locks the door, shattering my heart in one move.

17

NIK

It didn't have to be like this.

Night falls outside, and I struggle to stay still. I push away from my desk for what feels like the hundredth time in the past hour to pour myself another drink. But even as it burns down my throat, the amber-colored liquor provides very little comfort or distraction.

Unable to force myself to sit back down, I aimlessly and pointlessly pace in front of my desk instead.

For a moment, I consider turning my computer back on and trying to get some work done. An instant later, though, I admit there's no point in wasting my energy. I know I'm worthless right now, completely and utterly incapable of focusing on anything for more than a few seconds.

A particularly uncomfortable tightness has settled in my chest since I left Kat in the bedroom. The most horrible sensation has taken hold of me as the muscles around my ribcage and abdomen feel as if they begun to freeze into place, stiffening and losing elasticity. With each passing second, it gets harder and harder to breathe. As the minutes tick by, I almost fear that soon my heart won't be able to beat, as my core clutches it still.

Paradoxically, my skin feels clammy as I start to sweat despite feeling cold to my bones.

After rolling up my sleeves, I check the thermostat, surprised to see it's set to a balmy sixty-five degrees.

I walk over to the windows behind my desk, hoping that their less than stellar insulation will help adjust my confusing body temperature.

Unseeingly staring out the windows, I force myself to take a deep breath, slowly inhaling and exhaling. I even attempt to center my roaming thoughts, purposefully focusing on the mechanical aspect of simply breathing for a moment. All of it is a waste of time. Intrusive thoughts find their way back into my mind almost immediately.

Over and over again, Kat's face—as she looked when I locked her away—flashes in my mind. It doesn't matter whether I keep my eyes closed or open. I see her now almost as clearly as I saw her then. To make matters worse, as time goes by, the hurt and desperate look I saw in her beautiful eyes grows even more haunting.

I admit I have conflicting emotions about the chaotic way things escalated between the two of us earlier today. Truthfully, I can't help but feel a little justified in the course of action I took. After all, I pretty much begged Kat to be open and honest with me, and she refused. She didn't even bother giving me a good reason for her refusal. She can't expect me to trust her blindly under these extenuating circumstances.

It's not like I can trust Kat to take care of herself and be reasonable about her safety, either. Even if I disregard her long history of making reckless choices, I can't forget her little rebellious act. To sneak around like that—when she knows one of the most bloodthirsty men in the Seven Families is dying to get his hands on her—was incredibly foolhardy, even by her standards.

The mere idea of McGuire getting close enough to hurt her makes my blood run cold. I'm all for taking calculated risks, but this is one of the few instances where I will not roll the dice. If something were to happen to Kat, if McGuire were to take her from me as well... that would be it for me. There would be no surviving this loss. I simply wouldn't be able to function without her. Not anymore.

I've been around long enough to know that I'm not invincible or infallible. I know my strengths, just as I know my weaknesses. While McGuire remains at large and out for my blood, I'm more capable of keeping Kat safe when she's under my roof than when she is not. The man's a wild card on his best days. And ever since Erin went missing, I seriously doubt he's had many of those. For all his faults, it's no secret to anybody that he's a devoted father.

It's just a matter of probabilities. If Kat's here at home, where I know she's safe and sound, then her chances of making it through this nightmare unharmed are virtually one hundred percent. Out there, I simply can't guarantee these odds. There are too many variables. Faced with the choice between one hundred percent and anything less, I'm choosing the former every day of the week and twice on Sundays.

Unfortunately for Kat, who disagrees with my risk assessment, might makes right. At least in my world, which is where she is now. I tried to reason with her, to get her to see things my way. When that didn't work out, I had to do what was necessary to protect her, as I warned her I would. Kat and I may have different definitions of keeping one's word, but she must've realized that I don't make idle threats.

Today's events, while unfortunate, shouldn't have come as a surprise for her.

It all makes perfect logical sense. Still, I'm not naïve enough to mistake these dreadful physical sensations overtaking me for anything other than what they are—guilt and remorse.

At some point along the way, Kat's pain became my pain. Her suffering became my undoing. The sight of her dark blues eyes—which often stared back at me with warmth and passion—wide with horror and despair left a scar in my soul. For the rest of my life, no matter how long that may be, I'll never forgive myself for hurting her in the way that I did. My only hope is that, unlike myself, she might forgive me once this ordeal is over.

I'm startled by several loud, thundering voices outside my office. They yell frantically over each other in Russian before abruptly ceasing. Distracted from my anguished thoughts, I frown and listen carefully. That's when I hear a couple of hushed whispers just outside my door.

With a resigned sigh, I brace myself, wondering what new devastating problem will be dropped on my plate now. If only a *pakhan* could afford the luxury of personal days...

I hear a hesitant knock, and, in Russian, I order the newcomer to enter. The door opens, and to my surprise, both Dmitri and Vladimir stand outside. Their faces are the perfect picture of impassive deference, which tells me something truly awful happened.

While taking a fortifying breath, I drop my weight on my chair, momentarily closing my eyes. "What is it now?" I ask.

The two men exchange an anxious glance.

"Nik—" Dmitri says before pausing, seemingly searching for the right words. "I need you to stay calm."

Cold, slimy dread settles in the pit of my stomach. "Out

with it, Dmitri," I say impatiently. "I'm not in the mood for your games tonight."

"Nik..." Dmitri says slowly, buying time. "It seems Kat's gone."

I stare at him in disbelief. "She's *what*?!" I hear myself roar, feeling like I'm having an out-of-body experience. Intellectually, I understand the words must be coming out of my mouth, but it sure feels like I'm watching myself shout them from outside my body.

"Well, she's gone, Nik. She has escaped. After finishing my rounds, I came back here to check on her and you because I heard about your fight. When I unlocked your bedroom door, she wasn't there. Nobody saw her leave. She's just gone. Pretty much without a trace."

The only solid attachment I feel to my body is my heart, beating in my chest in an alarmingly vicious way I haven't felt before. I can't tell if it's caused by adrenaline, cardiac arrest or a panic attack. Most likely a combination of all three.

"How can she have escaped? What kind of backyard operation am I running here that this woman can leave without any of my men noticing two fucking days in a row? Should I expect McGuire to greet me in my own fucking kitchen tomorrow? I'll have your heads on a spike after I find her. Clearly, if I need something done around here, I have to do it myself."

I know my words are harsh and I'm glad they are. I hope they sting. As a matter of fact, I hope the other dozen idiots scurrying outside my door hear me, too. Once I'm done finding Kat, I'll take great pleasure in painstakingly dealing with every single one of the useless lot.

Through gritted teeth, I say, "Stop staring at me and get your worthless asses out there. I want the two of you to spread the word that every single man in my *bratva* will scour this city until we find her. No one will rest, stop, sleep, or eat until she's found. I don't want to see either of you until she is returned to me. And if any harm has been done to even one hair on her head, I will personally ensure that the same is done tenfold to every single man on watch today, including the two of you. No one has ever known pain like what I will unleash upon you if anything happens to her. Now get the fuck out of here."

The first thing I do is try to track Kat's phone. But it's a waste of time. The tracker tells me it's still at the penthouse, so she didn't bring it with her when she left.

After grabbing my car keys, I race down the stairs to the garage, too impatient to bother with the elevator.

I consider calling her friend A.J. for a moment but ultimately decide not to bother. It's extremely unlikely she'd share anything with me, and I don't have time to waste forcing her to tell me all she knows.

So I roam the city, checking any place Kat could be. As I drive almost aimlessly, adrenaline is the only thing fueling me and keeping my fear and despair at bay. I don't know what I'll do if McGuire finds her before me.

As we learned from Connor, Patrick McGuire has eyes on the penthouse, dutifully observing everyone who comes and goes. My only hope is that he'll contact me to ask for some sort of ransom—preferably not a demand for the return of his daughter in exchange for Kat. That would prove to be a problem, considering I didn't abduct the girl. McGuire can have anything he wants as long as Kat remains unharmed.

My chances of finding Kat are very slim. I have no idea how long she's been gone, and there's no shortage of places where she could be hiding.

Why does she have to be stubbornly careless? Why can't she understand I'm just trying to protect her as well as I can?

I knew I couldn't trust her. From the start, I worried Kat would turn out to be unreliable and untrustworthy, someone who relents to every whim that strikes her fancy regardless of the consequences. She's done nothing in the past forty-eight hours to prove me wrong.

After everything she and I have been through, how could Kat do this? Does she relish causing me pain? She must know by now how precious she is to me. The woman has me wrapped around her finger, and she isn't afraid to wield her power, toying with me as she pleases. Why wouldn't she, when she knows I'm utterly incapable of ever truly hurting her?

Hours pass, and I finally admit I'm wasting my time and energy. I need to focus and use my fucking brain. Kat is nothing if not clever, and I won't find her by pointlessly roaming the city. I can only catch her if I'm smart about this. Besides, if McGuire has her and sends out a ransom demand, I must be available to receive it and promptly respond. So I drive home, struggling to concentrate on what needs to be done instead of letting my despair and sense of defeat distract me.

I ride by myself in the elevator to the penthouse. Once the doors slide open, I'm met by darkness and deafening silence. No one's back. Kat hasn't been found. My phone didn't ring. There are no promising leads. No good news.

Defeated, I head to my office, a bit disturbed by how empty this place is. There are no signs of life. It's so eerie that I shut my office door, hoping it will push this unsettling feeling out of my mind. I can't deal with this nonsense right now.

As I sit on my chair, I think of Lucien. I don't have the

time or the energy to explain to him everything that has recently happened, but knowing him, I might not even have to. Lucien has a way of knowing all about everyone and everything without ever being told anything. It makes him the perfect choice for where to start my search. If anyone can help me, it's him. I grab my phone and search for his number, praying he'll pick up immediately. But before I can call him, my office door is kicked open.

Startled, I look up.

And just like that, I can't breathe. My heart must be still beating, or I would've dropped dead, but I could swear it came to a screeching halt.

Kat stands in the open doorway, haloed by the bleak darkness outside the room.

I stand up at once, gracelessly bumping into my desk as my chair rolls away. My legs turn to rubber, and I have to support my weight with my hands on the desk's warm mahogany surface. I exhale with relief. "Kat..." That one word a prayer, a benediction and a thanks—all rolled into one.

"*You*," she says through gritted teeth. Her blue eyes burn hotter and brighter than I've ever seen before.

I want to run to her, wrap my arms around her body, and never, ever let her go. I want to drop to my knees and beg her for forgiveness while promising I'll spend the rest of my days making up for my stupid mistake—as long as she stays forever.

But the adrenaline that's been keeping me upright since I heard the devastating news of her disappearance has abandoned me. I don't trust my legs to carry me over to her. As relief floods my veins, I don't even trust myself not to pass out at any moment now. I can feel myself growing lightheaded like a fucking idiot as Kat glowers at me from across the room.

"*You*," she repeats.

She looks so different. I can't quite put my finger on what exactly has changed in her appearance, but I've never seen her more beautiful. Somehow, Kat's both fire and ice as she glares at me. Her flushed skin glows, which I take as an indicator of a recent physical exertion episode. Her long dark hair—usually so smooth and meticulously in order—now frames her face in a breathtaking explosion of waves.

Kat has never looked more alive. It's an awe-inspiring sight, even though I've never seen her look less put-together. Or more stunning. I feel positively thunderstruck by her presence. She looks so heartbreakingly amazing as she scowls at me, radiating pure life, power, and chaotic energy.

Amidst my wonder, my heart aches because it dawns on me the severity of what I've done. Even if I live to a hundred, I'll never stop regretting my mistake. Kat offered me all of herself, all her beauty and wildness, and I tried to tame her. I tried to lock her in a gilded cage and clip her wings.

Kat's blue eyes are as dark as the duskiest depths of the ocean, and they never leave my face as she approaches me intently.

All words escape me as I watch her in awe. I can't move, I can't breathe. All I can do is admire her and drink in the sight of her all in one piece, back home with me. In some obscure part of my mind, alarm bells sound as my brain faintly registers that she's livid. But I pay them no mind.

Kat halts mere inches away from me. After squaring her shoulders, she searches for something deep within her pockets. Her slender fingers wrap around it, and with one graceful flick of her wrist, she launches it at me.

A small, solid object bounces off my chest. Reflexively, I

catch it with my left hand. Dumbstruck, I glance down, and, as it frequently happens whenever Kat's around, my world comes to a stop again. Somehow, in the palm of my hand lies the Flame of Mir.

A thousand thoughts cross my mind. I don't understand how this came to be. I have so many questions and so many things I need to say. But, once more in a daze, I can only stare at Kat, unable to even begin figuring out what to tell her.

"There," she says coldly. "We're even now."

Kat turns on her heels, heading towards the door again. There, she pauses before glancing at me over her shoulder.

Impassively, she says, "A few months ago, A.J. saw an opportunity to make good money by running game on Giuseppe Salvatore. I trust I don't have to tell you, of all people, who he is. Predictably, it didn't end well for her. He caught her red-handed. He had her right where he wanted her, which meant he had me at his beck and call. Long story short, he blackmailed me into doing all sorts of things, including infiltrating a certain museum gala and stealing the world's largest red diamond. He was very particular about the specifics of the whole thing. The details of this heist were nonnegotiable. It had to be done on that specific night, under his specific terms. I did what he wanted and gave him what he wanted, hoping it'd be the end of my involvement with the mafia. But little did I know what ironic little twist fate had in store for me."

With a humorless laugh, Kat smirks at me sardonically.

I stare at her, speechless and shocked, as fury like I've never felt before floods me. It burns as scorchingly hot as lava, irradiating through my body, inch by inch.

"Giuseppe Salvatore will die a horrible, painful death," I say through gritted teeth. "Even if it's the last thing I do.

McGuire can wait. I will find Salvatore tonight, and I will kill him myself."

Kat scoffs, shaking her head as sadness clouds her eyes. "You're missing my point entirely."

"No, I'm not. Trust me. I'm disgusted with myself. I don't deserve to even breathe the same air as you. I don't deserve to be in the same room as you. I'm not much better than that wretched fuck. Not after what I've put you through when you're innocent of any crime. But if you give me a chance, I'll spend the rest of my life atoning for my sins. I can never truly earn your forgiveness, but, Kat, on my life, I promise you I'll die trying."

Kat stares at me in silence for a long, endless moment. To my surprise, her anger dissolves from her face in an instant. She blinks rapidly as her eyes fill with tears and a sob escapes her lips. "No."

"No?" I ask, dumbly.

Kat shakes her head. "I warned you, Nik. I told you there was no coming back from what you did. But you went through with it, anyway. We are done. This is it for us."

With a sharp intake of breath, I shake my head frantically. "No, Kat. Don't say that. You can't mean that. I can't lose you. Hold on, just give me a chance to—"

"You aren't listening to me. I don't want to be with you. I have no interest in being with someone who needs to control me as much as you do. I don't want to be with someone who will quite literally lock me away whenever I disagree with him. Above all, I refuse to be someone who can't trust anything but his trust issues." Kat sniffs, trying to swallow her tears. "I don't need you to deal with Giuseppe Salvatore for me. I don't want you to go to war against the Irish *and* the Italians because of me. *This* is precisely why I couldn't be honest with you. I don't want you to spend the rest of your life atoning for your sins—whatever the hell that means for you. All I need and want from you is that you leave me alone for good. Don't come near me or contact me ever again. Stay out of my life."

Kat's words make me feel like I had the wind knocked out of me and took a blow to the head all at once. My head rings, I'm disoriented—I can't breathe. "*Dusha moya,* please don't do this. I'll give you anything. Anything, Kat. Just give me a chance to make things right. Please. I won't let you down, I promise. I'll devote every second of the rest of my life to making you happy. I'll give you anything your heart has ever desired."

While shaking her head, Kat studies my face. Something in her eyes tells me she's trying to take one last good look at me, expecting never to see me again.

She glances away. "The only thing I want is to be by myself. If you ever cared about me, you'll honor this one request of mine," she says, marching through the doorway.

A few steps away, Kat stops, turning to face me. Maybe for the last time. "I hope you find peace, Nik, instead of whatever it is you've been looking for this whole time."

She walks away, never looking back.

18

KAT

So much for home, sweet home.

After being away for so long, returning to my apartment feels surreal—especially considering everything that has happened to me since the last time I was inside it. Objectively speaking, not much time has passed since I was last here. Yet, it feels like a lifetime ago.

While sitting on my favorite spot on my cream-colored couch in my comfiest sweats in the middle of the day, I can't shake the feeling that something's seriously wrong. Even with a whole pint of chocolate chip ice cream in my lap and a generously filled wine glass, I cannot convince myself that everything feels right as I expected it would. Inwardly sighing, I force myself to face reality.

Nik and I are done. *C'est fini*. And somehow, I must forget him.

That's fine—more than fine. Everything is as it should be.

I may not have gotten my happy ending with Nik, but that's okay. I'll get it by myself, or maybe with someone else.

It doesn't even matter that the mere idea leaves a bad taste in my mouth.

Sure, it might be true that, after storming out of the penthouse, I thought I would feel better than I do right now. But that doesn't necessarily mean I've made a mistake. I just need some time to adjust to this change. That's all.

Of course, it's also completely normal to grieve what I have lost and what could've been. What I dreamed would come to be. What I now know will never be a part of my future.

It might take me a while to let go of all the memories of Nik, and that's okay. Like the night we first met at the gala—his dark eyes, hair and clothes. Or when he held me and comforted me through that horrid nightmare, tenderly whispering sweet nothings in Russian to me.

I can still recall the wonderful moment Nik and I shared during the aerobatic flight as if it had happened only yesterday. Especially when we became weightless, and he held my hands. And, of course—how could I ever forget?—the mesmerizing grin on his handsome face as we stepped out of the plane. Truth be told, I doubt I'll ever be able to forget that breathless kiss we shared on the airfield.

And how can anyone expect me to forget when Nik broke Vladmir's hand for me?

It's incredibly hard to accept that the man who's featured front and center in these wonderful memories is the same guy who quite literally locked me away in a tower. Yet, I can't escape this truth.

I shouldn't feel this miserable about never being in Nik's presence again. The mere thought of never feeling his skin against mine again or running my fingers through his silky, dark hair is unbearable. To think that I won't lose myself in the depths of his eyes again, or hear the rasp of his voice as he whispers something completely outrageous, for my ears only...

All of those titillating experiences are in the past now. And that's fine. It will have to be fine. After all, that was my choice—and frankly, that was the whole point. That's what matters to me, ultimately. I didn't get into my messy situation with Nik of my own volition, but I rectified that issue in the end. At last, I got what I wanted—I regained control of myself and my life. I chose to put an end to everything.

Everything is as it should be. All is well when it ends well. And I will repeat these words to myself over and over again as my mantra until I convince myself to believe them.

In the end, you have to always look out for number one. For me, that's always going to be me. That's why I had to kick Nik to the curb. As I've learned, he's bad for my health.

A soft, hesitant knock at my front door interrupts my pity party. Just in time, too, since I was getting dangerously close to no longer believing my own lies. And where would that leave me?

For a moment, I consider pretending I'm not home and ignoring my unannounced visitor. But I quickly dismiss the idea once I realize it's probably just A.J. checking in on me. My best friend deserves better from me, especially after everything she's done for me recently. I could also use the distraction of having some company around. She always has a knack for cheering me up, and I'm in desperate need of that right now.

I set the ice cream and the wine down on my cluttered coffee table and get up from the couch. After crossing the small distance to the front door, I unlock it, plastering a fake —but well-intentioned—smile on my face for A.J.'s benefit.

As it turns out, I shouldn't have bothered. Upon opening the door, my forced grin immediately falters as I come face-to-face with Dmitri. Perfectly calm, he gives me a half-smile that doesn't quite reach his eyes, leaning against the wall next to my front door.

"Hiya, Kat," he says, breaking my astonished silence.

"Dmitri," I say with a gasp. "What are you doing here? How do you even know where I live?"

He shoots me a funny look, raising an eyebrow. "Well, I thought it was obvious—I'm here to visit a friend. People still do that, right? As for your second question, come on, Kat. Please." He scoffs, rolling his eyes theatrically. "As if I didn't know your address all along. Who do you think went snooping around your life when Nik wanted information on the woman who stole his diamond? And, dare I say it, his heart. Yours truly, of course. Aren't you going to invite me in?"

I cross my arms, ignoring his question. "Didn't you hear? The Flame of Mir has been returned to its rightful owner. My debt to your boss has been paid. We have no business with each other, Dmitri. Not any longer."

"Right," he says, scowling. "Whatever you say, Kat. We'll go with that for the time being. Now, can I come in?"

"Why? Did Nik send you here? You're not here to kidnap me, are you, Dmitri? Because I swear, I'm not going down without a fight this time. No, sir."

His pale blues charmingly wrinkle at the corners as he laughs. "I'll keep that in mind. But no, I'm not here to kidnap you. Honestly, Kat, I'm a little insulted that you even have to ask. I thought we were friends. I feel like you should trust me more than that by now. For your information, Nik doesn't have the slightest idea I'm here. He'd probably have my head if he even suspected I came to see you."

I scoff. "Yeah, right. Nik lets you get away with virtually

anything. I wouldn't be surprised if he let you get away with murder. Knowing the two of you, he probably has, actually."

"I can neither confirm nor deny your accusations."

I roll my eyes, but I step aside to allow him inside my apartment. "Fine, come in. But I won't go easy on you if you try anything funny. You've been warned."

Dmitri strolls inside my apartment with his hands raised in mock surrender. "I'll be on my best behavior. As usual."

He pauses inside my living room, glancing around the place with an indecipherable expression on his chiseled face. "So this is where the infamous Katherine Devereaux lives."

With a sigh, I drop my weight back on the couch. "Take a seat." I wave my hand in the general direction of every surface in the room. "Or don't. I don't really care."

Dmitri shoots me a funny look, but he sits on the other side of my couch, directly opposite of where I'm sitting.

"I like your place. It's cozy," he says.

"Yeah. Well, it's no luxuriously designed penthouse, but what can I say? It's home. At least it's mine. I bought it with the labors of my own dishonest work."

Dmitri chuckles. "Won't you offer me something to drink, Kat? Not much of a host, are you?"

With a shrug, I point him to the fridge in the kitchen, visible from where we're sitting down.

"Knock yourself out. Make yourself at home."

"Famous last words," he says under his breath before getting up to fetch his beverage.

A moment later, Dmitri returns, a beer in hand. "Kat..." he says with a sigh, sitting down again. "We need to talk."

"No, Dmitri. We really don't."

"I'm afraid we do, Kat."

"Dmitri—" I say through gritted teeth, infusing my tone with every bit of warning I can muster.

He laughs. "That won't work with me, Kat. It doesn't work even when Nik does it, and he's much scarier than you. Especially now. And yet, here I am, right? So, save your energy. We need to talk. There's no point in trying to avoid the unavoidable."

"What do you mean by 'especially now'? What are you talking about?"

Dmitri's eyebrows almost reach his hairline. "Oh, right. You wouldn't know. Nik has been...particularly challenging since you left, which is why I'm here. It's time to come home, Kat. I'll have to insist."

I throw a pillow at him. "I *am* home, dumbass. And I warned you, Dmitri. I will not be kidnapped again. Ever. Are we clear?"

Dmitri sighs in exasperation. "Calm down, Kat. Nobody's kidnapping anybody. I'm merely here to persuade you to change your mind about this whole breaking up thing."

"Well, that's never going to happen. Ever. And no offense, Dmitri, but it's also none of your business. At all."

He rolls his eyes. "Come on. We've been over this so many times. It's totally my business. I guess we can agree to disagree on this, but I'm not leaving until you stop acting like an idiot. You're not getting rid of me until you promise to come back and give Nik another chance."

"A chance to do what? Lock me away again, throwing the key away this time?"

"That's a little dramatic, don't you think, Kat? Even for you."

"No, Dmitri. I don't think I'm being too dramatic. Before you get to decide what's an appropriate response to being stripped of your freedom, why don't we lock you away against your will first? Just to give you a little taste of what Nik put me through that day."

"Look, I'm not saying you should pretend nothing happened. I happen to agree with you—Nik fucked up big time. Hell, I bet you wouldn't get an argument from him on that one. Trust me when I tell you he's painfully aware of how badly he fucked up. If you don't believe me, check it out yourself."

I scoff. "Nice try. But I think I'll pass."

"My point is that no one expects you to forget what he did. I promise you he hasn't forgotten it and probably never will. But you can't just give up on people when they disappoint you or when they fuck up. Not if you know that there's something special there. Something unique, wonderful, and rare."

I sigh as my eyes tear up. I am *so* not strong enough to deal with this right now. "Dmitri, it's not as simple as you make it sound."

"But it is. You love him, and he loves you. That's all that matters. Everything else is just details. You can't lose sight of what's truly important. So let me take you home, Kat. Put Nik through the wringer. Make him work for it. But give him a chance to grovel. Allow him to make things right again, to make it up to you."

"Did he say that?" I ask breathlessly.

Dmitri looks at me, puzzled. "Did he say what?"

"That he loves me. Did Nik actually tell you that?"

Dmitri's expression softens. "He didn't have to, Kat. I know him. I know his heart. And deep down, you know it as well."

So Nik didn't say it.

"Well, I thought I did. I really did. But I was wrong, Dmitri."

"No, you weren't. You just think you were because you're afraid and confused, and I don't blame you. But I think I know you well enough by now to be sure that you are not someone who shies away from what scares you—not when it's something that you truly want."

I shrug, not meeting his too-perceptive eyes. "Well, maybe I don't want it, then."

"I don't believe that for a second. I don't think you do, either."

"You don't understand, Dmitri. Nik will never be able to trust me. You and I can argue until the heat death of the universe about who is to blame for that, but it will still be true. And if he can't trust me, then he will cling to me as hard as he can, always fearing and expecting the worst from me. He'll oppress me and crush me, and I'll die of misery, desperately trying to make him give me enough room to breathe. That's no way to live, Dmitri. No relationship can work under these circumstances."

"So you guys have problems. So what? Who doesn't? It doesn't mean that you get to give up on each other. You two are human, and you've made mistakes. Again, so fucking what? Get back on the horse and try again. The way I see it, the only thing that separates successful relationships from unsuccessful ones is whether people have given up on it or not."

"That's the stupidest thing I've ever heard. And possibly the most naïve one, too."

"I don't know about that," he says. "Maybe I'm speaking from personal experience."

"Dmitri..." I say, placing my hand on his shoulder.

"Listen, Kat," he interrupts me, uninterested in allowing the conversation shift to his own unfortunate love life, "Nik made a mistake. But you haven't been perfect, either. No offense. You guys have something special going on. Sure, in a moment of intense frustration, Nik decided it was a good idea to place you in captivity instead of talking it out with you. But he's the fucking boss of the *bratva*, Kat. One with control and trust issues, too. What did you expect? What did you think would happen once he finally lost his temper with you? It's bound to happen in any relationship. It's just a matter of time. If you ask me, what he did wasn't that bad, all things considered. It could've certainly been much worse —just think about all the other things he could've done instead."

I scoff, glaring at Dmitri. "I can't believe you just said that to me. Is any of this crap supposed to make me change my mind?"

"Come on, Kat, you know I'm making a good point here."

Mercifully, my phone rings, rattling on the coffee table. A welcome interruption to whatever nonsense Dmitri is about to say next.

"Hang on," I say. "It's my friend. I have to get this."

Dmitri nods, running his hands through his dark blond hair, and I get up, bringing the now-melted ice cream back to the freezer as I answer the call.

"Hey, A.J.," I say in greeting. "What's up?"

"*What's up?*" she says, her gleeful voice brimming with excitement. "I'll tell you what's up. I fucking did it, Kat."

I almost drop the ice cream container on the kitchen floor. Somehow, I manage to avoid disaster, setting it down on the counter instead.

The *stronzo*. She did it. We're free. At last.

"No way," I say, gasping.

A.J. scoffs. "Honey, please. It was only a matter of time. You know I'm that bitch. True, sometimes I'm the bitch that gets our asses in some serious trouble of the mafia variety.

But this time, I'm the bitch who cleans up her messes. Once and for all."

"A.J.—" I say, cutting her off. "I get it. Trust me, I've known for a while now that you are one bad motherfucker. Or bitch. But tell me—is it done? How did you pull it off? What do you need me to do?"

"We'll get to that in a minute, babe. All you need to know right now is that I finally have in my hands the paperwork Camilla told me about on the day your Russian fling's henchmen kidnapped you. And it's juicy, Kat. We were right—the *stronzo* does have a secret love child. When will men learn not to think with the wrong head? You'd think that a man who came from nothing would know better than to cheat on his wife, who's the only reason he became boss in the first place. But hey, he fucked around, and he's about to find out. I love that for us, Kat. I really do."

"Wow," I say, my heart racing. "I can't believe this is finally happening. I can't believe this isn't a dream. It's about fucking time. Our luck had to turn at some point, right? Where are you, A.J.? I think you should come over right now. Should we even be discussing this over the phone?"

"I'm fine," she says, so excited she's almost shouting over the phone. "You'll see me soon enough, Kitty Kat. Oh, I almost forgot to tell you—you'll get a kick out of this. The *stronzo*'s secret child? It turns out he's half-Russian! Isn't that a riot? His name is Dmitri Ivashkov. I got boatloads of documents tying him to the *stronzo*. Some go back twenty-something years."

With a gasp, I almost drop my phone. My spine straightens as I process what A.J. just told me. I touch the back of my neck as it grows uncomfortably warm.

I can't believe it... Dmitri, the *stronzo*'s bastard son?

Unable to help myself, I turn around nonchalantly,

desperately needing to look at Dmitri. Startled, I realize he's standing right behind me, merely a few inches away. At some point, while I was immersed in A.J.'s news, he must've closed the distance between us as quietly as a cat.

Dmitri is so tall I need to lean my head back to see his face instead of being at eye level with his chest. I do so as A.J. happily—and much too loudly—carries on over the phone. As soon as I see his face, I gasp again, loudly.

Every hair on my skin stands up as my body instinctively recognizes the imminent danger. One glance at Dmitri's pale blue eyes—the same shade as the *stronzo*'s, I finally notice—and I know he's heard every single word my friend just told me.

An unfamiliar, dark look comes over Dmitri's finely sculpted face as he reaches for me.

19

NIK

I MADE A GRAVE MISTAKE.

I was wrong.

I was so fucking wrong.

When Kat left me—not even bothering to glance back at me as she sauntered away, happily stomping my heart into a billion broken pieces—I was initially stunned and devastated.

Then, my distress gave way to anger. And my anger burned hot, boiling over and scorching everything in its warpath.

For so long, I held back, striving, for some reason, to be better than my baser nature. I denied myself the simple pleasure of surrendering to my instincts instead of worrying about pleasing a self-absorbed, untrustworthy woman. So if Kat wanted to leave me, that was fine with me. I had one less problem to worry about.

If she thought she was better than me, that was her mistake. I certainly didn't intend to mope around the place, suffering for a woman who didn't seem to give a fuck about what she was giving up on. Someone who couldn't be trusted to provide you the day of the week, let alone anything of actual significance.

If Kat wanted to end things, it was my pleasure to show her the door. Her loss would be my gain, I was sure —eventually.

Good riddance, I had thought to myself.

But then, night came.

Inevitably, as the hustling and bustling around the penthouse slowed down as my house staff ended their shifts and my men left to attend to theirs, I grew restless. Even worse, when the lights were dimmed, and all the noise went away, I grew lonely. I became painfully aware of all that I was lacking. Of my neediness. Not just for any company—which could too easily be arranged, especially of the female kind. No, my need was specific and unmistakable. Unavoidable and irresistible, too. With big, blue eyes and legs that go on for miles.

Big fucking deal, I told myself then. It wasn't the first time in my life that I craved or needed something I couldn't have. It probably wouldn't be the last.

So I didn't feel as good as I thought I should after this whole break-up nonsense. Who cares? It didn't have to mean anything unless I let it mean something.

So I turned on the news for background noise and listened to music once the TV's cacophony started to annoy me. After that, I exercised. Then, I worked. Long story short, I handled it—as I always do.

But then, the night grew late, and invariably, I had to try to sleep, which traditionally involves going to bed. As in, the bed I shared with Kat, where every morning I watched her sleep until she woke up and offered me her lazy—and seductive—smile. It was the bed where Kat and I fucked and made love to each other. On that bed, after, we held each other, whispering inside jokes and never-before-told secrets.

And that, as it turned out, was more than I could handle.

Still, I persevered. There were, after all, other bedrooms in this cavernous penthouse. And if none of them did the trick, there were always hotels or other houses and apartments.

Never—not even for a moment—did I entertain the idea of simply getting rid of the damn piece of furniture.

Shamefully, if the housekeepers hadn't replaced the covers before I could stop them, I'd have probably ordered that the sheets be left undisturbed. After all, Kat's scent would soon fade away forever.

Unthinkably, soon, it would be as if Kat had never been in my life.

To my great embarrassment, I eventually succumbed to the urge to cling to the remaining traces of Kat's presence in my world. It didn't take long for me to sink back under the covers that had once caressed her skin. After that, there was no point in stopping myself from doing what I craved, so I gorged myself on the breathtaking, luxurious fragrance her presence had left in my bed.

I didn't even dare move anything that Kat had left behind. Her makeup, her clothes, even her fucking toothbrush... Painstakingly, I ensured it all remained just as she had left it. God forbid I inconvenience her by misplacing her belongings—as if she might return at any moment.

It—I—was pathetic, and I knew it. Others knew it, too. Dmitri, in particular, seemed remarkably worried. It didn't matter. I didn't even care enough to pretend it did. Kat was gone, likely forever, and I couldn't give less of a fuck about anything except thoroughly enjoying the remnants of our time together—no matter how fleeting.

Soon after that, I stopped even bothering to leave my room. On my worst days, I barely got out of bed.

Because that's what they are now—*my* bed and *my* room. Not ours. Not anymore.

Now, instead of wasting my time and energy doing things I don't care about with people who don't matter, I spend the long days and nights with my memories of Kat. Over and over again, I fondly recall the first night we met and how impossibly mesmerizing she was in that velvet dress.

Repeatedly, I remember the night she desperately clung to me as I did my best to comfort her through her nightmare. I never even learned what it was about.

I can never forget that day on Yuri's plane, when he took us on that aerobatic flight. The way Kat giggled as we became weightless is forever branded on my brain... Just like the earthshaking way she kissed me after.

Of course, there's one thing I wish I could forget in its entirety: the stupidly reckless, heartbreakingly brave woman who retrieved my diamond from Giuseppe Salvatore himself.

Try as I might, I struggle to accept that the incredible person starring in these precious memories is one and the same with the one who deliberately misled me and lied to me. But I know it's the truth.

I guess I should feel thankful for the opportunity to escape this messy situation relatively unharmed. Instead, I can only think about how I'll never again feel Kat's soft skin under my fingertips or breathe in the scent of her freshly washed hair. I won't ever get to sink deep into the deep blue ocean of her eyes again, or hear the breathy, throaty way she gasps my name right before she climaxes.

Hurricane Kat and the devastating emotional turmoil

she evokes in me might be a thing of the past. She might never be in my life again. Without a doubt, it would mean that happiness would always and forever remain out of reach for me.

Forget about living a happy life—I'm not sure I'd have it in me to go on at all if that's how the rest of my life will be. I fail to see a reason to if Kat won't be in it. The *bratva*, Dmitri... None of it could be enough. The prospect of living out the rest of my days without the slightest possibility of Kat being in them is bleak and unthinkable.

There must be another way. Somehow.

The alternative is just inconceivable.

I have more money and power than I could ever have dreamed of, and yet, what I truly need is just out of reach. I can't go back in time and stop myself from breaking Kat's trust. She relied on me to keep her safe and care for her, as I promised her I would. And I failed her so thoroughly.

In the end, I was the one who didn't keep his word, the one who didn't deserve to be trusted. The irony of that isn't lost on me.

All along, Kat was true. Through it all, she only cared about was protecting others, including me. She constantly put me and those she loves above her interests, and I repaid her selflessness with betrayal and selfishness.

At the slightest hint of uncertainty, I transformed into Kat's worst nightmare: a possessive, controlling, and unreasonable tyrant. I let my past and my fears block my ability to trust. Despite everything Kat did for me and all I learned about her heart, I couldn't stop myself.

Even if I'm unlucky enough to live to a hundred years old, I will never forgive myself for what I did to her. It would be a miserable, unbearable existence, and it would still be less than what I deserve.

Unfortunately, even though I know with absolute certainty that I will never, ever be worthy of Kat's forgiveness, I'm too much of a selfish bastard to stop trying to get it. The only other thing I know for sure is that I can't waste more time than I already have. I've lost so much already. I can't lose her, too.

So I call her. Repeatedly. All along, I worry that my damned epiphany may have come a little too late. The incredible feat of winning her back might be impossible at this point. But I will try anyway, for as long as it takes. Even if Kat never takes me back, I'll still keep trying. I will never give up on us—not as long as there is anything left in me.

Around the time I reach over fifty unanswered calls, it becomes obvious to me that Kat'll never pick up the phone or call me back.

Naturally, that was when I decided to track her phone's location, thinking it might be time for us to speak in person. Admittedly, it feels a bit stalker-ish, but I don't let this bother me for too long. Compared to all the horrible things I've done, this one barely registers. It doesn't even break the top one hundred. Very mild, indeed.

For the first time in days, I'm eager to get out of bed. After quickly showering and dressing, I race downstairs to my car. Then I race to her, frustrated beyond measure by the daytime traffic. I knew I should've taken the chopper, but I didn't want to wait for it to be readied.

I rush to get to her, driving as fast as possible. But someone else beat me there. The door to Kat's apartment is wide open. As I stand outside, I hear somebody ruffling through her belongings.

Intrigued, I step inside the apartment, carefully avoiding announcing my presence to the mysterious individual by making too much noise.

Usually, nothing would have delighted me more than thoroughly examining Kat's place and the things that make it her home. But as I observe the ransacked state of the living room and the strange woman inside it, snooping around is the last thing on my mind.

The woman has her back turned to me, so I can see nothing but her light-colored sweater and jeans, plus the back of her blonde head. She turns around and gasps, startled by seeing me.

"Who the fuck are you?" she asks, breathlessly clutching her chest.

"Who the fuck am *I*? Who the fuck are you? Where's Kat?"

She huffs indignantly. "That's what I would like to know, too." While narrowing her brown eyes at me, she says, "And, unlike you, I am a concerned party with the keys to this place and a right to be here. I will only ask you one more time, mister. Who the fuck are you, and what are you doing here?"

I'm tempted to call her bluff, but I let go of the idea. The last thing I need is to antagonize this woman. In fact, getting her on my side would be an impressive coup in my current circumstances.

"You must be A.J.," I say under my breath. I hold my hand out to her. "My name is Nikolai Stefanovich. I'm looking for Kat."

A.J. raises her eyebrows so high I'm mildly surprised they don't disappear behind her bangs. With a scowl, she shakes my hand. "Oh, I bet you are, Nikolai."

Her tone surprises me. "What's that supposed to mean?"

"Oh, I think you know. I've heard *all* about you."

I laugh humorlessly. "I sure hope not."

"Obviously. And I don't blame you. If I were you, I'd be embarrassed, too."

I spot a cell phone on the floor, just outside the kitchen. Wordlessly, I walk towards it and pick it up. "No wonder Kat didn't answer my calls," I say.

A.J. gasps over my shoulder. "Shit."

I turn to look at her. "What is it? Tell me," I ask.

A.J. needs no further encouragement, talking a mile a minute. "The reason I came here in the first place is because I was on the phone with Kat—sharing some pretty spectacular news, by the way—when she just became unresponsive. The call dropped. I called back a bunch of times, but she never picked it up. She never called me back, either. That's not like her. I just had a bad feeling about it."

I have a bad feeling, too.

"Tell me everything you discussed with her," I say with urgency. A.J. hesitates, and I ask, "Is this about Salvatore?"

Eyes wide, she gasps before scanning me from head to toe. "You know about the *stronzo*?" she asks, sounding surprised.

I frown, puzzled. "Who?"

"Giuseppe Salvatore. The Italian family boss. Kat and I call him the *stronzo*. It means asshole in Italian. Did she tell you about him?"

I nod. "Yes. I know about the fucker. Were you two discussing him?"

A.J. shrugs. "In a way. Earlier today, I finally got my hands on the motherlode—a couple of boxes of records concerning his dirty little secret. As I'm sure you're aware, the *stronzo* is only the boss of the Italian family by the grace of his good wife, Gianna. If her father hadn't passed the mantle to his daughter's worthless husband before dying, maybe we'd never have the displeasure of dealing with him.

You'd think that would keep him from straying, right? But it didn't. Rumors have always run amok, but until recently, they were just that—rumors. Until today. I'm proud to say that I now have hard proof of his misstep. And I'm not afraid to use it, trust me. As soon as I find Kat, my next move will be to let Gianna Salvatore know all about her husband's love child, this guy named Dmitri Ivashkov."

My heart screeches to a halt inside my chest, painfully contracting. "What did you just say?" I ask, holding my breath.

"I said I have to find Kat ASAP so I can pay Gianna a call. Then maybe Kat and I will go to Ibiza. You're not invited, of course, and—"

"No, the son's name. What did you say it was?"

"Oh," A.J. says, blinking. "It's Dmitri Ivashkov. Why? Do you know him? I didn't want to be rude and ask you outright. I didn't want to imply that all Russians know each other or anything like that."

"You must've heard it wrong," I say. "The name. That's not him. It can't be."

A.J. shakes her head. "Nope. I'm sure of it. Dmitri Ivashkov. Early twenties, super hot in a himbo kind of way. His mother was one Elena Ivashkov. The *stronzo* unfailingly sent them money every month for over eighteen years. I have tons of other stuff, too. Trust me, it's him. I can back it up. Here, take a look."

A.J. hands me her cell phone, and, to my horror, I verify she is right. She opens file after file, photo after photo, and the documentation is undeniable. Dmitri is the son of Giuseppe Salvatore, the Italian family's hateful boss.

After handing the phone back to A.J., I stare blankly ahead, unseeing. I can't believe this, and yet...

I pick up my phone and call Dmitri, the man I love like a brother. To my dismay, he doesn't answer. I call Vladmir then. Maybe there's an explanation for this whole madness…

Vladmir picks up at the first ring. "Nikolai," he says.

Not wasting time with pleasantries, I ask, "Is Dmitri with you?"

After a brief pause, Vladmir says, "No. I've been wondering where he is. He was supposed to meet me an hour ago, but he hasn't shown up and isn't picking up his phone. No one's seen or heard from him since early this morning."

No, Dmitri. Not you. Anybody but you.

"Okay. If you see or hear from him, call me immediately. In the meantime, I need you to stop whatever you're doing and find him for me. Text me his phone's last known location as soon as possible."

After Vladmir acknowledges my orders, I hang up.

I turn to A.J. "Is there somewhere safe you could go to?" I ask. "If not, I'll drop you off at my home. You can wait there until I bring Kat back. You'll be completely safe."

She scowls. "What are you talking about? What's going on here? If you know Kat's whereabouts, you must tell me right now. And you're not dropping me off anywhere. Not a chance. If you're going to search for her, then I'm coming with you."

The last thing I need right now is someone else to worry about, but I don't have time to argue with her. So, with a sigh, I relent. I shut my eyes for a moment, steeling myself for what will follow next.

I finally understand it now. It all makes sense. At last.

Once again, Kat was right. As always.

McGuire never had anything to do with Maxim's untimely demise. He didn't kill my best friend.

Dmitri did.

20

KAT

I can't deny it any longer. It's obvious now—I must've been a naughty girl in one of my past lives. There's just no other explanation.

People often say that when it rains, it pours. In my case, I think it's more of a deluge situation.

At first, I had to deal with the *stronzo*, Giuseppe Salvatore, the head of the Italian mafia. That, of course, led to Nikolai Stefanovich, the *pakhan* of the *bratva*, deciding he had beef with me. Because of Nik, I found myself on Patrick McGuire's bad side. Then Dmitri Ivashkov, Nik's right-hand man and the *stronzo*'s secret love child, demanded that we go for a ride. And by ride, I mean suicide mission.

Dmitri sighs beside me. "I wish it hadn't come to this, Kat," he says under his breath. His hands clutch the steering wheel tightly. I don't know whether it is to keep them from shaking or from doing something even worse. "I did my best to avoid it. For what it's worth."

"Nothing. It's worth nothing, Dmitri," I say.

Dmitri wipes the sweat off his brow with the back of his

hand. "I don't blame you for feeling like that. I hope you can understand I don't have any other choice."

I sigh, staring out the car's window. "Trust me, Dmitri, there's always a choice."

We are leaving the city. Dmitri hasn't bothered blindfolding me, which tells me all I need to know about his intentions. He doesn't need to hide where we are going because I'm never returning.

"I wish that were true, Kat," he says, his voice breaking. "I'd think that you'd know better than most that sometimes we must do unspeakable things to protect those we love. Once you learned who I am, who my father is, I had no choice but to take you."

"I cared about you and thought you cared about me. I thought we were friends."

"We were, and I still care about you, Kat. There's just someone I care about more, that's all. You know as well as I do that now that my secret is out there, it's only a matter of time before I'm put down either by Nik or my father. I'm too much of a liability to both of them. I don't have much time left, and I'll be damned if I go down before setting her free."

Dmitri's mysterious girlfriend. He won't even dare uttering her name. It's almost like he thinks he isn't worthy of saying it out loud, as if he might sully her by the meaningless act.

"I would have helped you, Dmitri. I would have done my best to help you because we were friends. Or at least I thought we were before you kidnapped me after I welcomed you into my home."

"I'm so sorry, Kat—more than I can ever say. If there had been any other way... I wish I could promise to make up for this, but that would be a lie. I won't have time." Dmitri's eyes dart from side to side, unseeing. He's in full desperation mode, controlled by the adrenaline raging through his veins.

"Funny you should say that, Dmitri—I doubt I will, either. Now that I've taken the Flame of Mir from your dad, he will kill me on the spot, and you know it. You're sending me to my death."

Dmitri's shoulders sag, and he clenches his jaw. "I'm sorry," he says, his words barely more than a whisper. "You don't deserve this. I wish there was another way, but I'm out of time. My father will release her in exchange for you. And if Nik catches up with us before I can make the trade, you'll be my only leverage. He will do anything to get you back."

I open my mouth to retort, but then I think twice about it. There's just no point. Dmitri won't change his mind. He is too far gone to release me. I'm just wasting my breath and energy by arguing with him.

Dmitri's words about Nik make me want to weep, because I realize I will never see him again. I won't ever be in his arms again, feel his skin against my lips, or breathe in his scent...

Even worse, the last shared moment we will ever have will be one of hurt and regret. I'll never hear his laugh again. Our last kiss will be our last. If only I had known then...

I wish I had realized before that my fear of losing control was the only thing standing in the way of my happily ever after. I wish I had understood that by choosing to hold on to it, I was sentencing myself to live out the rest of my days with no chance of true love and happiness. If only I could return to the moment when I burst into his office to throw his diamond at him... I would tell myself that holding on to that fear would only bring me misery.

The irony is that I now realize I've been clutching to something imaginary. There is no such thing as complete control of your life or yourself. All this time, I've been clinging to an illusion, and it only brought me pain and anxiety. Now, I must accept that however much time I have left before Dmitri ends me will be full of nothing but regret. I lived a full life, I suppose. I did things my way, on my terms, for the most part. But, when it truly counted, I fucked up.

I didn't understand then that real love is so rare and magical that life puts you to the test before awarding it to you. I had to prove I was worthy of it. I had to pay a price for this kind of magic—the type that only comes around once in a lifetime—by sacrificing something of myself. Something that made me unworthy of it, even though I've been clinging to it like it's worth something.

I failed my test horribly by allowing my fear of letting go of nothing but a stupid illusion of control make me lose Nik. Unlike that pretense of control, Nik is real and capable of making me happier than I knew was even possible.

By a turn of fate, I came across someone who is every dream I have ever had made flesh. Everything I have ever wanted was on the other side of my fear, and I made the wrong choice. I chose to hold on to what needed to be lost, and now it's too late. I will never get a chance to get Nik back. And I have nobody but myself to blame for it.

While sweating profusely, Dmitri glances at his phone, harmlessly displayed on the console. Again and again, his eyes return to the device, and it makes me nervous. His frazzled state already makes him a careless driver. I don't like our chances of getting out of this car alive if he won't stop taking his eyes off the road.

"Expecting a phone call?" I ask with sarcasm. "If you untie me, I can check your phone for you."

Dmitri briefly looks at my wrists, painfully tied together by a zip tie. "No. I'm just... debating something."

"Are you having second thoughts about this plan of yours? I don't blame you. Why don't we pull over at that gas station and take a moment to think this whole thing through again?"

He shakes his head. "No. I'm torn about whether to keep or toss the phone. Nik can track it. If he suspects I might've taken you, he'll sniff us out in a heartbeat. But I need the phone to find her because it's the only way I have to locate her right now. I don't have the time to figure something else out before Giuseppe learns what your friend discovered about me."

"Why are you telling me all this?" I ask.

Dmitri shrugs. "I guess I'm just thinking out loud. But believe it or not, Kat, I still think of you as a friend. Even though I don't expect you to feel the same way about me right now. Also, in the end, it doesn't really matter if you know this stuff or not."

"Because I'm as good as dead, right, *friend*?" I ask, almost yelling as I struggle against the restraints around my wrists. But it's a waste of time and hurts like hell.

Dmitri doesn't bother giving me a response. With a resolute expression, he stares ahead through the windshield. The unwavering look in his eyes tells me my fate is as good as sealed.

The two of us sit in tense silence as he drives for what seems like hours. After an eternity has passed, Dmitri slows down. As he pulls over, the unmistakable sound of gravel being crushed under the car's wheels startles me. A moment later, we come to a stop in front of an abandoned-looking warehouse.

The building looks like it has no business still standing.

It's massive, wide enough to cover an entire block, and at least five stories high. Its once-blue paint has almost completely faded to a pale gray. Multiple spots over the facade have been stripped of it, replaced by a thick layer of rust.

I glance around, but I don't see any signs of life or anything else. The warehouse is the only structure occupying the massive lot.

"We have to make a quick stop. We won't be long," Dmitri says, unbuckling both our seatbelts. He comes around the car to open the passenger side door and drag me out of the vehicle against my will, while I drag my feet—quite literally.

Dmitri says nothing, and neither do I, as he forces me to walk into the decrepit building. Somehow, it's even more massive looking inside. It's damp and cold, too. Almost no sunlight makes it through the crumbling structure, but the interior is illuminated enough for us to see the way ahead.

Unable to contain myself any longer, I ask, "What are we doing here?"

I fully expect Dmitri to give me the silent treatment, but to my surprise, he answers my question. "I need to grab something with more of a kick than my pistol before we meet my father. This is one of the *bratva*'s armories. We won't be long."

While clutching my upper arm, Dmitri moves forward deliberately, clearly familiar with the place's layout. We stop before a set of double doors—a closet, if I had to guess. A thick metal chain is wrapped around the door handles, and a padlock larger than my fist secures it.

Still holding on to me, Dmitri digs around his pockets, searching for what I can only presume is the key that unlocks the doors. But before he is able to locate it, the startling sound of the warehouse's metal front doors opening and closing echoes through the air.

I don't have the chance to even muster a reaction since Dmitri's hand closes over my mouth almost instantly. I can barely breathe, let alone scream.

Quietly, Dmitri turns around, pressing his back against the doors to the armory. He positions me directly in front of him, drawing me close until my body practically covers the front of his.

A human shield. Nice.

A heartbeat later, I see *him*.

He's more breathtaking than ever—even more than I remember.

I thought I'd never see him again, but he's here. He's so handsome it almost physically hurts me. The mere sight of him makes me want to weep.

He came for me.

After everything, he still came for me.

Dmitri's hands grasp me painfully, but I barely feel the discomfort. All I see is Nik—his tall frame, those broad shoulders enclosed by his jet-black jacket, and that glossy dark hair arrestingly framing his gorgeous face.

I want to run into his arms. I want to hold him tightly to me and never let him go.

Dmitri tightens his hold on me and I realize I had been unwittingly struggling against him. I try harder to break free from him, but I might as well be pounding sand. Dmitri towers almost a foot over me, and he likely outweighs me by at least fifty pounds, too—I have no shot.

Nik's eyes land on us then.

"Kat..." he says hoarsely. "You're alive."

As Dmitri's palm keeps me from speaking, I frantically

nod, wordlessly attempting to convey to Nik everything I feel right now. All that's been left unsaid for far too long.

Nik scans me from head to toe. "Did he hurt you?"

I shake my head, and Nik's shoulders sag in relief. Instantly, his attention is diverted to the man behind me.

"Dmitri..." Nik calmly—almost placatingly—says.

"Nikki—" Dmitri says with a gasp, his voice quivering. "I'm so sorry. I didn't mean for any of this to happen. You have to believe me, Nik."

"I do, Dmitri," Nik says appeasingly, stretching his hand towards us. "Let Kat go, and we'll talk. Everything will be okay."

Violently shaking his head, Dmitri says, "No. I'm sorry, Nik. I can't do that. I'm sorry, but I need her."

Nik's voice remains impressively even. "You know I won't let you take her with you."

Humorlessly, Dmitri laughs. "I don't see how you can stop me. I have the girl and the gun."

Nik's gaze fixates on the pistol in Dmitri's hand. "Kat is not a part of this, Dmitri. This is between you and me. Let her go."

"You made her a part of this," Dmitri angrily says, clutching me tightly. "Her blood will be on your hands as much as mine."

Nik's eyes widen slightly at Dmitri's passionate tone. "No blood needs to be shed today. Why don't you let Kat go so you and I can sort this out between us? Peacefully."

Dmitri scoffs, rolling his eyes. "Come on, Nik. I know you too well to believe that. The moment I let her go, I'm a dead man. And I can't die just yet."

"You have the gun," Nik says. "You said it yourself. Let Kat go, Dmitri. You haven't harmed anyone innocent yet. No reason to start now."

"I realize this might not be my greatest moment, Nik, but I'm not that stupid. After what I've done to Maxim, to Kat... If I let her go, I'm done. You'll see to that."

Nik shakes his head, sighing. "Dmitri, you're like a brother to me. I could never kill you in cold blood. Let's talk. Let Kat go, and you and I will figure this out. I promise."

Dmitri's hold over me loosens a bit. I can't currently see his expression, but it's obvious that Nik's words have made him hesitant. Even now, the bond between the two of them is undeniable. Cruelly disregarding Nik's pleas isn't something that comes naturally to Dmitri. More than anything, he wants to trust his *pakhan*.

In the end, however, Dmitri's resolve wins. With a final shake of his head, he says, "Sorry, Nik. I'm taking Kat with me. I don't suppose you'd consider making my life easier and letting us go? I'd rather not have to hurt her in front of you. Or harm you."

Nik tenses up. For a second, he looks as if he might move towards us. But he hesitates. After taking a deep breath, he stares into Dmitri's pale blue eyes instead. "Why, Dmitri? Why would you choose this path for yourself? You and I were family. Is it true, then, that blood is thicker than water? I guess I wouldn't know."

Against my back, Dmitri's heart madly races. "No," he says in a horrified tone. "Nik, how can you even ask me that? My father is nothing to me. Less than nothing. Being related to him is the worst thing that has ever happened to me. He never cared about me or my mother. Not until you did. He tried to turn me against you once he learned of my connection to you. He's always despised you, Nik. You know that. He tried his damned best to play the part of the proud dad once he found out you and I were close. I wanted nothing to do with him. But then, the bastard learned about *her*. He took her from me, Nik. I had no choice—"

"You could've come to me, told me everything, and I'd have dealt with him for you—as your *pakhan* and friend. You should've trusted me, Dmitri."

"I wanted to, Nik—more than anything. But you have to understand... Even at first, I was deeply ashamed of my connection to him. I didn't want anyone to know that my blood is that bastard's blood. Least of all, you. You were always so good to me and to my mom. I couldn't bear the thought of disappointing you. I didn't want you to think we were on his side and toss us out. And then he took *her*, and I couldn't risk telling you everything. I had already jeopardized her life enough."

With a sigh, Nik says, "I never knew anything—"

"I know," Dmitri says. "And I hoped things would stay that way until I figured out how to get rid of my father. But Kat and her friend learned the truth about me, and I understood it was only a matter of time before you did. So I had to act fast. I hope you can someday forgive me."

"It doesn't have to be this way, Dmitri. It really doesn't. Let Kat go and let me help you."

With a sad laugh, Dmitri shakes his head. "I wish I could. I wish I believed you would actually do that. But I know you too well. You will never let me get away with what I did to Maxim and Kat. And I don't blame you. But I can't let you end me before I save *her*. I'll try to spare Kat of any pain I can."

Nik's eyes flicker to my face before quickly refocusing on Dmitri. Even from where I stand, I can see Dmitri's ominous statement's devastating effect on him. "Like you did for Maxim?" Nik's tone is measured but scathing, nonetheless.

Dmitri shrugs. "I am sorry about Maxim. I really am. For what it's worth, I made it quick. He didn't suffer long."

Nik's eyes darken, and my heart breaks for him. He never knew that on that single, eventful night, he lost the two people he loved the most in the world...

"What did you do with his body?" Nik asks.

"I had nothing to do with that. The last time I laid eyes on Maxim was when you saw his body on the ground in the museum."

Nik scoffs. "Right."

"I mean it, Nik. I have no reason to lie about this. Not anymore."

After the briefest pause, Nik asks, "How did you do it? Kill Maxim, I mean."

"The room was dark, and Maxim didn't hear me come up behind him. I wrapped *this* around his neck." Dmitri's fingers reveal from under the collar of his shirt the gold necklace with the emerald pendant he always wears. "And that was it. I left him where you saw him."

Nik conceals it well, but I spot the pain in his expression as clear as day. Still smothered by Dmitri's hand, I cry in silence. For Nik. For me. For Dmitri, too.

"I didn't want to kill Maxim, you know. I tried to resist my father for as long as I could. But he wouldn't be moved. He was adamant about Maxim being killed that night. Hell, during the party, he called me and ensured I could hear *her* cries over the phone... To make sure I'd follow through with his plan."

The gala's surveillance feeds. The call we saw Dmitri take...

With horror, I understand I was even more of a pawn in the *stronzo*'s hands than I had known. Just like Dmitri described, his father had been steadfast and specific about the terms of my assignment. He insisted I had to steal Nik's diamond on that fateful evening—nothing else would do. All of it is just a piece of this big puzzle...

"All of this because of Erin and Lorenzo?" Nik asks in disbelief.

"That's some of it, I'm sure, but not the whole picture. My father most definitely resents the humiliation Maxim—and, therefore, you—put him through with the whole mess involving Erin, but I always got the feeling that it was about more than that. He never got over the fact that the Russians and the Irish were running the show, even though he was the big, bad Italian boss. He'd love to have you and McGuire destroy each other. I think he knew there was so much bad blood between you and McGuire that it would be easy to start a war."

Nik sighs. "He wasn't wrong about that. But he doesn't have to win, Dmitri. We can turn it around. We can destroy him together and save your girl. Then we'll figure out how to clean this mess with the Irish. You and I are family. We'll work it out. Just let Kat go."

"I can't tell you how much I wish I could believe you," Dmitri says with a sigh. His voice is so sad it almost pains me. Almost. "But the truth is, I just know you too well, Nik. You can't possibly mean that, not after everything I did. You won't forget what I did to Maxim and Kat. I'd take a chance on you if it were just about me, but I just can't bet *her* life."

With a resigned, heartfelt sigh, Nik finally allows his glance to drift away from Dmitri. His dark brown eyes meet mine momentarily before he takes full measure of me. As lovingly as a caress, his gaze roams all over me. After a second, it returns to mine, and my breath catches. Something in his eyes makes me want to weep.

"I understand, Dmitri," Nik says, still looking at me. "Take me instead, then."

21

KAT

Dmitri's clammy palm contains my muffled scream of protest. Frantically, I shake my head, desperate to dissuade Nik from this horrible idea. His dark brown eyes glow with warmth and affection as he studies me for one final moment before diverting his attention back to my latest kidnapper.

"Think about it, Dmitri—you have no reason to keep Kat if you have me. I'm a much more valuable hostage to you. You'll still have plenty of leverage over me. Let her go and take me instead. I'll go with you willingly. You can tell Giuseppe to summon the Seven Families to witness me publicly surrender the *bratva* to him. As long as he agrees to release Kat and her friend from his service, of course. I'll even give him information he can use to fuck with McGuire. Your father will be compelled to release your girlfriend and do what you ask if you hand me to him under these terms."

As hard as I can, I struggle against Dmitri's deathly grasp over me. More than ever, it's vital that I free myself. But he is so strong. Mindlessly, he holds on to me with no issues.

"He will kill you, Nik," Dmitri says. "As soon as you surrender the *bratva*, he'll execute you."

"I understand."

"You'd have to lose your phone," Dmitri says with a sigh. "And disarm yourself, of course."

Without hesitation, Nik slides his phone and gun in Dmitri's direction.

"Done," the love of my life calmly says.

No longer holding back my tears, I sob against Dmitri's hand. This can't be happening. Whatever hell the *stronzo* could unleash on me wouldn't compare to what he would do to Nik, his rival, if he got his filthy hands on him.

"I'd like to restrain you, too, Nik."

Nik happily agrees to Dmitri's demand. "Of course. Just give me a moment to say goodbye to Kat first." Dmitri hesitates, and Nik says, "I promise I won't try anything, Dmitri. As long as you let her go, you have my word that I'll go with you willingly."

As it turns out, that's all the assurance Dmitri needs because he releases me without a second thought, pushing me towards Nik. I run into his arms, shaking.

Nik holds me tightly against his chest, leaning down to nuzzle my hair. He is warmth, strength and home. For the first time since storming out of his office, I feel the tension leave my body as if it instinctively knows I'm safe now.

I incoherently sob against the fabric of his shirt. "Nik..." I just got him back. I can't lose him again.

Nik kisses my head before tenderly tilting my head back until I look into his eyes. His gaze glitters with warmth and undisguised affection.

"Kat," he says with a small smile. His strong hands carefully and painlessly snap the plastic ties around my wrists without much effort. "Everything's going to be just fine."

"Liar," I say with an anguished sob, and he has the nerve to chuckle.

After pressing a too-brief kiss against my forehead, he says, "I want you to go out the door and find A.J. She's waiting for you outside. Somehow, I managed to convince her to stay in the car."

I frown. "No way. I'm not leaving here without you."

"Yes, you are. You're going to meet your friend, then you're going to find Vladmir, and you'll let him protect you—at least until Salvatore has a chance to end McGuire. After that, you'll be free, Kat—from all of us."

"I don't want to be free from you." Nik smiles.

"Nik..." Dmitri says with urgency.

While looking at Dmitri over my shoulder, Nik nods once before returning his gaze to my face.

"Now, listen to me, Kat," he says in a no-nonsense tone. "Whatever happens next, I want you to know how sorry I am for all the hurt I've caused you. I don't expect you to forgive me, but for what it's worth, I'd give away every cent I have to my name and every last breath I have left for a chance to try to make it up to you."

"Nik," I cry. "Stop. You can't go with him..."

Eyes ablaze, Nik ignores my protests. "If I don't see you again—if I don't get another chance to earn your forgiveness and your love—I need you to know that from the moment I met you, I was never the same. Meeting you was the greatest thing that's ever happened to me. If everything is to end for me soon, don't feel sorry for me. I got to be with you, and that made my life worthwhile. I don't want you to feel sad for me, *milaya*. So many people go through their whole lives without feeling how I feel when I'm with you. I'm beyond grateful that I was lucky enough to meet someone who makes me feel like you do. If this is my end, I'll die a happy man as long as I know you will thoroughly enjoy a very long, happy life. Promise me you will."

Uncontrollably sobbing, I somehow manage to say, "I can't lose you. There has to be a way—"

Nik's eyes don't leave mine—not even for a split second. "This is the way, Kat. If my life is the price for yours, I will gladly pay it any day or night. Now, promise me you will take care of yourself."

"Nik, I can't—"

"Kat." He gently shakes my shoulders once. "Promise me."

Nik's dark brown eyes mesmerize me, even as my heart shatters into a million pieces. Unable to deny him anything at this moment, I nod. "I promise."

With a small smile, Nik kisses my forehead. "Good girl," he says against my skin—one last time.

My voice wavers as I grab fistfuls of his shirt, unwilling to let him drift even an inch away from me. "Tell me this isn't goodbye, Nik. Tell me I'll see you again."

Nik's eyes crinkle as he smiles and studies my face, as if trying to commit it to memory. He tenderly caresses my cheek with his left hand, so gentle that I barely feel his touch. "Of course," he says under his breath. "I told you, remember? Wild horses couldn't keep me away."

The reminder of his passionate promise from not so long ago almost breaks me in half. Because this time, he doesn't mean it. He can't mean it. How could he? This *is* goodbye.

My expression must give my anguish away because Nik's eyes soften as he comforts me, pulling me back into his arms. "Shh. Don't cry, *milaya*. I can't bear it when you cry. You're going to unman me."

"And I can't bear to lose you."

"You won't," he says, kissing me. "Not now. Not ever. I'm yours until the end of time, Kat."

I sob against his chest with renewed fervor. "Nik—"

He cuts me off. "It's time for you to go, Kat. Go find A.J., and don't look back, okay? Now come here and give me a kiss."

Tears stream down my face, and I rise on my toes, touching my lips against Nik's as I wrap my arms around his neck. I kiss him with the strength of the agony inside me, with the force of all the words that will remain unsaid between us, and with the power of everything I feel for him—all the emotions he has evoked in me from the moment we met, all the yearning and devotion that will plague me until the end of my days.

As our lips meet with urgency, I breathe him in, willing myself to memorize every precious sensation—from the sound of his shaky gasp when our lips touch to the mouthwatering scent of his skin. I don't ever want to forget the feel of his body against mine and the warmth of his skin under my hands, or the feel of his hair against my fingertips—so different from the roughness of his scruff...

It's over too soon.

Too soon, Nik pulls away from me, breaking our embrace and untangling our limbs.

Forever wouldn't have been enough.

Nik's gaze meets mine one last time. "It's time, Kat. Go now." After one last look, he turns away from me to face Dmitri.

Unable to withstand the sight of what is about to unfold, I turn my back to them. The sight of Dmitri restraining Nik is more than I can take without breaking right now. I run outside instead, just like Nik wanted me to do. Before long, I locate his car, with A.J. sitting inside. Not long after that, in a haze, I find myself behind the wheel next to her.

My friend bombards me with a million questions about

what happened inside the warehouse, and somehow, I manage to fill her in on the awful turn of events that I witnessed.

"Well," A.J. says once I'm finished with my story. Minutes or hours might have passed since I escaped the warehouse —I wouldn't know either way. Time seems impossibly trivial and surreal now that Nik is gone from my life. "Let's call this Vladmir guy, then. Do you have his number? No? Well, that's fine. It doesn't matter. I'm sure I can find it easily enough. Can you hand me my laptop? It's in the bag I tossed in the backseat."

Shaking my head, I turn to face her, making my decision. "No," I say under my breath.

"No?" she asks me with a frown.

"No," I say with more certainty, handing her the computer as my resolve solidifies. "We are not calling Vladmir. At least not just yet. I need you to do something for me first. Do you think you can track Nik's phone?"

A.J. gives me a disbelieving look. "Track his phone?"

I nod, waiting for her to grab the laptop from my outstretched hand, but she just glares at me as if I have lost my mind. I can't blame her. I very well may have. I'd be lying if I said I feel completely sane right now.

"Now, why would you want me to do that, Kat? Not because you mean to go after him, I hope."

"A.J.—" I say with a sigh.

"Because that would be suicide. And you're way too smart to go on some crazy *kamikaze* mission for a guy. Right? Tell me you're too smart to be this dumb. I'm begging you."

"I have to save him."

A.J. sighs. "So, let me make sure I'm getting this right. You and I just got everything we've been working towards for the last year. We are finally free of the *stronzo* and all the other mafia misfortune we've encountered along the way. And you want to throw all of that away and get yourself into an even more dangerous situation with even more mafia families to save the *bratva*'s *pakhan*? Did I get it right?"

I shrug. "Yeah. I'd say that about sums it up."

"Are you out of your fucking mind?" A.J. asks, yelling at the top of her lungs, and I wince. The sound is particularly startling in Nik's locked up car.

I sigh wearily. "I won't lie to you. I might be. But it doesn't matter. I have to save him, A.J. I understand the odds are I will fail, but it doesn't matter. I have to try."

If I fail, Nik dies. So if I die, I die. A life without him hardly seems worth living, anyway.

A.J. gasps. "Who the hell are you, and what have you done to my best friend? You're just going to storm into a meeting of the Seven Families and save your boyfriend, who is now a hostage of the boss of the Italian family, with barely an hour's notice? Just like that? No planning, no scouting, no contingency plans, no nothing? You're just going to wing it. You'd have no control over anything. Every single detail would just be left to chance."

I nod. "Yep. Now, can you please track Nik's phone?"

Eyes wide, A.J. shakes her head. "You'd be putting yourself and your life at unbelievable risk—more than ever. Stealing the Flame of Mir from The Metropolitan Museum is nothing compared to this. And for what? Even if you succeed, you'll still lose everything you ever wanted and have been fighting for these past months. Scratch that—everything you've been fighting for your whole life! Even if you miraculously manage to save Nik and not kill yourself in the process, you'll never be fully in charge of your life again. You'll never be completely independent. I've met him, Kat. That man is too bossy, too possessive, too protective...

He's too much of a control freak to allow you to feel independent or exclusively in control again. And this time, if he gets his hands on you, he's never letting you go. Of that, I have no doubts. You can bet on that."

I sigh again. "God, I hope so. I'm counting on it. Now, can you please track him for me? I can't afford to waste any more time."

"Kat..." she says with a horrified groan.

Impatiently, I cut her off, raising my voice. "A.J.! If the choice is between my fear of losing control and my fear of losing him, please understand: it's no choice at all. I can't lose him. Nik is everything to me now. I love him. And if something happens to him, if he's taken from me forever... I don't know what I'd do. I don't think—no, I *know* I will never be happy again. Now, *please*, scold me all you want, but do it while you find him for me."

A.J. stares at me in shock for a second longer, and then, wordlessly, she reaches for her laptop. Blissfully silent, she powers it on and types away, shooting me sideways glances every thirty seconds.

I exhale in relief when she turns the laptop in my direction so I can view the screen.

"This is where he is," she says with a sigh. "Or at least where his phone is."

I stare at the blinking green dot on the map with a frown. It's not stationary, seeming to be moving further and further away from the city. There isn't much around where it is headed, so my guess is that Dmitri's probably taking Nik to the old financial district, which sends a chill down my spine. That can't be good, considering it's mostly deserted and abandoned nowadays.

After turning the car on, I take a deep breath, steeling myself.

"Thank you, A.J. I'll go get him now. If you don't want to come with me, I won't blame you. No hard feelings. I mean it."

A.J. scoffs. "Bitch, you have *really* lost your mind if you think you're doing this without me. Now, please tell me you have a plan. Or at least something that resembles it in the slightest."

My heart warms. I don't deserve her.

I smile at her with sympathy. "You're not going to like it."

A.J. sighs and closes her eyes before leaning her blonde head against her seat's headrest. "Fuck my life," she says through gritted teeth. After opening her eyes, she squares her shoulders.

With a final shake of her head, she turns to face me. "Just drive."

22

NIK

Even under the faint light in the vast, dark chamber, I have no trouble recognizing Giuseppe Salvatore a stone's throw away from where I stand.

While our peers gather around us in silence, I study him in his expertly tailored suit as the rage inside me begs me for release.

Never have I needed to kill as much as I do at this moment, knowing everything the man has done to Dmitri and Kat.

I've never wanted anything as much as I wanted to spend my life with Kat. But that will never come to be, thanks in no small part to Salvatore.

Even now, being kept from her makes me restless and uneasy. At least I have one consolation: in the end, Kat will be free and safe. After everything I've put her through, it's no small comfort to know that this will be my parting gift to her. My death will not be in vain.

Still, I would have liked to try to earn Kat's forgiveness. I would have cherished a long, happy life at her side.

Will she wonder about what could have been between

us? About the life we could have had together? A selfish part of me hopes Kat won't forget about me.

But in the end, I hope she does. I hope she thinks fondly of me now and then, but not too often. I'm not fond of the idea of Kat spending the rest of her days in any pain or misery, especially not over me.

Soon, it won't matter, anyway. Shackled and unarmed, I will die tonight at Salvatore's hands, and Kat will be safe.

Over the years, Dmitri often asked me about my past and my will to live and overcome my pitiful circumstances. He often marveled at it, amazed at how far removed I had come to be from the street urchin I once was. Moments ago, when he brought me before the heads of the Seven Families, memories of my trials and youth flooded me and I started to feel emotional.

I found myself reminiscing about the tortuous path that has brought me here. All the pain and suffering, the senseless violence... All the longing and yearning, and the undeniable desire to reach for something better than myself.

I have accomplished so much in a little over three decades on this earth, but I will leave it knowing I could have achieved so much more.

I have so many regrets... I wish I had done so much differently. There are so many mistakes I won't have the time to fix. But if anything had been different, maybe I wouldn't have known Kat. Perhaps I wouldn't have stumbled upon her at that party.

Even now, I can picture her so clearly—her lush lips curving into a tempting smile as her dark blue eyes sparkle at me.

By a serendipitous turn of fate, I came across the most fascinating woman ever born. Somehow, I was fortunate enough to have the opportunity to get to know her. I savored the feel of her on me, under me, and around me as I brought her pleasure over and over again. With my last breath, I'll regret the pain I've caused her, but I'll part this world knowing I protected her to the end.

If only I had known years ago that Kat would be in my future someday, even for a short time... How much more could I have achieved? What kind of man could I have become?

Throughout my life, the one thing I could always count on was my desire to survive, to seize the chance to carry on and become something better than I was the day before. Even during the darkest times of my early years, this yearning was the only constant I knew. I've never been willing to lay down my life for something more significant than myself. Truthfully, I've struggled to picture a cause greater than my need for survival. But I will gladly do it for Kat's life, for her future, safety and happiness.

Salvatore's pale blue eyes shine with unconcealed pleasure at the sight of me bound and powerless before him. His slick, greasy smirk twists his unbecoming features into a disturbing picture under the flickering lights above.

I shove my shoulders back, meeting his mocking gaze without hesitation. Even though my life is about to end, I know I have won. Kat will be happy and free of him and me.

The only regret I will take with me is that I hurt her so badly. If only we hadn't wasted so much time that we could've spent being happy together...

23

KAT

Hidden behind one of the ornate, crumbling marble columns, I survey the old bank with disgust.

No current of fresh air stirs down on the crumbling lobby, lending the area a mildewy stench. Without the slightest traces of a draft, dust has piled up since the decrepit bank last was in business. Sooty leather chairs and shiny bullet casings litter the gold-veined, black marble floors.

After almost a decade of vacancy, most of the building has decayed into ruins, and even the paint is peeling from the walls.

Even though I put the pedal to the metal to get here, the drive still took the better part of an insufferable hour, seeming interminable at every mile of the road leading to the bank. With each passing minute, I became more and more convinced that I was going to be too late and Dmitri and his father would have already executed Nik by the time I managed to get to their location.

A dozen yards from where I stand, I spot movement under the glow of a dim overhead light fixture. A handful of men start to gather in somber silence. Members of the Seven Families, no doubt.

Careful not to make noise and denounce my presence, I remain hidden, watching. My plan's minuscule chances of success depend on A.J. and I having the element of surprise. Of course, all our efforts could be in vain if Nik is already dead. But I can't allow myself to go down that path just yet. I need to focus on what I can control right now.

Barely daring to breathe, I observe a small crowd of finely dressed men standing in a semicircle around the faint light. Behind them, more of the same decaying Corinthian marble columns loom. Inside their expensively made jackets, tucked underneath their waistbands or cleverly hidden around their ankles, the bulges of weapons of different sizes are unmistakable.

Was that the fate that awaited Nik? To be shot to death?

Only over my dead body.

The men's shifty eyes and shuffling feet denounce their uneasiness at being here. My guess is that they are not too eager to hang out in a dark room with their worst rivals.

A shiver runs down my spine as I study their hardened stares and the cruel glint in their eyes. I can't even begin to imagine the horrible things they'd do to me and A.J. if they got their hands on us... But I force myself to remain focused on my task and continue looking for signs of Nik, Dmitri and the *stronzo*. I can't afford any distracting thoughts or emotions right now.

My heart threatens to slam out of my chest, and my breath catches as I spot Dmitri and his repulsive father leading Nik to the area where the other men are gathered. Relief like I have never known before courses through me, and I have to steady myself against a marble column as my legs start to give out.

Nik is still alive.

Unshed tears pool in my eyes, but I manage to keep them at bay, quietly drying them and taking deep, calming breaths to keep myself from unraveling into a crying mess of a woman.

Thankfully, as Giuseppe Salvatore steps closer to the light, my anger returns a hundred times stronger than before. He hauls Nik to a spot under the dim spotlight while slickly smiling in triumph.

The proud way Nik carries himself almost hides the desolate look on his face, but I know him better than that. Even under the abysmal lighting, it's easy to tell he has given up hope.

I glance around the room, searching, until I find A.J. standing across the bank's lobby from me. With a slight nod to her, I move through the darkness in Nik's direction. From the corner of my eye, I see A.J. shifting into position.

Dmitri pulls Nik along through the group of men, who exchange uneasy glances with each other. Some even whisper words too soft for my ears to catch.

The *stronzo* grins widely as he pulls out a shiny revolver from the inside pocket of his bespoke suit jacket.

Nik knew this fate awaited him when he surrendered to Dmitri, and he still went through with it because he wanted to save me.

Dmitri maneuvers Nik into the center of the semicircle until they stand under the spotlight. Quite literally. My former friend stands behind Nik, and they both turn to face the *stronzo*.

One look at Nik's expression of resignation, and my heart shatters for the millionth time in the past twenty-four hours.

My eyes meet A.J.'s again, and she nods, giving me the

sign I was waiting for just as the Italian boss smirks at Nik. "*Don* Stefanovich. Kneel before me."

Not in this lifetime.

A.J. kills the overhead lights while triggering the old building's fire alarm and sprinklers. On cue, the ear-splitting sound of police sirens echoes outside, and I fire my gun up in the air. It's the same pistol Nik gave me all those nights ago. On my way here, I found it in his glove box and thought it would add a poetic touch to this daring rescue.

Chaos, of course, ensues.

More gunshots follow, and my stomach churns as I anxiously hope for the best. It was clear from the start that this plan would require vast amounts of luck to work out. I can do nothing but hope that A.J., Nik, and I are not the target of a stray bullet.

Fortunately, my eyes adjust to the darkness in an instant, so I hasten to reach Nik, staying as close to the ground as possible. He is staring straight ahead, likely stunned by the cacophony of sounds and the sudden darkness A.J. unleashed upon us.

As I close the distance between the two of us, my gaze lingers on him, handcuffed and covered in gashes with his fine clothes sullied and torn.

Nik is so much better than these men. He has an undeniable, innate nobility about him that the others could never hope to achieve. Whatever lousy deeds my Russian may have committed throughout his years in the *bratva*, I have no doubts he had good, justifiable reasons for them.

I exhale with relief once I'm right behind him, touching his shoulder lightly. "Nik."

He stiffens, straining against his restraints. He swiftly turns to face me, and something like pure joy crosses his expression once his eyes land on me.

Almost instantly, that emotion and expression are followed by one I'm too familiar with. Nik makes no effort to disguise his unmistakable rage. As I could've guessed, he isn't thrilled that I'm risking myself to rescue him.

Well, tough luck, *miliy*.

"It's me," I say, panting with exertion. "Your very own knight in shining armor. Let's get out of here before your mafia buddies realize this daring rescue has been brought to them by me and my army of one."

Nik's eyes narrow at me. "You won't be able to sit for a week after I'm done spanking you for this stunt," he says through gritted teeth.

Delighted, I laugh. "Oh, Nik... Don't threaten me with a good time. Now, we have to go. No. Really. Let's go. Here, hold this. You know guns make me nervous."

Without another word, Nik takes the pistol from my hands to follow me as I lead the way. The frantic look in his eyes and the tense line of his jaw tell me all I need to know about his frazzled state of mind.

"I'm guessing there are no cops outside," he says, his disapproval plain and obvious.

"Nope. I'm afraid it's just A.J. and me, but Vladmir is on his way, for whatever that's worth. You know how I feel about that man." I shrug. "But I figured backup of some kind couldn't hurt. He was too far behind us for me to wait for him, though, so I devised a plan."

"A plan? You use that word too liberally, *dusha moya*."

Just hearing the Russian term of endearment, I have to restrain myself from wrapping my arms around his neck and kissing him until we are both out of breath.

"I had resigned myself to never laying eyes on you again," Nik says in a hurt tone. "I hoped you would turn your back on me and go home without looking back. To hear your voice again, to see your face once more—"

I sigh, melting completely. "Listen to me, Nik. For as long as I live, I will never turn my back on you again. Ever."

Nik angrily mutters something in Russian. I don't need to be fluent in the language to get the idea that it was a dirty, filthy curse. "Of all the stupid, foolish things, Kat... You shouldn't be here. Best-case scenario, you end up dead."

I scoff. "Don't be silly. Best-case scenario, I'll get you back. And as you should know by now, I deserve nothing but the very best."

Nik's dark brown eyes burn into mine, and it's obvious he's torn between the desire to kiss me and the urge to strangle me.

"Damn it, Kat. You shouldn't have come."

"Well, I'm here now, so let's focus on getting out of here so you can spend the rest of our days berating me for my recklessness, shall we?"

His immediate response is a pained groan, but I never get to find out what new form of outraged reprimand he planned to delight me with because the bane of my existence intercepts us. Giuseppe Salvatore, the *stronzo*, stands proud and indignant directly in front of us.

"Well, well, well. Look who stopped for a visit. Someway, somehow, I'm not surprised to see you had a hand in this charade, my dear Ms. Devereaux," he says with his best slimy smirk. "And you, Nikolai—what is it about you Russian men that you just can't resist meddling with the women who belong to your betters?"

"You are not his better," I say through gritted teeth. "And I will never belong to you."

"I guess we'll see about that, won't we? I'm assuming our

friend A.J. is close by. What a merry gathering this is!" Salvatore sighs in feigned delight. "Why don't we go find her?"

"Leave her alone," I say as Nik gently pushes me behind his body.

"Don't worry, Kat. He'll leave us alone now," Nik says, rising to his impressive height. "He won't be bothering any of us anymore. Isn't that right, Salvatore? Not Kat, not A.J., not Dmitri."

"And why would I do that, Nikolai?" the horrid man asks mockingly. "Because you say so?"

Nik smiles his gigawatt grin, but his dark eyes remain cold. "Yeah. That's exactly right," he says. "Because I say so."

Without another word, Nik unflinchingly fires my gun between the *stronzo*'s pale blue eyes.

24

KAT

HE HAS COME for me at last.

Even through the bedroom's closed solid wood door, I hear Nik's voice and muffled footsteps on the marble floors. He pauses outside the doorway, and I hold my breath.

Soon after Nik ended Giuseppe Salvatore's miserable life, Vladmir and a sizable contingent of *bratva* soldiers arrived at the scene. By then, most of the non-Italian representatives of the Seven Families had made themselves scarce, but the cacophonous mayhem A.J. and I caused carried on for at least another hour. It took the *bratva* a while to figure out how to end our orchestrated chaos. Thankfully, they managed it before we attracted any undesired attention, especially of the law enforcement kind. Or so I was told.

The *stronzo*'s body had barely hit the floor before Nik had me whisked away from the crime scene. Upon arrival, Vladmir was immediately dispatched to bring A.J. and me to the penthouse, even before dealing with Dmitri.

My protests were for naught. Just thinking of leaving Nik behind put me on the verge of a panic attack, but he wouldn't let me have my way with this. After he promised me at least a dozen times that everything was under control and that he wasn't in any danger, I had to accept defeat. It became clear that disagreeing with him was a waste of time. Over and over again, Nik pointed out that he wouldn't be able to think right until he knew I was safe at home. According to him, the sooner that happened, the sooner he'd be able to return to me.

After A.J. and I were dropped off at the penthouse, she immediately demanded that I give her a tour of the place. Even though my heart wasn't in it, I obliged her, thinking to myself that I could use the distraction.

A.J. oohed and aahed at every luxurious detail. Once we reached my former bedroom, she promptly shooed me away so she could enjoy a long soak in the guest bathroom's jacuzzi tub. With a final warning to not disturb her slumber for the next twelve hours, she made me take my leave.

Truth be told, I felt the need to wash up, too. After being kidnapped—again—and having to scramble to come to Nik's rescue, a hot shower seemed just the thing. Afterwards, I waited for Nik to return, dressed in only his fluffy bathrobe while fretting about his well-being. Until I finally heard his voice through the shut door.

The undeniable confirmation that Nik is still alive and well makes me relax for the first time in days. My legs turn into jelly, and I have to lean against his massive bed to keep myself from falling.

As his steps stop outside the door, my breath catches in anticipation. I laugh at myself. After everything we've been through, somehow I still get butterflies in my stomach just thinking about him.

Wordlessly, Nik opens the door and enters the room.

One look at him, and my mind goes blank—nothing but

pure static. My earlier worries and nervousness turn into yearning, then breathless excitement, and then an undeniable urgency to be in his arms again. If I'm not touching him in the next heartbeat, I might lose my mind.

I drink in the sight of him—so tall, dark, and handsome.

Once Nik sees me, he sighs loudly, and the tension in his shoulders leaves his frame. His eyes devour me from head to toe, his feelings so clear and undisguised in his gaze. His every emotion is displayed on his face, yet he seems unconcerned about it.

A bit clumsily—and entirely desperately—I run for him. Without even the slightest hesitation, Nik opens his arms, and I leap into them, wrapping my arms and legs around his body. He steps back to absorb my momentum while his arms clutch me almost painfully tight.

"I missed you," I say into his ear.

For a second, I wonder if Nik will joke about how I just saw him a couple of hours ago. Instead, he says, "Fuck. I missed you more."

I gasp when everything I thought I would never get a chance to tell him rushes to the forefront of my mind. Suddenly, I can't wait even a second longer to share it with him. I push against his chest, and, with obvious reluctance, Nik sets me down, but his arms linger around my waist.

I take a deep breath. "Nik, we need to talk. There's something I must tell you."

Nik's shoulders stiffen, and his eyes become guarded as a saddened expression washes over his handsome face. "What is it?"

The words rush out of my mouth. "We've wasted so much time. You and I have spent way too much time letting meaningless things and worries get in the way of our happiness. It's time we stop this nonsense. After the challenges we've been through since we first met, we deserve it more than anyone. I say it's our turn to be madly, ridiculously, embarrassingly happy. I know it won't be easy, but I'm game if you are."

"What are you saying?" he asks, his voice slightly unsteady.

I shrug, smiling. "You know I hate feeling powerless or like things are spiraling out of my control. And, sure, at this point, it's fair to say I have something of a traumatic history with controlling mafia bosses. If I never see another mobster for the rest of my life, it will still be too soon. But you are my exception. And I never want to let my fears stand in the way of our happiness again. I don't want to hold on to them. Nothing but misery awaits me if I make that mistake again. I want to hold on to you instead. For the rest of my days. And if you feel the same way—"

"I do," he quickly says.

I squeeze his biceps, grinning. "Let's not waste another precious second with our useless emotional baggage, then. Let's be outrageously happy instead."

Nik's dark brown eyes frantically search my face. "Kat, do you mean that?"

After wrapping my arms around his neck, I pull him closer. "Nik, I need you. Even if I hadn't been forced to confront my mortality and yours today, I would still have returned to you." I smile at him. "Eventually."

"You would have?" he asks incredulously.

I sigh, rolling my eyes. "Of course. I was having a hard time staying away from you before Dmitri even knocked on my door. Mind you, that does *not* mean you get to lock me away in a tower or browbeat me into giving in to your every whim and dictate. You will need to curb your urges to boss me around, mister. In turn, I will share all my secrets with you. I'll become the proverbial open book. Get ready, Nik, because I'm about to give the term *oversharing* a whole new meaning."

Nik scoffs, his lips twisting into the most captivating smirk. "Kat, please. Don't threaten me with a good time."

I raise an eyebrow at him. "I'm warning you. You don't know what you're signing up for. Before long, you'll be begging me to shut my mouth."

"Unlikely," he says, unabashedly amused. "But if somehow that day ever comes, I know just the thing you can do with your lips instead."

I hook my finger around the collar of Nik's shirt and pull him closer and closer until our faces are a mere inch apart. His breath mingles with mine, and he shudders.

Suddenly, I become entranced by his mouth. "Speaking of which, will you shut up and kiss me already?"

"In a moment. First, there's something I need to tell you, too."

"What is it?" I ask impatiently.

Nik studies my expression before brushing his lips over my ear. His breaths warm my skin as, with a trembling hand, he cups my face. "Kat, I love you with all my heart."

My heart skips a beat, but with a shrug, I wink at him. "I know."

"Do you think—could you see yourself one day feeling the same way? Before you answer, you should know how deeply sorry I am for hurting you. I will never, ever be able to apologize enough for locking you in here and forcing you to stay. Or for losing my head that day, or for dragging you into my mess of a life. I'll always be profoundly ashamed of what I've done to you and the pain I've caused you."

I sigh. "Nik, you aren't listening to me. I wanted to run back to you after less than a day apart. Yes, locking me away was despicable—and the other stuff didn't make you look great either. But I still fell in love with you!"

Nik blinks twice, tilting his head as if he can't believe he heard me correctly.

I almost can't resist the urge to roll my eyes. Men are so freaking clueless...

Amused by his dumbstruck expression, I say, "Come on. You know I've had a crush on you from the start. Even when you were mean to me and I wanted to hate you, I couldn't help craving being around you. With every word we exchanged, every moment we shared, it grew harder and harder to remember why I wasn't supposed to fall for you. And when you kissed me or touched me?" I sigh, theatrically fanning myself. "Let me put it like this: you don't play fair, *miliy*. I never stood a chance."

Nik shakes his head with a flattered, bewildered expression. "I can't believe this is my life."

"What do you mean?"

"Come on. You know exactly what I mean. You're the most excruciatingly beautiful woman I've ever seen. From the moment I first saw you, I was a goner. Every single thing about the way your mind works seems like it was designed to drive me crazy. And you did. Repeatedly. Whenever I'm around you, I fall deeper and deeper under your spell."

My lips curl into a delighted smile. "Well, good. Add that to the list, along with all the other reasons why we should be together. It's ranked somewhere below the fact that you were so freaking eager to give up your life in exchange for mine. But be warned, Nik—if you ever even dream about trying that again, I'll kill you myself."

"There was no other choice, *milaya*. I'd have done it, no hesitation."

I narrow my eyes at him, scowling. I'm about to question

his insane statement when he pulls me closer. So I relent for now, craving the feeling of being in his arms, wrapped by his warmth and scent.

Nik nuzzles my hair. "I can't quite believe you actually love me. Even after everything?"

"Yes, but you'll have to spend the rest of your life loving me in return."

He pulls away just enough to gaze into my eyes. While cupping the back of my neck, he studies my face before smiling at me. "*Milaya,* your wish is my command."

Still smiling, Nik curls his finger under my chin, drawing me closer for a kiss. A shiver races down my spine as he brushes his lips against mine, touching his tongue to them. I sigh, breathing in deeply, and he grows more aggressive in his caress, sinking deeper into the kiss with his mouth firmly slanted against mine.

Nik's hands cover my breasts over the thick fabric of the robe. My nipples harden from his touch, and he hoarsely groans into my mouth. I can't help squirming against him in response, my hips instinctively pressing against his erection.

"Spread your legs for me, Kat," Nik says against my cheek, at the corner of my lips.

Eagerly, I follow his command. Unhurriedly, Nik drags his hand under the robe, down my stomach, until he is cupping me between my thighs. Maddeningly slowly, he pets me.

"You are wet, *kiska.*"

I nod, trembling. My eyes slide shut as his fingers lazily part my lips.

At last, Nik strokes me where I crave him the most, his lids going heavy as he languidly pleasures me. A moan escapes my lips, and pure, undisguised, masculine satisfaction washes over his gorgeous features.

I moan, sighing. "Oh, Nik...I want you. I need you, all of you, right now."

"Not yet," he says against my lips, kissing me. His finger sinks deeper between my folds, all the way inside of me, as his thumb circles my clitoris.

I cling harder to him, leaning all of my weight on his shoulders as my legs grow weak, practically giving out under me.

I throw my head back in ecstasy, softly moaning as he lazily thrusts and circles. He watches me briefly before his lips descend upon my neck, showering me with open-mouthed kisses.

I gasp. "I'm close..."

At once, Nik's attentions come to a stop. He withdraws his finger and ceases his kisses, making me cry out in protest.

While holding my hand, he leads me to the side of the bed. He sits on it, then he taps his upper thigh. "Come here. Straddle me."

I glance at him before disrobing myself. At the sight of my completely naked body, Nik hisses in a breath. He shudders. "*Kiska.* My woman is a work of art. A vision. A present from the gods."

I smile, slowly approaching him. "Sweet-talker."

Before I can lower myself onto his lap, he makes quick work of his clothes, undressing with lightning speed. Once I am poised above his cock, he wraps his hand around its base, fisting it. "Come closer. Take me inside you, *kiska.*"

I lower myself. Once the crown of his member enters me, he throws his head back as a pained groan escapes his lips. His hands roughly cup my breasts, his thumb and finger immediately pinching my nipples.

I want to savor the moment, but it's more than I can take. I can't hold it back.

"Oh, Nik," I cry out.

Even with only the tip of his shaft inside me, I start to come. The slickness and strength of my climax demand that I slip down his length. I sink my fingernails deep into the flesh of his shoulder before throwing my head back in pleasure. A breathy, raspy scream escapes my lips, and one of Nik's hands drifts from my breast to the back of my neck. He grips me and forces me to look at him. Nik stares into my eyes as every inch of him invades me, deeper and deeper, while I pulse around him.

He's so thick. So warm. So hard.

I stare into Nik's eyes as I come, and it makes me feel as if no part of me can be hidden from his all-seeing gaze. In this scorchingly intimate moment, I can't shake the notion that there's no part of me he doesn't see, no part of me that hasn't been bared before him—no part of me he hasn't studied. No part of me he doesn't love unconditionally.

By the time my spasming orgasm ebbs, Nik is throbbing inside me. He raises his hips as he pulls me down harder onto his lap. While clutching the flesh on my ass, he guides us through a steady, languid pace. Not long after, I'm on the brink of a second climax.

Nik wraps my hair around his wrist, making sure my eyes never leave his. "I'm not done with you yet."

This time, when his maddening rhythm takes its toll and I'm seconds away from coming again, he allows me to throw my head back and grind against him to my heart's content. The tips of my hair brush against his legs as I cry out in ecstasy, and he leans forward, kissing my breasts as I sigh his name repeatedly.

When I'm able to open my eyes and look at him again,

panting, I find his mesmerized eyes raptly watching me, maddened by the pleasure he is wrecking on my body.

After grasping his hand, I pull it to my mouth and suck his index finger. I drag it down my neck, between my breasts, past the valley of my stomach until it rests against my clitoris. "Touch me, Nik."

We both stare at his hand, sunk between my folds as I grind down on it, swirling my hips at an unhurried pace. Nik groans, his eyes riveted to where we're joined.

"I want all of you, Nik." I cup my breasts, teasing their tips as he watches, seemingly enthralled. "Every single part of you. I need it just as much as you need to give it to me."

Nik groans, pained, before he lifts me, brusquely laying me down on the bed. Still deep inside me, he raises himself in his arms to look at me. His gaze is fixed on my face as he rolls his hips between my legs. "You're more than I could've ever dreamed of, *kiska.*"

"Fuck me. Take me as hard as you want. I'm all yours."

With a sigh, he wraps his hand around my throat, pressing my head to the side until the column of my neck is bared to him. He leans down to press his face to the sensitive skin, inhaling profoundly while practically growling against me. Then, he nibbles the sensitive area where my neck and shoulder connect before sucking it hard.

I pant as his hips pound against mine, struggling against the urge not to orgasm again. "Nik! It's... oh, Nik..."

Nik rides me relentlessly, and ecstasy courses through me, reaching all the way down to my bones. He grabs the back of my knees, pulling me closer against his hips before bringing my ankles to rest atop his shoulders. Before increasing his riveting pace, he turns his head to press a kiss against my left ankle.

When I begin to quicken around him again, Nik roars

with pleasure, throwing his head back in abandon before spreading my legs wide. He leans forward, resting his forehead against mine. As his hips rock against me, his eyes stare intensely into mine.

"Kat, I'm close," he says. He is so deep inside me that I feel his words as much as I hear them.

I struggle to catch my breath. "Come inside me. I need to feel all of you inside me."

My request proves to be his breaking point.

Nik slams his body against mine. "Can't fight it any longer," he grunts, taking me so hard I know I'll be sore for a week. As he is sent over the edge, he roars. "*Kat!*" Over and over again, he thrusts deep inside of me.

Warmth fills me to my core, and I moan. "I can feel you inside me. So hot..." My knees drop to the bed, and all tension leaves my body as I come for him again.

Nik groans, feeling me contract around his cock. He grinds his hips against mine again, ejaculating the last of his come.

Long moments pass as we lay together, striving to catch our breaths. It's a struggle even to begin formulating thoughts—my body and mind have been rendered utterly useless by the havoc of sensations he wreaked over me.

"Kat," Nik says at last, dazedly.

I sigh. "I never even knew pleasure like this was possible."

At last, I am satisfied. At last, I feel complete. Whole, even. All these years spent yearning, craving, dreaming... No more.

Nik raises his head from where it rests between my breasts. His eyes find mine, and he studies my expression.

As I gaze at his dear face, all these now-familiar emotions throb inside my chest. Before, I had fooled myself into thinking it was nothing more than attraction, an infatuation... I didn't know then and couldn't discern what I felt. But I understand it now.

Nik rubs his nose along mine. "I love you, Kat. I am completely, hopelessly in love with you." He presses a soft, tender kiss against my lips.

"Nik, I love you so much. With all of me." My eyes glisten as he presses feathery kisses all over my face.

"I will love you every day of my life. And if there's an afterlife, I will love you there, too."

I lose myself in his beautiful eyes, and I see the truth of his words reflected there. I see all the love he has in him—all mine for the taking.

Once upon a time, I had despaired at my misfortune, wishing for all I thought I could never have.

Now, as my heart feels as if it might burst from all the love it tries to hold in, the truth finally sinks in.

At last, I have everything I've ever dreamed of. It's all mine.

25

NIK

"Easy-peasy!" Kat whispers to herself as she quietly steps into the dimly lit chamber, swinging a large, nondescript cloth bag over her delicate shoulder.

She hasn't spotted me sitting in silence in the empty room. As far as she is concerned, I'm supposed to be over a hundred miles away—and I was. But my meeting ended earlier than expected, so I returned home and decided to sit back and relax until Kat returned from her outing.

"Did you get anything nice?" I ask her, my voice loudly rumbling through the penthouse's empty foyer.

With an almost imperceptible gasp, Kat freezes mid-stride before slowly turning to face me, a far-too-wide grin plastered over her face.

"Nik..." she says, concealing her shock at seeing me. "You're home early, my love. What a wonderful surprise!"

While eyeing the bag she is now subtly hiding behind her legs, I dryly say, "I'm sure you paid for all that."

After blinking twice, Kat seems to decide there's no point in denying the obvious. With a sigh, she rests her free hand on her hip. "Maybe not with money or anything of the sort, but I'd say that I earned it fairly. In a way. I mean, I certainly paid for it with the sweat off my back."

I study her for a moment, from the top of her head—where not a hair is out of place—to the tip of her designer six-inch heels. She rolls her eyes at my incredulous expression. "Figuratively speaking, of course, *miliy*."

With a tired but amused sigh, I rub my hand over my jaw. "Who did we steal from today, Kat?"

"No one you need to worry about," she says, with a dismissive wave of her hand. "This guy A.J. told me about."

"This *guy*?"

Kat shrugs. "A.J. said he broke her heart and that I should knock myself out as far as he was concerned. Since we owe her through the heat death of the universe for saving our lives repeatedly, I figured the least I could do was oblige her. Just this time, of course. And since you were busy with work, I thought you'd be happy if I kept myself busy to ease the pain of being away from you."

"I am. But I also have half a mind to heat your ass for endangering yourself. Again."

Kat scoffs, rolling her eyes. "Oh, please! Nobody even saw me. The fool probably won't even know I took something of his for months. You should've seen his place, Nik. What a mess."

I sigh. "Let me see what you have," I say at last. It's the damnedest thing—no matter what kind of new havoc this madwoman wreaks around me, I can't stay mad at her to save my life. Especially not now, with our new life together, when she's all smiles and kisses whenever she sees me around the penthouse.

This isn't Kat's first heist since we officially moved in together. I strongly doubt it will be her last. I might as well make peace with my fate, pleading to all deities listening to help me keep her unharmed. And to grant me the serenity to accept the things I cannot change—like Kat's devil-may-care attitude when it comes to her personal safety. At this point, Kat knows I'll let her get away with anything. That's why I had no choice but to spread the word that if even a hair on her perfect head is harmed, somebody is going to beg me for the mercy of a quick death. She's perfectly aware of this fact, of course. And she doesn't hesitate to take advantage of it at the slightest inconvenience or provocation.

Kat saunters over to me, practically skipping across the marble floors before dropping her lush ass on my lap. Barely containing her grin, she proudly offers me the bag.

Curious, I glance inside. The small collection of colorful gemstones—diamonds, emeralds, sapphires, and even a few blood-red rubies—astonishes me.

My perplexed expression delights her, and she shrugs, placidly saying, "What can I say? He and I are in the same line of work. I guess there's some truth to that saying about no honor among thieves, after all."

With an impressed whistle, I shake my head, returning her loot. "Not bad, *milaya*. Not bad."

"Right? Especially not for an afternoon of light work. What can I say?" She sighs with feigned modesty. "It's not much, but it's honest, dishonest work."

"Speaking of honest work," I innocently say, "did you give any thought to my suggestion that you should consider devoting some of your time to charity work?" Kat gasps in outrage, clutching her jewels to her chest. "I'm just saying—it could be a good use of your time. It's not as if you need to take on any more jobs, *milaya*. I have more money than even you can ever spend."

"Is that a challenge? Because it sounds like a challenge."

I ignore her interruption. "And who knows? You could find a cause that is dear to your heart. Maybe helping young girls with an attitude problem who can't seem to stay out of trouble to save their own lives? I feel like that could be your calling."

Kat narrows her eyes at me. "You're teasing me," she says accusingly.

With a small laugh, I nod. "Unless, of course, you happen to agree with me."

With an outraged huff, Kat lightly slaps my shoulder. "Can you imagine?" she asks, horrified, nibbling her bottom lip. "Me, gainfully employed, doing some good, old-fashioned honest work?" She shudders. "I don't think so. No, sir!"

"Call me sir one more time, and I won't bring it up again," I say in a whisper, and Kat rolls her eyes before laughing. She leans forward to kiss me, unwittingly awakening my insatiable hunger for her. It's been too long since I made love to her. At least eight hours by now...

She pulls away too soon, and I groan in protest. Mercilessly ignoring my starving pleas, she asks, "So, how did your meeting go?"

Patrick McGuire and I have been meeting periodically for months now. In the aftermath of the Salvatore ordeal, McGuire finally accepted that the *bratva* and I had nothing to do with his daughter's disappearance. In an attempt to mend fences, we've been working together to find her. It was, if nothing else, a gesture of good faith.

Besides, Maxim would have wanted me to ensure Erin was safe and well. I owe him that—and so much more. Especially considering the mess involving the location of his remains, a mystery I still haven't been able to solve.

Kat insisted we should have a memorial service for him.

Diamond Dream 245

At first, I resisted her idea, thinking the whole thing would leave a bad taste in my mouth since we would be burying nothing but an empty casket. But in the end, as usual, she was right. It was time. Even though it was nothing but a symbolic gesture, it gave me the closure I needed to move on and start a new life with her.

"It went as well as it could be expected," I say with a sigh. "And by that, I mean it was a complete waste of time, but at least McGuire and I didn't come to blows. This time."

"Baby steps," she jokes. Then, gently, she says, "You'll find Erin. And Maxim. Don't be so hard on yourself. You're doing the best you can, and that's not nothing."

I sigh. "It sure feels like it sometimes."

"I know, *miliy*," she says, wrapping her arms around my neck before pressing a soft kiss against my forehead. "But I know you'll succeed at this as you have with everything else you've ever set out to accomplish."

"My greatest accomplishment," I say, squeezing the plump flesh of her ass, "is to be loved by you."

She winks me. "And I'll never let you forget it."

I laugh. "Don't I know it."

Kat smiles at me for a moment before a sober expression settles over her finely wrought features. Before she even opens her lips to form the words, I already know what she's going to ask me.

"Did you see him?"

I nod in response, still beyond words, even after all these months. "Lorenzo was there, too."

After the reigning Italian boss, Giuseppe Salvatore—or the *stronzo*, as Kat tends to refer to him—died at my hands, his nephew, Lorenzo, took his place. The young man was a breath of fresh air compared to his disgrace of an uncle. In all fairness, as Lorenzo likes to remind me, Giuseppe was only his uncle by marriage.

Lorenzo has been trying to step up to the plate and establish order within the Italian family's ranks. He has his work cut out for him, and I don't envy his position. But for whatever it's worth, he seems to be made of stronger—and better—stuff than his predecessor.

"How is he doing?"

I know she's not referring to the new young Italian boss.

"Dmitri's...condition hasn't improved much since I last saw him. He barely seemed to recognize me this time. Or at least I felt that way because all he does is ask about her."

His girlfriend. Shortly after Salvatore died, we found Dmitri's girlfriend in a deplorable state. We freed her, and we've been trying our best to help her recover since then, but understandably, the young woman is still profoundly damaged and traumatized.

Somehow, Dmitri is in an even worse state.

His betrayal cut me deeply, more than anything or anyone else before him. Still, I just couldn't bring myself to kill him. The best alternative had been to have him incarcerated. Not in an actual, government-provided prison, of course. We always handle these things internally. Instead, I had him confined in our private lockup. Indefinitely.

Dmitri hasn't been faring well ever since. At times, I fear that keeping him away from the girl might be a fate worse than death for him. Every time I visit him, he seems to be further down the path towards insanity. I worry I will gaze into my friend's eyes one day, and nothing but madness will stare back at me.

Kat sighs. "Poor Dmitri. I wish there were another way."

I rub my hand over her back. "I know, *milaya*. I do, too."

She stares blankly ahead, frowning slightly. But to my

Diamond Dream

surprise, after a moment, she seems content to drop the subject, shrugging before turning to face me.

"After you left this morning, I thought about the night we first met. As monumental of a night as it was for you and me, we had no idea everything would change. Forever." With a teasing glint in her eyes, she brushes her lips against mine. "I bet you didn't even know what hit you when you first saw me across the room."

"It was the stuff of legends, Kat. The earth moved. Even if I live to be a hundred years old, I'll still perfectly remember the way you looked that night and the devastation you caused in my life. You stole my diamond and my heart—and I was better for it."

"And now you have me *and* your diamond."

I rise from my seat and set her down on the chair. "Speaking of which, there's something I've been meaning to ask you."

Kat stares at me in confusion as I walk over to where my suit jacket hangs, fishing around the pockets for the item I've been carrying for a while.

After grabbing the small velvet box, I take my time walking back to her, and she watches me with unmistakable curiosity.

"This belongs to you," I say, referring to the object within my hand. "I've been dying to give it back to you since you threw it at me. I've had it with me this entire time, waiting for the right moment to return it to its rightful owner."

I drop to one knee in front of her, and she gasps, her eyes widening. "Nik—"

My heart thunders inside my chest. "Kat, I've been yours from the first moment I saw you. I would do unspeakable things to make you the happiest woman in the world.

There's nothing I wouldn't do for you, and there's no one I love, cherish, or trust more. I never, ever want to be parted from you again. Please make me the happiest man on this earth by giving me the honor of loving, protecting, and treasuring you with all of me for the rest of my life. Marry me, Kat."

I flip the ring box open, revealing the ring I commissioned for her months ago—days after she stormed into my home office and rightfully flung the red diamond at me. Before I had any reason to believe there was hope she would miraculously forgive me. Before I knew she would ever take me back. One look at the red diamond, and I knew there was only one acceptable fate for it.

It was appropriate, after all, that the gemstone that brought us together in the first place should be the one to symbolize our eternal bond.

Kat stares at the ring with wide eyes before gasping. "Is that... is that the *Flame of Mir*?"

"Yeah. Do you like it?"

"Do I *like* it? This is the most stunning ring I've ever seen in my life! It is, of course, scandalously, outrageously extravagant—but, oh, Nik! I love it! It's perfect."

"Does that mean you will marry me?" I ask her impatiently, barely daring to breathe.

Kat finally averts her mesmerized eyes from the ring to my face, her expression changing from confused to exasperated. "Of course I'll marry you! Nik, I love you. Marrying you is a no-brainer."

I slide the ring onto her finger before she can take the words back. She dreamily gazes at it for a moment. Then, before I have a chance to react, she launches herself at me, sending both of us tumbling to the ground.

My delighted laugh echoes as she enfolds me with her

arms, showering my face and neck with the most delectable, feathery kisses.

"Nikolai Stefanovich..." she says, sighing. "You're the man of my dreams. You're the answer to my every prayer. You're more, so much more than everything I've ever wanted —you're everything I've always needed. Being loved by you is the greatest thing that has ever happened to me. There's nothing I'd love more than to marry you. I love you, you know."

The look on her exquisite face almost unmans me. "I'll never get over hearing you say that."

She smiles at me with a playful glint in her dark blue eyes. "That's fine with me. I'll never stop saying it."

"Maybe one day you'll somehow love me as much as I love you."

"As it happens, I already do. Scratch that—you can't possibly love me as much as I love you. I'm positive I love you more."

I bite back a groan as Kat's luscious body rubs against mine. As always, the slightest friction between us is enough to make me crave her to distraction. "In your dreams, Kat."

"While we're at the subject of my dreams," she says, her gaze fixated on my lips, "I think it's time we seal the deal."

I couldn't agree more. Still, I can't resist teasing her. "Ask me nicely."

Kat's maddening mouth curves into the most sensual smile. Her eyes darken before she whispers, "Kiss me, Nik. Kiss me, and I'm yours."

BONUS

Thank you so much for reading *Diamond Don* and *Diamond Dream*!

Miss Nik and Kat already? Catch up with them as they celebrate their first anniversary.

Scan the QR code below to receive the epilogue (*exclusive for newsletter subscribers*):

I would also be incredibly grateful if you would take a minute to share your thoughts about Nik and Kat's story by leaving a quick review on Amazon, Goodreads, BookBub, or wherever you prefer. Your review could help other readers discover this book. Thank you!

DMITRI IS NEXT...

EMERALD DUET

EMERALD ENEMIES & EMERALD EMBRACE

Dmitri's story is coming out this fall!

MAILING LIST

Sign up to my newsletter for exclusive bonus content and updates on upcoming releases! **New subscribers get an exclusive epilogue.**

Scan the QR code to subscribe:

COMING UP NEXT...

Emerald Duet
(*Dmitri's story!*)

Sapphire Duet

Ruby Duet

ABOUT THE AUTHOR

Anna Cole writes thrilling, steamy romance stories about fierce, unapologetic heroines and the larger-than-life, possessive antiheroes who are crazy about them. She spends her time on the East Coast, plotting out all the delicious pain and suffering she will put her characters through on their quest for true love and a happily ever after.

When she's not writing, Anna enjoys sunsets, long walks on the beach, and spending time with her favorite book boyfriends—and her husband and dog, too.

Made in the USA
Monee, IL
22 August 2024